THE FINAL MESSAGE TO ROME

A Tale of the First Persecution

DANIEL GOPPELT

Copyright © 2014 Daniel Goppelt
All rights reserved.

ISBN: 1502430231
ISBN 13: 9781502430236

This book is dedicated to believers around the world who suffer for their faith. Two, specifically, who have impacted me: Ivan (Vanya) Moiseyev and Rifqa Bary.

Foreword

WHAT YOU ARE about to read is a form of historical fiction with a spiritual lesson, essentially a parable. I did not make up this story or sit down with the intention to write a story. This story was given to me by the Lord. I hope you will not misunderstand me. Nothing I have written in this story should be taken as inspired by God on a level footing with the canon of scripture. While I do know that God led me to write this story, and the lessons of the story are defensible from scripture, I have not dishonored God by adding to his infallible, inspired book, the Bible. I have taken care to ensure that everything I have written agrees with scripture, and I pray that God will be lifted up and will draw anyone who reads this writing to himself.

 The historical account of the events surrounding the martyrdom of the apostle Peter is based largely upon the ancient accounts of the historians Hegesippus and Jerome. Their historical account has also been alluded to in the Apocryphal books and was referenced by the author John Foxe in his classic work, *Foxe's Book of Martyrs*. Though John Foxe noted that some doubt the account of Peter's martyrdom in Rome, and that their doubts are not entirely unfounded, he proceeded to use the account in his writing. This is the account that God has led me to use as the stage for the story he has given me.

 I have not done an exhaustive amount of research into Roman culture and history, though I have done a fair amount to ensure that the story is compatible with historical fact. I have also done some research into the history of the first-century church. When the Lord gave me this story, he did not want me to write a book on the history of the first-century church. He wanted me to write a story, a parable that would explain the truth he had given to me in a way that was both exciting and thought provoking.

There has been a lot of trailblazing in writing this story. When I began, I knew roughly where the story would begin and end but not what would happen in between. Writing this story has been, frankly, a strange and wonderful journey, and it has taken me in directions that I had not thought of. As I wrote this story, my thoughts turned to the many believers around the world who endure persecution and suffering for their faith in Jesus Christ. Since this is an issue that is very close to my heart, I think it is appropriate that God led me to tell a story that reminds us of our brethren who are in bonds. I think more about this issue as I see world rulers become increasingly lifted up in pride and hateful toward the Lord and his people.

The Lord allowed me to write this story over a period of four years. During those years, I faced a great deal of spiritual opposition, discouragement, and frustration in the writing of this book. The enemy, the devil, often tempted me to quit and give up writing this story that God entrusted to me. Through the whole challenge, I had to remind myself that God gave me this story; I had to tell it. God invited me to follow him into a great adventure in writing this story, or parable, as I always called it, for that is what it is.

While readers may see some striking parallels between this story and the best-selling novels *Quo Vadis, Martyr of the Catacombs: A Tale of Ancient Rome,* and other writings, no plagiarism is intended. Any similarity between this book and other writings or actual people who have endured persecution is unintentional. Other critics may call into question the names of the characters in the story. All the names used in this writing endeavor were chosen solely for their meaning and ethnic origin, especially the two main characters, Anthony and Ariel. The name Anthony is Latin meaning "praiseworthy" and Ariel is Hebrew meaning "lioness of God." No intention of plagiarism was ever present in the selection of the characters' names.

The ultimate lesson of this story was given to me when I was praying to God and questioning him as to why he does the things that, from our perspective, make no sense. This is especially true in the areas of sorrow and suffering, both of which we encounter so frequently. The Lord gave me this lesson and a story to communicate it in a way that will hopefully let us see life from his perspective. While I do not pretend to have a complete explanation for the grief and disappointments we endure, I do offer a hope, a reason to trust the heart of the one who is rich in love for us.

I hope that you will be both inspired and captivated by what you read, and may God receive all the glory.

Yours sincerely,
Daniel Goppelt

Table of Contents

I.	The Fire	1
II.	Kidnapped	11
III.	A Midnight Meeting	23
IV.	Into the Alleys	33
V.	The Secret Tunnel	51
VI.	A New Assignment	65
VII.	The Nightmare Begins	81
VIII.	A Plot Discovered	93
IX.	Rescue and Tragedy	105
X.	Surprise for Ariel	117
XI.	In the Dungeon	129
XII.	On Trial	143
XIII.	Escape	159
XIV.	In Hiding	171
XV.	Return to the Catacombs	183
XVI.	Reunited	199
XVII.	A Last Request	211
XVIII.	The Secret Revealed	219
XIX.	Persecuted, But Not Forsaken	229
Epilogue		235
Afterword		239
Acknowledgements		241
Bibliography		243

A Map of Ancient Rome

THE TWO CHILDREN would have used a similar map to navigate around Rome. Catacombs could be found along every highway going out of Rome at a distance of approximately a mile from the city and beyond. The catacombs mentioned in the story would have been located outside the city along the Via Latina and the Via Appia.

Historical Note: The section of the city outside the inner wall, was not in existence in 64 AD, nor was the Colloseum.

Map Legend:
1. The Senator's house.
2. The route taken by the children on their first trip out of the city at night.
3. The route used for the return trip.
4. The entrance to the secret tunnel.
5. The secret house where the tunnel comes up.
6. Return to the Senator's house.
7. House of the Indian family.
8. Ariel's escape from Rome.
9. Nero's Golden Palace.

Map of Ancient Rome at the time of the First Persecution.

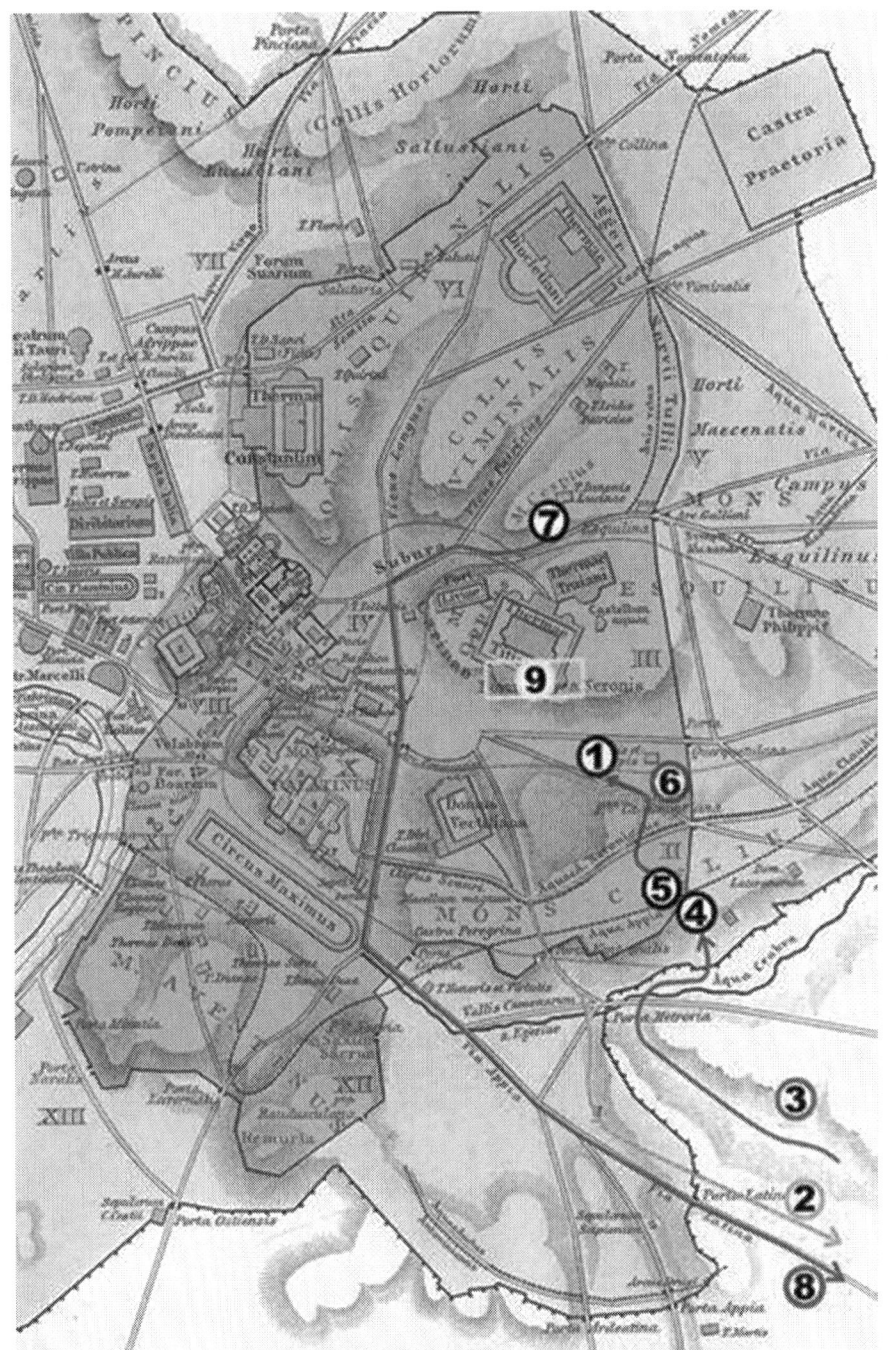

Chapter 1

THE FIRE

IT WAS DURING the last four years of the reign of Nero, emperor of Rome, from 64 to 68 AD, that the most horrific and terrifying persecution was unleashed against the followers of Jesus. During those terrible years, the believers were tortured and killed in multitudes like never before. Among those who perished was the apostle Peter, close friend of Jesus and one of the most prominent of the apostles. Many notable scholars of history report that he was crucified in the city of Rome. This is a story of a boy and a girl who lived in Rome at the time of his martyrdom. Their names were Anthony and Ariel.

Each had been born in the land of Asia Minor, located to the north of the Great Sea. Both of their families enjoyed the privilege of Roman citizenship. Tragically, neither had any other siblings. Due to the prevalence of disease and miscarriage, only half of children lived to see adulthood. Anthony's parents were originally from the city of Rome but had moved to Asia Minor shortly before he was born. As part of the high nobility and ruling class, they had been sent to Asia Minor to serve in a government capacity. At length, they grew tired of their life away from the place they had always considered home and returned to Rome.

As for Ariel, she and her family had lived in Asia Minor through most of her childhood and had moved to Rome just as she was entering her teen years. Ariel's parents were not Roman by birth. They had purchased their citizenship with a large sum of money. The heritage of her parents happened to be Hebrew, and her parents were devout followers of the Jewish religion, traditions, and customs.

Both families moved to Rome in the year 63 AD. At the time, Anthony was fifteen years of age, and Ariel was fourteen. They didn't meet until a year later, when Rome was struck by the great fire of 64 AD. The fire broke out at the southwest corner of the Circus Maximus and spread through the valley that ran north along the slopes of the Hills Palatine and Caelian.

The conflagration raged on for five horrible days before it was finally extinguished, or so everyone thought. Before anyone could so much as breathe a sigh of relief, a second inferno broke out. Fortunately, the casualties of the second fire proved to be far fewer than those of the first, at least in terms of human life. As for the buildings, the toll of the second fire was far greater than the first. When it was all over, three of the fourteen districts of Rome had been leveled, seven sustained only minimal damage, and four remained unscathed. No one knew exactly how many people perished in the fire, but the population of Rome was never the same after the smoke cleared.

As it happened, both families were living in an apartment building on the south side of the city, close to the Circus Maximus. This section of the city was where many of the city inhabitants lived, housed in multistory wooden buildings offering rooms for rent. Some of these buildings were only a few stories high, while others contained as many as six floors. The confined space of these buildings, and the wooden timber, provided ideal fuel for the fire as it raced on, driven by a fierce wind. To make matters worse, the buildings were overcrowded with renters.

The construction quality and living conditions of the buildings were also miserable. They were poorly built and unstable. Poverty and disease were rampant in these buildings as they were throughout the entire city. The families had intended the arrangement only as a temporary one. They were in the process of relocating and had been unable to find better accommodations.

When the fire broke out, much of the city was asleep. Tragically, no one was keeping vigilant watch that night. The fire crept up on them unawares. At last, a servant did spot the fire and sounded the alarm, but by that time, the fire was already upon them. All fled their homes in utter confusion and panic. It was absolute pandemonium and chaos in the city that night. The two children and their families escaped only minutes before the building they were staying in was engulfed in flames.

By the time the two families left their homes, the streets were crowded with people fleeing in absolute terror. Another element that made their escape difficult were the roads' themselves. The main highways that ran through Rome were paved with stone, straight and easy to navigate. By contrast, these streets, if anyone dared to call them that, were little better than tight alleyways or back passages. They were narrow, twisted, and irregular.

The smoke of the fire had already filled the streets, making them impossible to navigate. Many people turned down the wrong roads and quickly found themselves trapped by the fire. In the confusion and pandemonium of the fleeing crowds, the two children were separated and hopelessly lost from their parents.

Few buildings in Rome were made of stone or brick. Nearly everything was built of wood. Many of the burning buildings collapsed, injuring and even crushing people in the streets below. Both Anthony and Ariel were injured when one of these buildings came down, leaving them unconscious for over a day. They awoke to find themselves in a place they had never seen before, surrounded by people from many diverse nationalities, classes, and languages. It seemed a bit uncommon to the children that all these people should be together, though Rome was a city of many peoples and languages.

Upon inquiring as to where they were, the children learned that they were outside the city, in an underground network of tunnels used for burial purposes. These caves were known as the catacombs and were located alongside the major highways that ran in and out of the city. The wounds they had suffered from the fire had been dressed and bandaged, but both children were too weak to leave their beds. They asked the people watching over them who they were and why they had brought them to the caves. The people told them they had found them unconscious among the charred debris and rubble in the streets.

Knowing that they would surely die without help, they had brought them to the caves to see that they were cared for. Like the children, many of the other people present had also lost their homes in the fire. With no other place to seek shelter, they had come to the caves as a last resort. Other victims who had been fortunate enough to escape with their lives fled out of the city and collapsed in the surrounding fields.

The children were hurting more than they had ever hurt before, not only because of their injuries but because it was doubtful that they would ever see their parents again. The one thing that enabled them to bear the pain was the love that they saw in the people living with and caring for them. They had seen servants and physicians express concern for the people they waited upon, but these people had something entirely different. There were children of all ages living in the catacombs. They showed them an unbelievable amount of care and kindness.

Quite often the people would group together in a certain chamber or tunnel to talk, or listen to a story or some other form of teaching. At first glance, the children might have perceived these gatherings as similar to the religious ceremonies and customs they were familiar with. However, there was nothing religious about these gatherings or these people. They were from all different ages and races. Some were slaves, and others were free, but in each one of them, they could see a mark of love. Anthony and Ariel had only seen glimpses of such love in their past life, something that each of them had yearned to see and experience.

One such man who often came to these gatherings, Ariel recognized as being of Hebrew descent. The man's name was Simon Peter, but everyone knew him simply as Peter. Both the children could tell that he commanded significant influence, but his influence was not as a governor, priest, or rabbi. He was not over them in authority. If anything, he was everyone's servant. Of course, this could be said about almost any of these people. Anthony and Ariel were told by the people that Peter had been a fisherman in the land of Israel. He had spent most of his early life working on the Sea of Galilee, until he met a man called Jesus.

Anthony and Ariel could tell from the way the people talked about this Jesus that he was more than just a man. Often at night, when the two of them would be lying awake in bed, they could hear the people, especially the children, praying to him on behalf of Anthony and Ariel, asking him to heal them from their injuries. They also prayed that he would heal them from the inner pain that they were feeling. The two children could tell that they were praying, but not like the prayers with which they were familiar. The prayers that they had known were recited as if from a book or an established ritual. These people, and the children especially, simply spoke to this Jesus, as if they knew him personally, just as if they were talking to him face-to-face.

They called him Lord and God. This was very confusing for the two children, referring to a man as God or a god. Ariel had been raised in a Hebrew family. They believed that someday their Messiah, who was also their god, would come and deliver them from all the oppression from which their people were suffering. Her family believed that their Messiah had not yet come. She had heard the name of Jesus a few times among her family members, but they never spoke of him as their Messiah or even a prophet. Anthony had been raised in a Roman household, where he had been taught the worship of many gods. This Jesus was certainly not one of them.

Both the children saw something different in this Jesus, something that they had not seen in any other god or teaching. He had been a man, and yet he was so much more. He was for all people, regardless of gender, race, wealth, nation, or strength. He had a love for and an interest in each and every person. The stories that were told of him seemed so unbelievable and yet so real. His mother, a young girl called Mary, had conceived him when she was still a virgin. They knew that this was impossible, but for this god, nothing was impossible. They said that he could heal the blind, the deaf, or the crippled by simply touching them or giving a command. There were other stories about him that were even more fantastic, stories that said he had walked on the water of a stormy lake and had even calmed a storm by commanding it to cease.

Even more amazing than the stories that other people told of him were the stories he told himself. They were all very real, even mundane, but they were more than just stories. There was something far deeper to them. A shepherd who left ninety-nine sheep so he could rescue one that was lost, a father who forgave a son who brought him so much shame, an outcast who had compassion for the people who had rejected him. In everything that this Jesus did or said, there was a love greater than anything the children had ever heard of.

His life had ended thirty years prior, when the Romans crucified him. Both the children had only heard stories about this cruel form of torture being used in lands on the Roman frontier. It was the worst fate a man could suffer. To the death, all the way to the very end, this Jesus did not stop loving people, all people, even the ones who were killing him. He bore no hatred for his enemies. He had commanded his followers to love their enemies. He showed that same kind of love as he pled with God, whom he called his Father, to forgive the people who were killing him.

His enemies still seemed to be afraid of him even after he was dead. Roman soldiers were given the bizarre and unheard of task of guarding his grave to "make sure that nothing happened."

Three days after he was buried, his body mysteriously vanished from the grave where it had been laid. His friends said that he had indeed been killed but that he was not dead anymore. They said that they had seen him, alive, and that they were not just seeing things; he had truly risen from the dead. He continued to live among them for several more weeks. Then one day, he left. He left the land of Israel; he left the earth itself, but not by death. His followers had seen him ascend from the ground and disappear into the clouds.

He did not leave them hopeless. Two angels appeared and confirmed what he had said even before he had died, that he would come back to Earth again. He had warned them that difficult times lay ahead, but he also comforted them with a promise never to forsake them or abandon them when they needed him.

He had left them a code to live by, and he set the example by living his life as he said they should. Among his instructions were to love others as he had loved them, to serve others rather than demanding to be served, and to make whatever sacrifice was needed for God or for others. The one thing that could be seen in all his commands was his love; it seemed to be his life's story. Anthony and Ariel could see this love very clearly in the lives of his followers. This was greater than anything they had ever known. No other god they had ever heard of was so loving and yet so holy. No other god had cared for humankind enough to become a man and die in such a horrible way. Rising from the dead was impossible. No man or god had ever given his life for someone else and still managed to triumph by returning to life, but for Jesus, nothing was impossible.

Anthony and Ariel were awed by such love and power. As they heard and saw more of this god, they started to see themselves differently. Even though their parents had been proud of them as good children, that didn't seem important anymore. It did not matter how other people saw them, but how God saw them. Jesus had said that he had come into the world to save sinners. He had compassion for all men, for all men were the slaves of sin. By listening to the words of Jesus and their own consciences, they understood why and how much they truly needed him and what he had to offer, true life. He was not offering them a chance to live a life that was better or happier but to actually live life as it was meant to be, more abundantly, as only God could offer. This life would never end and could not be taken away by anyone or anything.

Overwhelmed by the awesomeness of God and his love for them in spite of their sins, Anthony and Ariel, each on their own, knelt before the Lord and spoke to him as they would to another person. They did not use the same words, but they each gave themselves fully to the same person, to Jesus Christ, the Son of God. He had always been God, but now he was their god. They gave themselves to him, believing that he would do what he said he would do, forgive them and receive them as his own. There was great joy in the catacombs that night and even greater joy in heaven. It had been a little over two months since the great fire.

During the time that they stayed in the catacombs, the children saw many other people who had been severely burned or injured in the fire. Before they had heard about Jesus, they were very worried about the injuries they had suffered, but now their injuries no longer seemed to matter. They were more concerned with the pain that other people were feeling. They had prayed to God that he would be heal them, but now they spent more time praying that God would heal the other people who were suffering. They rejoiced with the others who, like them, had found peace simply believing in Jesus Christ. As for the injuries the children had suffered, they managed to stand up and walk about after a week or two, but they were very sore and stiff. They had suffered quite a few cuts and bruises along with several burns. They regained their strength much faster than either had expected, and with the exception of a few scars, one would never have known about their injuries.

One night, a few days after giving their lives and hearts to Jesus, they and forty other people went down to the Tiber River, which flowed through Rome. The group gathered on a bank of the river a mile or so south of the city to ensure they would not be observed. The two children and ten others publicly confessed that they were followers of Jesus, the Son of God. They were baptized, immersed in the waters of the river, by Peter. They returned to the catacombs in high spirits, but very quietly so they would not attract attention.

Anthony and Ariel devoted their lives to serving the victims of the great fire and telling them what God had done in their lives. Sometimes they served in the catacombs; on other days, they would go out into the city, which they could scarcely recognize as the same one they had known before the great fire. Wherever they were, whatever they were doing, he, Jesus, was with them, and they were focused on pleasing him. This was how their life went on for about five months.

Each of the children returned to the place in the city where their families had been living, but there was nothing left but rubble and ashes. They asked around to find out if anyone knew what might have happened to their parents, but no one could tell them anything. Their hearts were almost broken with grief, fearing that their parents may have died and knowing the fate that awaited them in eternity. Still, they clung to the hope that somehow God had spared their parents' lives, and they trusted that their heavenly Father would care and comfort them in the middle of their sorrow. They continued to serve the people in the catacombs and the people in the city of Rome.

The children were joyful and content in their new life. The believers still had to work to provide for their basic needs, and many had lost their homes to the fire or because of their faith. Other believers who still had a house to live in generously opened them to those who had no place to stay. The believers in Rome—or followers of the Way, as they sometimes called themselves—met frequently to motivate, encourage, and pray with and for each other. They met in small groups wherever they could, usually in their homes. Meeting in the burial caves was not their first choice of assembly, but in the absence of any other alternative, they would meet in the catacombs. The conversation of the people as they met was intimate and personal. Though they gathered together numerous times in any given week, they were especially glad to meet on the first day of the week in remembrance of their Lord's resurrection. There was very little regular or official reading that went on among the followers of Jesus. Books were often difficult to acquire, and barely ten percent of believers could read. On occasion, one of the more educated members would read from some of the inspired writings the believers did have. When reading was done, it was often drawn from the writings of the Lord's prophets in Israel, and the law he had given them. Ariel was very familiar with these. Some of the more recent writings included a chronicle of the life of Jesus Christ, written by a man named Luke, who had written it while he was living in Rome. Another was a letter that had been written to the believers in Rome several years ago by one of the influential leaders of the Way, an apostle named Paul.

Jewish synagogues could be found in the city, as Rome was home to people of many different races. Many Jews lived in Rome and actively practiced their religion, which was recognized and protected by the Roman government. Descendants of Israel were not the only ones who practiced Judaism. Many Romans themselves had adopted Judaism as their religion and had even gone so far as to become Jews by way of circumcision.

The children were always glad to be in the company of their friends and brethren. The time was inspiring and refreshing. As time passed, the city gradually began to recover from the catastrophe of the fire. More of the believers who had been taking shelter at the catacombs were able to find better lodging and moved out. The area outside the city walls was home to a large percentage of the slave and lower-class population. This was not surprising considering that half of the population of Rome itself was comprised of slaves. The children had made some connections in the homes of people who lived outside the city. However, they had been unable to find a believer's house where they could obtain permanent residence. They were content living the life they knew God had provided for them, and they were passionate about the role he had given them in the story he was writing. Then one day something very extraordinary happened, an event that would change their lives forever.

Chapter 2

Kidnapped

It had been seven months' time since the great fire, and things were starting to look up for the city. Rome was able to provide some temporary food and shelter for the victims of the fire, and they were beginning to rebuild what the fire had destroyed. The emperor, Nero, had taken ownership of a large parcel of the land that had been burned out and was using it to build a palace. In the few weeks after the fire, the children had been working with the believers to reach out to the victims of the fire. Now several months later, they were able to find work helping the believers in their labors wherever they were needed. Some days they would be working in the city, alongside one of the believers in a shop, while on other days, they would be outside the city, tending crops in the field. On other occasions, they were needed to deliver food, clothes, and other essentials to people who needed them. They were also delivering messages to and from the catacombs from people who needed assistance. They informed the Christians of where the believers would gather and general news of what was happening throughout the city. Although accidental fires were common throughout the city, there were some rumors going around that the great fire had been set intentionally. The children and the other believers took little notice of rumors and gossip, being preoccupied with more important matters.

On this evening, the children had completed their tasks in the city and were on their way back to the catacombs. Their work today had kept them a bit later than usual, and only a few other people were on the streets traveling home.

Suddenly, as the children were passing by the entrance to a narrow alley, three men leaped out upon them. Before the children could react, the men covered their mouths to prevent them from screaming and pulled them back into the dark alley, where they bound and gagged Anthony and Ariel. The three men dragged the children back through the alley and into a small dilapidated and abandoned building. The three men were exceptionally strong and they overcame the children's best efforts to break free with ease. The men kept the children in the building, bound and gagged, until the sun had gone down. Then they dragged Anthony and Ariel out and began moving them through the alleys. It was completely dark outside, and the streets were deserted. The children knew that there was little chance of anyone coming to their rescue. With the children's hands tied behind their backs, and one man holding each of them, the three men led them away into the city.

Anthony and Ariel noticed that the men kept to the alleys and shadows as much as possible to avoid being seen. Whenever they were coming out of an alley, into the open, the lead man would look in all directions and then motion to the rest of the group to move on. After about fifteen minutes of walking, the group arrived at a small, dark house. It was one of several houses along the street, all of which were very small and showed no signs of being lived in. Neither of the children could tell where they were.

The lead man walked up to front door, knocked, and then whispered something through the keyhole that the children could not hear. The door was opened almost immediately, the children were hurried inside, and the door was barred behind them. After locking the door, the man who had been waiting inside the house lifted a torch stuck in a crevice of the wall and led the group through the house, carrying a ring of keys in his other hand.

The man led the group into a small room with two chairs and a table with a small oil lamp burning on top of it. There was not enough light for the children to distinguish anything else in the room except a solid wooden door in one corner.

The man carrying the torch strode over to the door and unlocked it. Anthony and Ariel were pushed into the room, and the door was shut and locked behind them. The floor and walls of the room were built of solid stone, and the door was made of strong wood; escape was impossible. Both children were still very confused as to why the men had seized them in this manner and then, instead of trying to rob or kill them, had chosen to imprison them. What were they planning to do next?

Both of them kept their ear to the door and listened for anything that might help them understand their situation. Two men remained outside talking for several hours. Unfortunately, the door was far too thick for them to hear anything that offered an explanation for their being kidnapped. It was very uncomfortable for the children lying there in the dark, with their hands tied behind their backs, and very frightening, as neither of them could see each other. They whispered to each other a little as they sat there in the dark but they were unable to get more than a few words out. The gravity of the situation had left them both, especially Ariel, in absolute shock. It was as if they were paralyzed in mind and in body. Still, they made themselves as comfortable as possible lying against the wall. Ariel fell asleep after they had been in the room for several hours, but Anthony kept on listening with his ear on the door. Nearly an hour after midnight, he faintly heard another man enter the room and address the two men. They spoke in much louder tones than they had been speaking, and Anthony was able understand what they were saying.

"Stay alert tonight," he said, "and make sure that those two children don't escape. The overseer will be here early in the morning. He will likely want the boy."

"And the girl?" one of the men asked.

"We will see," the man responded. "Maybe, maybe not."

Anthony kept on listening, but he heard nothing else. He decided that it would be best not to tell Ariel what he had heard.

He looked up toward the ceiling in the darkness and whispered through the gag, "Oh Lord, hear me now. Please don't forget us. Keep us strong for you. I believe that you still love us no matter what happens."

The night passed slowly. Anthony continued to listen at the door. He could hear the murmurs of two men talking to each other in low voices but could understand nothing of what they said. Eventually, he, too, fell asleep, leaning against the door. Even though the two children were frightened, they were also exhausted from the day's work.

They were awakened when the heavy wooden door swung open with a groan and a shaft of light fell upon them. Three men appeared; two of them entered the small room. Each man seized one of the children and escorted them out of the room. The third man stood by the doorway, holding a torch. It was morning, but the sun had not yet risen. With the man holding the torch leading the way, Anthony and Ariel were forced to walk through the house with the other two men holding them by the arm. From the dim light of the torch, they could see that they were in a house made of wood and brick, rather crudely built and in serious need of repair. The house was dirty and disheveled, with no furniture or any other normal household articles. They passed through several rooms, looking for something that might suggest where they were, but could see nothing that suggested anything, except an old abandoned house.

The man with the torch led them into a room with considerably more light coming from several lamps burning along the walls. This room had a table with several chairs around it. The chairs were a bit more elegant than the rest of the house and seemed rather out of place. Seated at the table were two other men, who appeared to be members of, or at least servants of, some upper-class household. The two men rose from their places. One of them stood by the table, while the other approached the two children. He fixed his gaze on Anthony for about a minute and then shifted his focus to the man carrying the torch.

"I accept," the man said. "He will work very well. Take him to the house, and tell them that I sent you. They will see that you are paid."

"What about the girl?" the man with the torch asked.

"Take her to the house too," the man said. "Show her to the master's daughters. I think they may be able to use her."

Anthony and Ariel were taken from the room and through a low doorway, which led out into an alleyway. Still exercising their usual caution, the men led them through a series of alleyways and passages, always keeping in the shadows and avoiding people as much as possible. The children could see from the surrounding buildings that they were in a rather run-down part of the city. They passed through an area that was under construction, and the children recognized it immediately. They were on the southeast side of the city, where the fire had done most of its damage. After about ten minutes of walking, they found themselves in another section of town that was far more beautiful and had escaped the devastation of the fire. The buildings were well kept and even a bit majestic in their construction and decoration. They reminded the children of some of the homes they had once lived in.

Just as the sun was beginning to make its full appearance on the horizon, their captors halted in a narrow passage just opposite a spacious and elegant house. Two of the men kept Anthony and Ariel in the shadows of the alley, while the third ventured across the street and knocked on the door of the house. They could not see who answered it, but after a minute or two of talking, the man turned and motioned to his friends to advance. The two men hurried the children across the street, into the house, and the door was quickly shut and locked behind them.

They were in a large, well-furnished room. The floor, walls, pillars, and ceiling were all made of finely cut and polished stone. It was still a bit dark inside, as another servant was just lighting the oil lamps. The lead man left the group standing by the door. He crossed over to the corner of the room and ascended a flight of stairs there. The two who remained removed the gags from the children's mouths. The third man returned shortly after, accompanied by two middle-aged men and a woman who looked to be about thirty years old. Judging from their dress, they were all members of the household staff. The three men crossed the room and stood before the two children, with their gazes fixed on Anthony.

Anthony felt the man who had been holding him release his grip. The older of the two men addressed Anthony and told him to follow him. Anthony walked after him with the other visitor from the empty house walking behind him. They led him through several halls and down a flight of stairs to a small room with a table and a chair behind it. The man seated himself at the table, seized a pen, and began to write on a parchment. Anthony stood opposite the man, waiting in silence.

After about a minute, the man looked up and told the second man, standing behind Anthony, to unbind his hands. After Anthony's hands were released, the older man began to question him. He asked Anthony his name, who his parents were, where he lived, and what work experience he had. Anthony answered all the questions honestly, explaining his life history up to the previous night. He was very careful to leave out that he had been staying at the catacombs with Christians, as the Romans called them. When he had lived with his family, he had heard them speak of Christians as seditionists and conspirators against Rome. Anthony was relieved that the man did not ask him any questions about Ariel. The man listened quietly to his story, wrote down a few more lines on the parchment, and continued with his questioning. He seemed a little surprised that this young boy claimed to be the member of an influential Roman family.

"Can you supply any proof that you are a member of this family?" the man questioned.

"No, sir, I'm afraid I cannot," Anthony replied.

"Do you have any relatives or reputable friends who can validate your claims?" the man inquired.

"I'm afraid not, sir, Anthony answered. "I have been unable to find any of my relatives or friends since the great fire."

"I will investigate your claims, but until then, can you be content to remain here as a servant to a Roman senator?" the man asked. "We will treat you well and see that your needs are met."

Several thoughts flashed through Anthony's mind. If he said no, they still wouldn't let him go unless he could prove his identity. They would only confine him, punish him, and guard him more closely. Worst of all, they might sell him to someone else, and being separated from Ariel, the only friend he had right now, was the last thing he wanted. If he agreed to serve them, he would have much more freedom. It was at this moment that Anthony heard something inside him saying to agree to what was being offered.

"I am yours," Anthony replied humbly. "I will serve you faithfully in any way I can."

The man smiled. "You say you come from a Roman family. Can you read and write?"

"I can read and write both Greek and Latin," Anthony replied. Greek was a more common language that was spoken all throughout the empire. Latin was not widely spoken except among Roman citizens.

The man suddenly rose from his chair and motioned Anthony to sit down. "Sit here, and write as I tell you," he ordered.

Anthony sat down and wrote several lines of Greek and Roman poetry as the man dictated to him. He wrote first in Greek, and then the man told him to write what he had written in Latin. Anthony completed this with no trouble at all. After about five minutes, the man told him to stop.

"Excellent, Senator Marcus may be able to put that skill to good use. My name is Claudio. I am the overseer of Senator Flavius Aurelius Marcus's house. Go with Rufus," he said, motioning to the servant standing behind Anthony. "Today you will be helping him in the household gardens."

Anthony bowed respectfully, as he had seen many of his family's servants do, and followed Rufus to the gardens. He had eaten nothing since the previous morning and was feeling a bit faint. When they reached the gardens, he respectfully asked Rufus if he might have some water. Rufus told him to start working and that he would receive water later. Like all traditional Roman palaces, the garden was located at the back of the house and was the chosen place for a family to spend the evening after a day of work. Anthony noted the size of the garden that it was much larger than any other garden he had ever been in.

It was midmorning, nearly two hours later, before Anthony received some water, and he continued working in the garden with Rufus and two other servants, Titus and Alexis. He was not given any food the whole day, and by midafternoon, he was nearly exhausted. Still, he worked on, praying to God that he would be given the strength he needed.

At last, Rufus noticed that he was becoming faint and permitted him to eat a small amount of fruit and bread. As the evening was drawing near, Rufus told Anthony to stop and go with the two other servants to wash themselves, change their clothes, and serve at a feast for the senator's family and their distinguished guests. Anthony followed Titus and Alexis to a small room where they found a washbasin. After Anthony had finished washing himself and was given some more formal clothes for serving at the banquet, he assisted the two other servants in decorating and assembling the banquet hall for the feast. They had just finished making the last finishing touches to the hall when the guests began to arrive. Anthony was quite familiar with the internal workings and schedule of a Roman household. The family would rise early in the morning as the sun came up and quickly be off and about their business. Business and work activities came to an end in the midafternoon, after which they would return to their homes to eat dinner, the largest meal of the day, with friends and family. All members of the household retired when night fell. Almost no activity went on after sundown.

The activities of that evening kept all of the household servants very busy. Anthony and Titus were tasked with bringing platters of food to the banquet hall located just in front of the garden. After bringing in the new dishes of food, they removed those that were empty. They also carried new jugs of wine up from the cellars when more wine was needed. Like all other upper-class Roman houses, this one had been built with special passages for servants to go here and there throughout the house without disturbing their masters. Anthony and the other servants would slip quietly into the dining hall and back out being as inconspicuous as possible.

All the guests and family were seated on couches set up in a rectangular pattern. The couches were large enough to seat as many as three people. The guests all ate their meals half lying on their sides, resting on one elbow. There were no utensils used in the course of the evening, as Anthony well knew there wouldn't be. The Romans ate all their meals with their bare hands.

Each time Anthony was called into the hall, he scanned the room, hoping to spot Ariel, but she was nowhere to be found. At first, he began to worry that their kidnappers might have taken her to be sold somewhere else. The very thought made Anthony sweat. Worried and distracted, he collided with Rufus as he was carrying a platter of meat from the kitchen to the senator's couch.

Anthony had just set the tray down before the guests, and was returning to the kitchen with an empty dish, when he suddenly stopped dead in his tracks, his mouth wide open. *There she is,* Anthony said silently to himself. *At least I think that's her.*

Anthony had to look three times before contenting himself that it was indeed Ariel. She had been standing in the hall, behind one of the couches, the whole time, but she was dressed in such elegant clothes that Anthony had not recognized her. She was working a fan for three young women seated on a couch on the opposite side of the room to the senator's couch. Ariel turned, looked him straight in the eyes with a smile and then motioned him on with her eyes. Hastily regaining his composure, Anthony strode out of the hall and breathed a sigh of relief. Ariel was still here, and no one had noticed how he froze upon seeing her.

Rufus had told Anthony that several members of the Roman Senate would be present for this feast and that all servants must perform at their best. Anthony knew a good deal of what took place at such an event and was able to keep his head and carry out his tasks without too much trouble. He was still a bit afraid of what was happening but continued praying that God would give him the strength and faith he needed. He also thanked the Lord that both he and Ariel were safe, at least for the moment.

After the meal was concluded, the guests moved out to the garden for the final festivities. It was a cool, breezy evening, and the leafy canopy that shaded the outside garden made for quite a relaxing atmosphere. At one end of the garden, there was a group of musicians playing for most of the evening. At intervals, one or several fairly dressed young girls would come out and dance for the guests while the musicians played on. Magicians, poets, and other entertainers also played a part in the festivities as the sun descended to the edge of the western sky.

The stars were just starting to come out when the guests finally began to take their leave. The servants were exhausted from the demands of the feast, and after the guests had departed, the banquet hall still had to be cleaned and reset. Anthony noticed that Ariel had been paying special attention to two of the young women who had been sitting opposite the senator's couch. They two young ladies were dressed in radiant clothes, and Anthony presumed them to be in their middle or late teen years. He had observed that at a certain point right after the guests had departed, Ariel and a few other maids had left the banquet hall. Then, half an hour later, they had returned and assisted with resetting it.

Anthony assisted some the servants with cleaning the dishes used in the banquet. Nearly all the dishes were made of metal and cleaned by rubbing them down with sand. The servants must have been at work until nearly nine o'clock before Claudio told them that they could retire for the night. Anthony followed the servants to the second floor of the building, where they all would spend the night. The senator and his family slept on the second floor of the house, as did the servants, though in separate quarters. This was a common practice in nearly all of the Roman households. Anthony did not see where Ariel or any of the other maids retired and still wondered what was to become of the two of them. The servants washed their hands and faces in a washbasin and hurriedly collapsed into their beds. Anthony was given a blanket and a corner in a room with several other male servants. As he lay down, he spoke to God one more time before falling asleep.

"Why here, Lord? What do you have for us here? You gave me the strength to keep going; now I need the strength to trust you. Watch over us and give us favor in this house. Oh Jesus, I am afraid. Please, don't leave us now."

He fell asleep and did not wake up again until the next morning.

The sun was just starting to come up when the servants arose for the duties of the day. Anthony was ordered by Claudio to continue his work in the gardens. He pressed on, hoping that soon he would have a chance to speak to Ariel and learn more of their situation. He continued pleading silently with the Lord for strength and for understanding of what was going to happen.

The Final Message to Rome

A little before noon, a few other servants were called away to serve the senator's family their midday meal. The meals at morning and midday in a Roman house were comparatively small to what was eaten in the evening. Rufus told Anthony to continue his work until after the meal was over, and then he would be called to the kitchen to receive his portion. After he had eaten, he was to return to the garden. A little before the noon meal was served, Anthony was walking to the garden fountain to draw some water for the plants, when he came upon two elegantly dressed young women sitting on one side of the fountain, relaxing on a couch. He recognized them as the same two that Ariel had been paying special attention to at the feast and remembered what their kidnappers had said two nights ago about the master's daughters. Ariel may have been assigned to them as a maid-in-waiting. Roman families often had servants who were assigned to specific members of the family. If so, then Ariel would likely be somewhere close by. As he filled his water jug for the plants, he looked quickly around the garden to see if he could spot Ariel, but she was nowhere in sight. Returning to his assigned task, he continued on to the section of the garden where he had been working. Just then, one of the young women rang a small bell. Anthony immediately slowed his pace; they could be ringing for Ariel. His suspicions proved correct. Ariel appeared a few moments later from a garden entrance concealed by a hedge just behind where the ladies were seated.

Upon seeing each other, Ariel slowed her walk into the garden, and Anthony almost dropped his water jug. Fortunately, they both managed to regain their composure and proceeded with their duties. Ariel approached the women who were seated on the couch, bowed, and stood before them in silence, waiting for their instructions. Anthony walked by quickly, going to the section of the garden where he had left off watering. After emptying his jug, he returned to the fountain to draw more. On his way, he met the two women, followed by Ariel, coming down the garden path. Anthony, familiar with household procedure and courtesy, stepped off the path and bowed respectfully as they passed him. He looked up again to see Ariel walking by. As she passed, she dropped something that looked like a crumpled piece of paper into the bushes beside the path and then looked back at him with a smile. After the party had passed, Anthony picked up the water jug and ventured back onto the brick pathway. He looked over at the bushes to see what Ariel had planted. Among the plants and leaves, he spotted a small, wadded piece of parchment or something very much like it. He was about to pick it up, when out of the corner of his eye, he spotted some other people coming down the same path: a middle-aged man and woman, both very finely dressed. Anthony immediately stepped off the path and bowed. He decided to go back to the fountain, refill the water jug, and then come back for the paper. Hopefully by then, the path would be deserted.

When Anthony returned, the path was clear. He found the spot where Ariel had dropped the parchment and pulled it out from among the bushes. On the parchment, written in Greek, were the words "Tonight at the fountain." Anthony quickly hid the message under his clothes, picked up his water jug, and proceeded to his duties.

Chapter 3

A Midnight Meeting

Anthony did not see Ariel again for the rest of the afternoon. As the evening approached, he began to get a little worried. How would he get to the fountain at night without being seen? He completed his work in the garden and assisted with the evening meal, which was much less formal and simpler than the previous evening. When the meal was over and the hall had been cleaned and reset, the servants returned to their sleeping quarters. Anthony lay down in his corner but made sure that he did not fall asleep. He waited for about half an hour, until he was sure that all of the servants had retired and were fully asleep. Then he rose up quietly and crept out of the room. Crouching down at the door, he looked around the corner to make sure that no one was outside. Then he slipped out, barely making the faintest sound. Once out, he stood pressed up against the wall in the shadows and listened. The house was completely still, no noise whatsoever. Taking care to stay in the shadows, he snuck back downstairs to the garden and hid behind some bushes where he could see the fountain and still keep out of sight.

He had not been there for more than a minute when he saw a figure emerge from behind the thick hedgerow on the other side of the fountain. It beckoned him to come over behind the hedge. He could not tell for sure if it was Ariel but ventured out quietly and ducked behind the hedge where he had seen the figure come out, taking care not to make any noise rustling or crunching any leaves. Ariel was there. With the illumination of the night sky, Anthony could see her as she stepped out of the shadows. What a joy it was to see her, her face tender with a radiant smile and her blue eyes shining in the starlight. She had let her thick brown hair down flowing over her shoulders. Something had changed; something was different about her. Never before had Anthony seen her as being so beautiful. The two embraced each other, overjoyed that they were back together. Both the children felt a little more comfortable and safe now. They were well concealed behind the hedge; the house was totally quiet and best of all there was no one on the ground floor who could overhear them. Everyone was asleep upstairs. In Roman households all members slept on the second floor both master and slave. The whole house had been exhausted by the long day of work and it was unlikely than anyone would wake up till morning. Still they were both careful to keep their voices to a whisper.

"What happened to you?" they both asked at the same time.

Anthony related his story first, as briefly as possible. He told her about his interview with Claudio, the house overseer, and his work with Rufus and the other servants in the gardens and at the banquet. Anthony had collected as much information as he could by asking the other servants about the senator, what went on around the house, and what was happening throughout the city. He had also observed as much of the layout of the house as he could.

Ariel listened attentively as Anthony told his tale. Once or twice she stopped him and asked him to clarify some fact that he had learned about the house, the senator, and what was happening in Rome. She also asked if he had overheard anything important during the feast on the previous evening. Anthony told her that he had not overheard anything that might interest them, only the guests making merry of themselves, laughing and joking. Ariel nodded slightly and then began to explain what had happened to her since they had been separated.

"After they took you away, the men who captured us kept me in the front room for a few minutes. Then the man who had left us for a moment came back down the stairs along with that woman you saw, about twenty or thirty years old. The lady looked at me quietly for a few moments and then motioned for us to follow her. We followed her up the stairs to one small storeroom. My hands were still tied. The woman crossed over to the other side of the room, opened a chest that was full of clothes, and began looking through it. After a minute or so of searching, she pulled some clothes out of the chest, walked over to me, and began asking questions.

"She started out by asking my name, where I was from, who my parents were, most of the same questions they asked you. I told her everything she wanted to know, but I made sure to leave out that I was a follower of Jesus.

"The woman asked me, 'Are you related to the boy you were brought in with?' I said no. I'm glad she did not ask anything else about you.

"She then asked if I could give her the names of anyone who could affirm that I at least had the rights of a Roman citizen. I told her that I hadn't been able to find any of my friends and family since the fire.

"After I answered all her questions, she told the men to untie me. They released my hands, and she led me across the room and into a closet. It was filled with elegant clothes and towels all hung up on hooks or bars against the wall. There was a little bit of daylight in the room, coming through a small window or a skylight. She handed me the clothes she had taken from the chest.

"'Put these on,' she said commandingly. 'You are now a maid in this house.'

Her manner seemed to have changed. She seemed a bit gentler than when she had spoken to me in front of the men.

"'My name is Julia,' she continued. 'I am in charge of all the woman servants in this house. We needed a young girl to wait on Senator Marcus's two daughters, Gloria and Floriana. You and I will be serving them their morning meal in the house garden. Change into these clothes, and wait here until I come back.'

"She left the room and shut the door behind her. I changed into the clothes, but I hid my old clothes under a chest where I could remember to find them. I was looking around the room, trying to learn what was kept in this rather large storage room or closet, when she got back. She threw the door open and told me to follow her quickly to the garden.

We hurried down to the garden and arranged a table and some chairs. After that, we hurried to the kitchen and brought the food for Gloria and Floriana's morning meal. We arrived just in time as the two of them were coming into the garden. Julia did most of the serving. She had me standing behind their sofa with a fan or running back to the kitchen to bring more food. When the two ladies had finished eating, Julia told me to remove the dishes and return them to the kitchen. After I had cleared everything, she told me to come and stand in front of the two sisters. The two of them looked me over for a few seconds and then at each other. They smiled. Julia told them a few things about me and that they had brought me here thinking that I might serve well as a maid. They then asked me my name, my age, and if I had any previous experience as a maid-in-waiting. I said that I did not.

"One of them turned to Julia and said, 'We'll see how she does.'

"Julia nodded and told me that from now on, I was to act as their personal attendant for whatever they needed. I smiled and nodded. 'Gladly.'

"The two sisters got up and motioned me to follow them. 'This way,' they said as they made their way out of the garden.

"I waited on the two of them for most of the morning, with Julia observing now and then from a distance. I brought them whatever they called for and worked the fan. In the afternoon, they sent me to help decorate the great hall for the feast. They came down to the hall shortly before all the people arrived and told me to wait on them personally. I waited on them for the evening and helped them prepare for the night by bringing clothes and putting out the lights. They told me to go back to the hall and help reset it after they retired. I saw you helping in the hall, and I wanted to talk to you, but there was too much to do and too many people around. After a few hours, Julia told me to retire for the night and to be ready to serve the senator's daughters early in the morning. She showed me where I was to sleep and then left.

"I have been serving as a maid-in-waiting to the senator's daughters ever since. They have been very kind, and even patient with me, as I am still growing accustomed to serving in a Roman household. It is very tiring constantly being on call for whatever they may need. I have certainly received strength from the Lord that I have not had before."

Anthony smiled. "I have been praying for strength too," he said. "There is just enough for today, but I have to trust God for tomorrow."

Ariel smiled back. "I saw you working in the garden," she said. "I could tell that you were struggling to hang on."

"I was," Anthony replied, "but I was also praying for God's strength and his presence, for both of us. He allowed us to be brought here, and he promised that he would not leave us. I still wonder why he brought us here and what is happening to the rest of our friends."

At this, Ariel's expression changed to a very serious look, and Anthony could tell that something was really bothering her.

"I think I know why, Anthony," Ariel said, "and that is also why I asked you to come here tonight. I had to speak to you as soon as possible. Something very bad is about to happen."

"Tell me," Anthony said. "What is wrong?"

Ariel continued, "Last night at the feast, while I was waiting on the senator's daughters, I overheard some of the other guests talking. It would seem that Senator Marcus is a very influential member of the Roman Senate. Several of the guests last night were also Senate members. They were talking about some future plans of the emperor, Nero. Everyone in Rome is wondering how the fire got started. Some rumors have been going around that Nero may have started the fire for some political or personal reason. The word has spread very quickly around the city, and while most people may not believe the rumor, they have become very suspicious.

"The word has gotten back to the emperor, and he intends to divert suspicion by putting the blame on all the Christians in Rome. Then he plans to have every Christian tortured and killed as an enemy of the state. That means us, all our friends back at the catacombs and inside the city. I have heard from Peter and others about what has been happening to the church around the world. We have suffered some terrible things since Jesus returned to his Father, but judging from what the guests were saying, what Nero plans to unleash will be far worse than anything we have ever faced. I'm worried about our friends; I think we need to warn them so they can be prepared for what is about to happen."

Anthony was very surprised and was silent for several seconds before regaining himself.

"Christ warned us that this would happen," he said quite solemnly as he hung his head. "He said that if they hate me, they would hate you. They crucified him. Why wouldn't they do the same to us? I remember hearing my parents talk a little about Christians. They spoke of them as rebels who were trying to overthrow Rome. Nobody in the world will ever truly love or accept people like us."

"I know, Anthony," Ariel replied, "but from what the guests said, this is going to be unlike anything we have ever seen before. My parents lived in Jerusalem right around the time Jesus returned to his Father. They saw what the Christians suffered at the hands of Saul of Tarsus. They could not believe the reports from Damascus that Saul the Pharisee had become Paul the Apostle. The religious rulers have especially hated us, but just like Jesus, it was difficult for them to turn the people against us. This was because of all the miracles, the loving works that the disciples did, and especially the way God spoke through Peter and the other apostles. Jesus told them to 'let their light shine before men, that they may see your good works and praise your Father in heaven.' The disciples did just that, and it worked. The religious leaders were also doing good works, but they were doing it so they would be praised for it, and the people saw through the whole thing. Jesus called them hypocrites, and he proved it to everyone. All he had to do was be himself. This is why they hated us."

Ariel went on, "The leaders in Israel and Rome have hated us, but the fire in Rome is just the opportunity that they have been waiting for. It's the perfect excuse for them to justify their real plans. Rome has accused Christians of being enemies of the state for years, but they have never been able to prove it. We have never started a riot, tried to overthrow the government, or done anything that really qualifies as an act of treason. Rome has never been able to really convince its citizens, or even the slaves in Rome, that we are enemies of the state. Now things have changed. If the emperor can convince the citizens that the

Christians started the fire, they will start believing that we are dangerous people. They will cry out for us to be killed everywhere. They will hunt us down like animals.

"I have heard from Peter that Rome has been persecuting Christians, but this would be much worse than anything Rome has ever done. Nero plans to wage war on us, a real war, unlike anything we have ever seen or heard about. Now our only hope is the Lord. Before Jesus returned to heaven, he promised that he would always be with us, even to the end of the world. He would not leave us or forsake us. We need him now more than ever, and so do our friends."

Anthony and Ariel were silent for a long time. They both knew full well the danger of going out into the city at night. Nearly all the people of Rome returned to their houses well before dark and didn't come out until morning. They had good reason to. The streets were incredibly dangerous after dark; it was then that all the robbers and thieves would be about. No one in their right mind would go out when the criminals had free rein of the city. Though the city did have night patrols, only a small portion of the city could be protected, and anyone who went out without a very large armed escort would be attacked, robbed, beaten, or even killed. Thinking of the danger, Anthony hesitated, but when he thought of his friends and what would befall them, he nodded in agreement.

"You are right, Ariel," he said. "We do need to warn the others, but how? We don't know where we are or how to get back to the catacombs."

Rising to her feet, Ariel peeked out from behind the hedge into the garden. She looked this way and that. Once she was sure that there was no one watching them, she stepped out into the moonlight. Motioning to Anthony to follow her, she led him back into the main house, toward the front room. She led him into a small storeroom.

It was dark in the room, and Ariel kept the door open to let in what little light there was from the house oil lamps and the moon. She began searching through the various articles of fabric, jugs, and other household tools and supplies. Finally, she found what she was looking for, a small oil lamp. With a small piece of steel and a flint stone, she lit the lamp, set it down on the floor, and closed the door. She and Anthony knelt, holding a large blanket around the lamp to prevent its light from showing under the door. Ariel reached under her clothes and pulled out a folded piece of parchment. When she spread it out on the floor next to the lamp, Anthony saw that it was a map showing a very detailed outlay of the city. He guessed that a professional mapmaker must have drawn it up.

"I found this in the household library," Ariel said. "It shows the whole city, and I was able to figure out where we are. The senator's house is right here in the southeast section of the city." She pointed to a place on the map. "The catacombs that we were living in are also on the south side. It's a little over two miles away. You and I are fairly familiar with that area of the city. We worked there helping people who had been hurt by the fire."

Ariel refreshed Anthony's memory to some of the things that had happened to them in the past few months, mentioning certain roads, buildings, statues, and other landmarks. Anthony quickly recognized the places that Ariel was referring to.

"I know the area you're talking about, Ariel, but it will be very difficult for me to get back to the catacombs in the night," he warned.

"Anthony, I know it is dangerous, but I think we both should go. We'll have a better chance of finding our way there and back if we go together. Besides, I want to see our friends again," Ariel said.

Anthony nodded. "Very well, we'll go together. Which roads should we take?"

"The best way to get back without getting lost is to follow these roads," Ariel said, pointing to two roads on the map. "We'll follow this road east. Very soon we will come to a crossroads just inside the city walls. From there we turn right and follow the road heading southwest. This road leads to another crossroads on one of the major highways going out of the city. You and I have used this road many times to get in and out of the city. You should recognize it. At the crossroads, we turn left and follow the road out of the city; it's not far. Once outside we will be out of the dense part of the city. The land slopes downhill outside the city walls. We should head south along the road to a ridge running south and follow that to the Via Latina. Once we find the Via Latina it will lead us straight to the catacombs."

Anthony nodded, "I just hope we don't get caught."

"I have thought of that," said Ariel as she got up and started looking through some of the items in the storeroom. "Here they are. I found the clothes that you had on when the men kidnapped us. I kept them hidden with the clothes that I was wearing. Put them on. They are not as fancy as the ones we have to wear in the senator's house. Hopefully, we won't attract as much attention, but even with these clothes, we still have to stay hidden. The criminals rule the streets at night. If they find us, we're dead."

Ariel handed Anthony his old clothes. "Change into these. I'll watch the door."

Ariel moved the lamp farther back in the closet, behind some chests, in order to give Anthony enough light to change his clothes and still prevent the light from being seen from outside. She kept watch at the door while he changed clothes, and then he watched while she changed.

Once back in her old clothes, Ariel blew out the oil lamp. The two children slipped out of the storeroom very quietly and closed the door. Walking softly, they crept through the house, taking care to stay in the shadows and listening for any noise. They made it to the side door of the house, close to the garden; no one had seen them. Ariel pulled a key out of a small pouch she was wearing and unlocked the door quietly. The two children slipped out into the alley, and Ariel secured the door behind them. They then crept down the alley toward the street. The moon was full that night, and the stars were out.

The two paused before going out into the street. Anthony took Ariel's hand, lifted his gaze skyward, and whispered, "Dear Lord Jesus, protect us. Guide us through the darkness, and show us the way back to the catacombs. Hide us from anyone who might see us, and strengthen all of us to endure what is about to happen."

Chapter 4

INTO THE ALLEYS

There was no noise to be heard from where they stood, so they crept out into the street. They turned left, heading east down the road, still taking care to stay in the shadows of the buildings. The road the children traveled down was very narrow, as they knew it would be. All the streets in Rome were narrow; even the main highways rarely exceeded sixteen feet in width.

Although the street was quiet and deserted, the children kept their eyes and ears on the alert. The city of Rome was without streetlamps. Fortunately, there was a full moon out, giving just enough light for the children to navigate the streets and still escape detection. The streets were littered with debris, and they had to watch where they stepped for fear of slipping or making noise. As there was no established system for the removal of garbage, the citizens simply tossed it and their waste out into the streets, where it remained until a heavy rain washed it away.

The first set of crossroads Ariel had mentioned was just a little over two hundred yards from the senator's house, but because the children were proceeding in such a cautious manner, it took much longer than usual to cover the distance.

They were about fifty yards from the crossroads when Anthony, who was in the lead, suddenly stopped.

"What's wrong?" Ariel whispered.

"Look at the crossroads," Anthony replied. "It's too wide. We'll have to go out into the open to get around the corner. We can't risk being spotted."

"According to the map, the road turns sharply to the right," Ariel responded. "Let's get over to the other side of the street and see if we can get around the corner without going into the light."

"All right," Anthony agreed, "but quickly and quietly."

Ariel nodded. She and Anthony looked both directions and then crossed the street. The two kept close to the walls of the buildings and continued edging their way up to the crossroads. They stopped approximately ten yards from where the roads intersected. They did not dare go any farther for fear of walking into the light. The two waited for several seconds, listening and looking around for anyone who might be about. Both considered whether they should take the risk.

"I don't see or hear anyone," Ariel offered. "Following the roads is the best way to get out of the city without getting lost. Hopefully, no one will see us if we go quickly."

Anthony exhaled a deep breath. "I guess you're right. We'll just have to—" Anthony strained his eyes, gazing across the street. "Wait. Get back up against the wall."

"What's wrong?" Ariel asked.

"There, in the shadows," Anthony replied, pointing across the intersection.

Ariel looked. At first she saw nothing, but as she strained her eyes, she saw something move. Anthony was right; something or someone was moving in the shadows on the corner opposite them. In a few seconds, a Roman soldier stepped out of the shadows, into the dim light. He scanned the crossroads and streets that led into the intersection and then stepped back into the darkness.

"He's a sentry," Anthony whispered, "and he's not alone. There are others with him. We'll never get around the corner without being spotted."

"Then what should we do?" Ariel pressed. "We have to warn the others."

"I don't know how we'll get out," Anthony said, "unless..."

Anthony paused in midsentence again. As he did this, he turned his gaze back along wall they had been sneaking along.

"Move back along the walls of the buildings," said Anthony. "I have an idea."

The two turned and began edging their way along houses that lined the street. Several houses down from where they had stopped, the two children came upon a dark alley that ran between two of the buildings.

"This is it," Anthony said. "I remember this street. This alleyway leads down among some of the houses and away from the main road. Then it connects with another passage that links with the road going south out of the city. It should take us around the corner and past the guards."

"Do you think we can find our way in the dark?" Ariel asked.

"It's the only way we can get past those guards," Anthony said. "We have to hurry if we want to make it out to the catacombs and get back before everyone wakes up. Follow me."

With Anthony leading the way, the two slipped into the alleyway and moved through cautiously, watching and listening for any danger. Once they were a good distance from the road, Anthony quickened his pace while still keeping alert.

After about two or three minutes of walking, Anthony slowed his pace and began looking to the left side of the alley. Suddenly, he stopped and held up his hand as if he had heard something. His gaze shifted this way and that.

"Ariel," he whispered gravely, "there is someone else in the alley with us. I don't know where or how many, but I think we are being followed."

The two children glanced back down the alleyway but could see no one. Anthony gently grabbed Ariel's arm.

"They're almost certainly thieves, and they know this alleyway better than I do. Let's get out of here as fast as we can," Anthony urged.

The two children stole along as quickly as they could, still listening intently. Anthony was right, they were being followed, and by more than just one. Although it was too dark in the alley for them to see, they could hear the sound of footsteps growing closer and closer. Sensing a growing feeling of panic, Anthony took in and released several deep breaths to regain his composure. Having sufficiently calmed himself, he glanced about, looking and listening for a possible escape.

"Ariel," Anthony whispered, "Pick up some stones as you walk. I have an idea."

Both of them grabbed some small rocks lying beside the walls of the passage, still moving as fast as they could.

"There it is," Anthony whispered at last. "This is the passage that should take us back to the main road."

Ariel breathed a sigh of relief, but the next moment, her heart stopped. The side alleyway was several yards up the passage, but directly beyond it, she and Anthony saw a group of shadowy figures step into the dim light of the passage, walking in their direction. If those men got between them and the side passage, they would be trapped between two groups of men who intended to rob them or do them harm.

The group before them had almost cleared the side alleyway when Anthony whispered, "I don't think they have seen us. Throw your rocks at the men in front of us, and then pick up some more; let's see if we can drive them back."

With their hands trembling, the children hurled the few missiles in their hands at the shadowy figures before them. Shouts of pain were heard as the men in front of them were met by the barrage of stones. Having exhausted their supply, the children grabbed up more from the pavement and continued the attack. The strategy proved effective; the group in front of them began to fall back. Anthony and Ariel advanced quickly, still throwing more stones and keeping in the shadows to conceal their position. They continued forward until they made it up to the passageway. Ariel was just about to run for it, when she felt Anthony grab her arm.

"Don't run just yet," he said. "Push them back a little farther, then throw a few rocks at the men behind us, and then we'll run, but quietly."

Ariel did as Anthony said. They kept moving forward, hurling stones down the alley. By now the men in front of them were out of the light and could not be seen, but the children kept throwing stones into the darkness, hoping the rocks would find their intended targets. The plan worked. The men in front of them had been so surprised by the sudden attack that they had not thrown any stones in their defense but had retreated instead.

After the two children had passed the entrance to the passageway by about three yards, Anthony whispered with urgency, "Now."

They turned, and each threw no more than three rocks at the figures who had been following them and who had also gained on them significantly. This surprise attack stunned their pursuers, who also quickly retreated. This gave the children just enough time to slip out of the alleyway before both groups of men began hurling stones down the alleyway at each other, supposing that they were pelting their intended prey. The children could hear the rattle and clink of a barrage of the rocks hitting the walls and floor of the passage, accompanied by shouts of pain. They rushed back to the main road as fast as they could. They had spent no more than seven minutes in the alleyway, but it felt like an hour to them.

With Anthony leading the way, the two children hurried down the alley, knowing that at any moment, their pursuers could be upon them again. Fortunately, after a few minutes of running, they came out of the passage and found themselves back on the road heading south. They emerged with caution, still keeping in the shadows and looking for any soldiers who might be patrolling the streets. They still had a good distance to cover before reaching the second set of crossroads that they would have to navigate through if they were to make it out of the city.

The road they were on intersected the other highway almost perfectly at a right angle. At the intersection, the highway split into four directions, heading north south, east and west. They would be heading south. They approached the intersection, listening and gazing intently over the road and the surrounding buildings. They saw nothing. The road showed no signs of being under guard, but both knew that a soldier could step out of the shadows at any moment.

"What shall we do, Anthony?" Ariel whispered.

Anthony was silent for a few moments. He surveyed the road for a few seconds and then looked down to the ground, contemplating what they should do next; then he spoke. "This set of crossroads is not as well lit as the last one. I think we can get around the corner without going into the light."

The children took a second look at the crossroads and then began edging their way closer along the buildings beside the road. Anthony was right; they were able to get around the corner at the intersection without exposing themselves. They maneuvered around the corner, and were off along the road heading south out of Rome.

Because this last leg of the journey would be the longest, nearly half a mile, the children hurried along as fast as they could, still keeping their eyes and ears open. The time passed quickly. The two children did not encounter any other people on the road as they hurried along. They were getting closer to their destination, but they both realized that they had yet to overcome the most formidable obstacle they would encounter.

The senator's house was located inside the city walls. According to the map, the road they were following would lead them to one of the city gates, but how would they get through? By now the gate would certainly be locked and heavily guarded. Any guard would be suspicious of two children sneaking out of the city in the dead of night, and at present, the children knew of no other way to get out of the city. The city wall was around thirty feet high. Scaling it and climbing or jumping down the other side would be fatal, especially in the dark. The two slowed their pace to walk as they considered this problem.

Ariel looked up at Anthony with a shadow of fear and anxiety on her face. "Anthony, how will we get through the gate?" she asked. Anthony's expression showed that he was wondering the same thing.

"I don't know," he said. "That gate is our best hope of getting out of the city. Still, getting past the sentries and opening the gate without being seen is absolutely impossible."

Anthony's assessment proved correct. With some difficulty, the children made it within thirty yards of the gate and halted, puzzled and frustrated over the obstacle standing before them.

The area around the gate was well illuminated by multiple torches. They did not dare venture any closer for fear of exposing themselves to the light. Judging from the size of the gate, the children knew that it was far too heavy for them to open by themselves. Two sentries were clearly visible standing on either side of the gate, and Anthony was certain that there would be more up on the wall.

Anthony exhaled a deep breath and shook his head; they would not be getting out this way. Seeing his response, Ariel reached down and grabbed his hand. Anthony looked over at her.

"I think I know what we need to do," she said.

Looking into her eyes, he knew immediately what she meant. Both the children bowed their heads for a few seconds and then lifted their gazes skyward, wondering and silently asking their Lord to give them a way out. They stood there waiting to see if anything would develop. After about five minutes, they sat down with their backs against the stone wall of a building, waiting and hoping.

Another ten minutes passed, but nothing changed. The torches continued burning, and the guards remained at their posts; there was no possible way for them to approach the gates without being spotted.

Then, just as both of them were about ready to give up hope, Ariel heard a noise approaching from the direction of the road they had just traveled. The city had been serenely silent, so it caught her attention immediately. Anthony heard the noise too and rose up quickly, as it seemed to be coming closer.

"Wheels, I think some kind of wagon is coming this way," Ariel offered.

Anthony nodded. "A chariot, to be exact."

The children stepped back into a gap between two buildings, still watching the gate. The two stood against the wall as the soft rumble of wheels and the clicking of horses' hooves approached. It was a chariot, carrying two Roman soldiers in full armor, one driving the horses and the other standing by. The one standing by clearly appeared to be of high rank and esteem from his age and decorative armor. The other was a very young soldier wearing armor that was standard for a normal legionnaire.

The chariot stopped in front of the gate, and the sentries saluted the officer. The officer motioned for the gate to be opened, and the two sentries immediately scrabbled to remove the locks and bars.

The children saw that even the guards found opening the gate very difficult. The chariot was just about to drive on, when suddenly the two horses pulling the chariot reared up as if frightened by something and dashed forward, braying in a very disturbed manner. The sudden action of the horses caught the officer and the driver by surprise, causing them to lose their balance and fall backward out of the chariot. The horses continued to run forward, pulling the empty chariot with them. The two sentries tried to stop the horses, but to no avail. The two steeds dashed straight out of the city gates, knocking both the sentries to the ground. All four soldiers rose up quickly and rushed out after the chariot. Just a stone's throw outside the gate, the horses paused and the soldiers caught up with them. Just as the soldiers thought they had regained the horses, they reared up yet again and dashed off at full gallop.

For a moment, the children stood completely dumbfounded by what they had seen. In less than ten seconds, all the men at the gate were gone. Seeing their opportunity, Anthony and Ariel regained their composure and ran as fast as they could toward the gates. They cleared the archway with no trouble and were exhilarated to be outside the city walls.

Thinking of the guards watching from atop the wall, Anthony grabbed Ariel's hand and ran off the road heading southeast. They had only covered a few paces when Anthony suddenly grabbed Ariel and pulled both of them to the ground. This shocked and frightened Ariel, and she was about to cry out, when Anthony covered her mouth. Then she saw why. Two of the soldiers, those who had been guarding the gate, had turned and were running back toward it. A moment or two later and they would have been caught. The two buried their faces in the earth, hoping the soldiers hadn't seen them.

At that moment, they heard the angry shouts of the general. "Get back here, you two!" he bellowed. "Catch those horses!"

The two soldiers heading back for the gate did not question the order but turned swiftly and raced after the chariot.

They must have realized that they left the gate unguarded, Anthony reasoned to himself.

Both children breathed a sigh of relief; that was close. They stayed down on the ground for a few more seconds before looking up. Everyone was running down the road after the horses. They rose up quickly and ran as fast as they could, away from the city, still bearing off the main road. The children had run nearly two hundred yards when they saw that the runaway horses had stopped and the soldiers chasing them had caught up with them.

Just then, Anthony, who was in the lead, suddenly slowed his pace and held up his hand to tell Ariel to do the same. The children came to a stop and crouched down, still watching the soldiers on the road ahead of them. The Roman officer and his driver climbed into the chariot and continued down the road, but at a very slow pace. The soldiers who had been posted at the gate turned and began to walk at first and then run back toward the city. The two children lay facedown on the ground, hoping that they would not be seen. After about a minute, they looked back up in the direction of the city. By the light from the lamps, they saw the two figures pass through the arch, and the light disappeared as the gates were shut.

Both the children looked at each other with the same question in mind. "How will we get back in?"

Ariel shrugged her shoulders. "I guess we'll just have to find another way back in, after we warn the others," she said.

Remembering the urgency of their errand, they rose up quickly and continued southward to the catacombs, following the road but taking care not to travel on it. The children were very familiar with the road leading to the catacombs south of Rome, but it was a challenge navigating them at night. It would have been even more difficult if the moon and stars were not out.

The children ran quickly yet quietly, knowing that the catacombs were nearly a mile and a half away. They encountered no one else on the road as they proceeded southward. After about twenty minutes, they reached the low foothills where the caves were located. The entrance was at the foot of a small hill. A large stone covered the entrance, but the children had expected this. Knowing the hatred that the Romans had for the Christians, they always kept the entrance covered when no one was coming or going. Anthony was the first to come to the entrance. He picked up a rock from the ground and tapped on the boulder as he had done many times before. After a few moments, the children could hear the murmur of voices. A minute passed, and then the stone began to move. The children lent their strength, and the stone was rolled aside.

The people inside the cave moved the stone just enough to permit the children to enter, and then replaced it. Even though they had been away from the catacombs for only a few days, it seemed like much longer. In the few months since the fire, the children had developed a deep bond with the people here. These passages and tunnels were the closest thing to home for them. It was good to be back.

The men who had come to open the door remembered them and greeted them warmly. The children asked the men briefly how everyone was doing and if anything significant had happened in the past few days. For a few minutes, the children forgot about the urgency of their visit.

Recollecting his thoughts, Anthony asked how many people were present, particularly the elder believers.

"There are about thirty people here tonight," one of the men replied. "They've come from inside the city and from the other caves. Peter has been teaching as we share a meal. We were just finishing now; then we'll be going to prayer."

The children were glad to hear that Simon Peter himself was visiting this catacomb and that he was even now speaking with a group of believers from other catacombs and the inner city of Rome itself.

"We have come here to deliver a message," Ariel said. "It is of the utmost importance. Where are they all gathered?"

The watchman directed them to a large room where the people usually met to hear the teachings of Jesus. Hurrying along through the passage, Anthony and Ariel found the room where everyone was gathered. Sure enough, Peter was still there, standing in the middle of a small crowd. There were nearly thirty people seated on the floor, listening intently to what he was saying. A few were clearing away plates and baskets. Anthony and Ariel sat down at the back of the group and listened to the stirring words of the apostle.

The Final Message to Rome

Anthony leaned over and whispered in Ariel's ear, "We'll wait till he stops and before they start to pray. That will be the best time to tell them. You should do the talking, since you actually heard what was said."

Ariel nodded in reply and then went on listening to Peter. He finished speaking after about five minutes, and the believers prepared to join in prayer. Now was the time. Both children rose to their feet.

"Sirs, sirs, please hear me," said Anthony, projecting his voice. "Forgive my interruption, but please listen. I have something very important to say that I think should be said before we kneel and pray to the Lord."

The people parted and allowed him and Ariel to come to the front of the crowd. Turning to face them, Anthony cleared his throat, took a deep breath, and began.

"Ariel and I have been gone for several days, and the reason is because we were seized by some men in the city. They held us prisoner and sold us as slaves into the house of Senator Marcus, a prominent member of the Roman Senate. Last night, there was a feast at the senator's house. Several other senators were present, and Ariel overheard some very disturbing news concerning the emperor and his intentions concerning us, and all followers of Jesus. Ariel, tell them what you heard."

Anthony stepped back as Ariel recounted the events of the evening and precisely what she had seen and heard at the banquet. A slight murmur of voices was heard among the crowd as she mentioned the emperor's intentions to blame the Christians for the fire and use it as an excuse to completely stamp out all believers in Jesus. The children could see that the people understood the seriousness of the emperor's intentions to persecute like never before. The citizens and governors of Rome had always detested the followers of the Way. For their refusal to worship the Roman gods, they were denounced as pagans and atheists. For their memorial of Jesus's death, in which the believers ate a meal where the bread and wine were taken in remembrance of the body and blood of Jesus, the Romans considered them cannibals. Last of all, for their refusal to give absolute loyalty and worship to the emperor as

Lord and God, they were denounced as traitors, enemies of the state and all humanity. Now the emperor had an even greater motive, his own reputation.

After Ariel had finished speaking, the talking in the crowd grew as people looked at and spoke to their neighbors with surprise and concern.

Sensing the need to prevent their friends from being taken away by terror and anxiety from their news, Anthony stepped forward again.

"Please, do not misunderstand us," he said. "We took the risk of sneaking out of the city not to frighten or discourage you but to warn you so that you may be ready for what is about to happen."

Anthony and Ariel both felt a gentle, strong hand on their shoulders. They turned to see Peter standing behind them with a tender smile on his face.

"Thank you," he said, "both of you. You have taken a great risk to come here and deliver this important message. Also, for your willingness to remain as slaves to protect us, we thank you. For your courage and devotion to us and to our Lord Jesus, we are in your debt."

Peter motioned to the two of them to sit down in front of the small crowd of people who were listening. They sat down and looked back up as Peter prepared to speak again.

"Brothers and sisters, what shall we do?" Peter asked. "Many of us know well what it means to suffer for claiming the name of Jesus, and now we must face it again, worse than ever before. What shall we do?"

The believers thought to themselves how they would answer. Many things came to mind, but none of them could think of the best way to answer the question. A few people looked up at Peter and, with some shyness, prepared to offer their response.

Yet, before any of them could speak, Peter raised his hand and said, "Wait, before you answer, there is one thing you must do first. Tell it to Jesus. Whatever has come to your mind, speak to the Lord first, as you would to each other or a friend. Tell him everything. Whatever you are thinking, whatever you are feeling, your thoughts, your fears, questions, feelings, and anything else. Lay them all before the Lord, but don't forget to thank him for all the things that he has done for us. Then be silent, and wait to hear what he has to say to you. We must all do this right now."

The believers rose to their feet and began to cry out to God in their hearts. They all had a lot to say, and it took a while for everyone to finish pouring out their hearts to the Lord while remembering to thank him for all the blessings that he had given them. When each person had finished, they one by one sat down in silence.

After everyone had sat for a while, Peter stood back up. "What has the Lord said to you?"

The people did not know how to answer. They were not sure how to put into words what they felt. Finally, one man stood up.

"For some reason, it doesn't seem to matter anymore. When I first heard the news, I was a bit concerned, but now, in spite of what is about to happen, I am not worried."

Peter smiled. "Well done. That was the very reason that I asked you to do it. No matter where we find ourselves, we should not worry about anything. Rather, we should commit whatever is in our hearts to him through prayer, without forgetting to thank him for all the things that he has done but that we so often take for granted. Our Lord promises that his peace will guard and rule our hearts. We no longer have any cause to be afraid. Yea, our Lord has commanded us time and time again, 'Do not be afraid.'

"Our hearts should always be ruled by his peace, especially in tribulation. Tribulation should not come as a surprise to us. Sorrow and suffering are terribly painful, and no one escapes them. We brought sin into the world, and suffering with it. The two will always be with us, until our Lord makes a final end to them.

"From the very beginning, when we were with Jesus, he told us that because we are not of the world, the world would hate us and war against us. All those who have stood for him have been persecuted, even the prophets who came before our Savior, Jesus. We can expect the same treatment. He warned us that our lives would be difficult. He never promised us that our lives would be pain-free; he promised just the opposite. However, he has given us some very precious promises for those times of need.

"He did not give us a way to be free from pain, but he does offer to share it with us. Yea, our Lord invites and calls to us to share in his sufferings, and he says it is a gift. It is through sharing in his sufferings that we learn to know him better. We cannot truly know him without knowing his sufferings. It is impossible.

"Sorrow and suffering almost never make sense. This is true even for those who do not know Jesus, but for us, we know that with Jesus, there are no accidents. He works all things together for our good even though we may not understand how or why. It is for this reason that we must live by faith, not by sight, as others do. Yea, if we do not live this way, we cannot hope to please him. For without faith, it is impossible to please him.

"We have the hope of eternal life that others do not have. Jesus is that hope. The Lord be praised that we do not have to suffer forever. Our suffering is only for a season, and it is not to be compared with the glory that is coming. We are not of this world; we do not belong here."

At this, Peter lifted his gaze skyward and raised his hands in front of him, palms up to shoulder height.

"Thank you, Lord, for sending us this warning by these two faithful servants of yours. Be with them, Lord, and may they continue to prove themselves faithful to the very end, when you welcome them into your joy."

Then he looked back to the people who were watching and listening intently.

"As you are accused as evildoers, do not grow discouraged and return evil for evil. Respond with good works instead. 'Love your enemies,' Jesus said. 'Bless them that curse you, do good to those who hate you, and pray for those who hurtfully mock and persecute you.' By this, it will be clearly seen that they are the real evil ones. Submit yourselves to the civil authorities knowing that civil authorities were ordained by God to fulfill his purposes. By honoring them, we honor him. Even though we may suffer wrongfully, endure to the end. It is commendable for an innocent man to endure suffering for the Lord's sake.

"Jesus commanded us to let our light shine. This light is a powerful weapon, and it must be used wisely. Always be ready to answer those

The Final Message to Rome

who ask you about what you possess. Do not forget to rejoice as you suffer, knowing that God counts you worthy to suffer for him. Entrust yourself into his hands; he is faithful, and he is with us always, even to the end of the world. Our Lord gave us this promise so that we may be bold and not be afraid of anything that men may do to us."

The crowd was silent for at least a minute after Peter finished speaking. No one knew what to say or what to do. At last, one man stood up. He maneuvered his way through the crowd and took his stand by Peter's side. He reached down with his right hand and grasped Peter's hand firmly.

Then he extended his other hand to the crowd and said, "This is our Lord's charge, and we will obey him. What about the rest of you? Will you stand with us?"

One by one, the crowd all stood to their feet and joined hands. After all the believers stood united, the man bowed his head and prayed, "Dear Lord, we commit ourselves into your hands. As we stand here for you, we ask that you would stand with us, your will be done. Amen."

After the man finished praying, other believers began to pray and voice both their fears and devotion to God. This continued for some time, how long or short no one knew, but as time went on, a strange sense of peace and hope came over the believers. All of them had heard about the persecution the church had faced since its birth, and some had friends who had experienced it firsthand. Yet, as they continued to pray, the Lord began to grant each of them courage, strength, and the assurance that they would be able to face whatever was about to happen.

Then, one by one, they began to offer prayers of thanksgiving and praise, rejoicing that they had a hope in Jesus that could not be destroyed or taken away. Their names had been written in heaven. God himself knew them and would never leave or forsake them. When everyone had stopped praying, a few of the believers began to sing a song of praise to the Lord, and everyone else joined in.

After the singing, Peter addressed the group and told them that he, along with a few others, had to go to another section of the catacombs outside the city. Each of the believers bade him farewell, and he and the others prepared to leave the cave. Some left alone and others in small groups, taking care not to leave all at one time.

As the people began to walk out, Anthony touched Ariel on the shoulder. "I think it's time for us to go back," he said.

Ariel looked back at him over her shoulder and nodded.

They both realized that getting back into the city would be much more difficult than getting out, so the two of them approached one of the elders who was about to leave and explained their problem to him. They had met him in the catacombs before they had been kidnapped. They also knew that he actually lived in Rome and had extensive knowledge of all the ins and outs of the city. His name was Justus.

"Sir, we believe that God may have allowed us to be brought into Senator Marcus's house so that we could warn you of what is coming. We are content to remain servants in the senator's house, as it may enable us to learn more information that could be helpful to everyone here and around the city. Still, it is essential that we return to the senator's house immediately, lest anyone should find we are missing. We both know that you have an excellent knowledge of the city. Can you help us find a way back without being discovered?" Anthony pleaded.

"Where is the senator's house located, and how did you get out of the city?" Justus asked.

They explained in detail where the house was located, recalling its position on the map that Ariel had found in the house, and the roads that they had followed coming out of the city.

Justus was silent for a few moments.

"There is a way to get in and out of the city without using the gates. There is a tunnel on this side of the city that we built many years ago. The entrance is concealed, and it is far enough from the city walls to prevent anyone from seeing us in the dark. A few others and I are sneaking back into the city tonight. If you will come with us, we can show you the tunnel and how to get back to your master's house."

"Thank you, sir," both of the children said.

"Go to the entrance, and wait there," Justus ordered. "I'll find the others."

As the children waited for Justus, they looked around the cavern that had been their home since the great fire. They had deeply missed this place and the people. Since they had lost their parents, this was the only home and family they had. Part of them longed to be at home, but they both knew the danger their friends were in, and the best way to help and protect them was to go back to the senator's house.

Justus returned in a few minutes, followed by five other believers: two middle-aged men, a woman slightly younger, and two other men whom they judged to be in their twenties.

There was a torch stuck in the wall, next to the stone that covered the entrance, and a clay water pot on the ground under the torch. Justus and the two older men stepped forward to remove the stone from the entrance, while another man, not among the group that was leaving, picked up the clay pot and covered the torch.

A fresh breeze of the night air brushed against the children's faces as the stone began to budge, revealing the world outside.

All was dark for about a minute. The men moved the stone just enough so one person could get out. Each member quietly slipped out, and the stone was replaced. Justus and the two men scanned the surrounding area and listened intently for several seconds before calling everyone together in a circle.

"Ariel, Anthony, I want you to stay close to Antipas," Justus said, motioning to one of the younger men. "Follow him, and don't leave his side until we make it back into the city. I don't want either of you to get lost."

The children nodded and moved over next to Antipas.

Justus continued, "It's a little over a mile to the tunnel's entrance. We are going to stay off the main road to avoid being seen. There's a valley between two hills that runs toward the city. We'll use that valley to get back to Rome. When the valley opens up, we turn right and work our way along the city wall to the corner where it turns north. There is a small, ravine leading up to the wall that is where we will find the tunnel.

Rome is not in danger of any attack, so there won't be any patrols outside the city, but there will be sentries on the walls, so we have to be cautious. We are not just in danger from the Romans. This area is full of thieves, so keep your eyes and ears open. Walk briskly but quietly. We cannot talk to each other as we walk back. Do not speak a word unless you see or hear something that could pose a danger. When we get close to the city walls, we will be going through some trees, bushes, and large rocks. They provide excellent cover, but go softly, and make sure that you do not get lost or separated from the rest of the group."

Justus paused for a moment. "Do you all understand?"

All nodded in agreement. "Yes."

"Then off with us."

Chapter 5

The Secret Tunnel

Rising stealthily, Justus turned out into the darkness with the small party following. The two children noticed that the people did not walk together as one group. They followed Justus walking two by two in a line, keeping a short distance between each pair. He was moving at a very brisk pace, and everyone in the group was hard-pressed to keep up with him. The night was quiet and still, but the children remembered what he had told them about staying alert. No one in the group said a word, as Justus had instructed them to do.

The children remembered the route that they had taken coming out of the city and noticed that Justus was taking a different route, one that was a bit longer. However, they soon judged that he was using a route that would keep them better concealed. He was careful to keep a good distance from the road while taking advantage of every bit of cover available.

The trees in the field provided good concealment, but the group had to be careful where they stepped. A soft but sharp crack as one of the group stepped on a fallen stick startled everyone for a moment. For a brief moment, the children lost their breath. With his characteristic vigilance, Justus calmly motioned for the group to move on.

Everyone had been so focused on keeping up with Justus and looking out for any danger that they reached the city before they knew it.

They could now see the outline of the walls and buildings dimly silhouetted against the sky. At this, Justus slowed his pace. Then he stopped for a moment and motioned for everyone to kneel down, doing the same himself. They waited there for several moments, watching and listening intently, but nothing moved, and nothing was heard. As they came out of the narrow valley and turned right, they crossed a small brook running parallel to the city walls.

With the city in sight, everyone walked with even more caution. Justus crouched, still on his feet but very close to the ground, as he crept forward. He placed his feet ever so softly, making no noise at all. The rest of the group followed his example. They proceeded in this manner for nearly five minutes. They were now almost two hundred yards from the city walls.

At this, Justus turned sharply to the left and crawled up a small ravine behind a thick clump of bushes. There they found a couple of large rocks protruding out of the ground on the right side of the gully. The four men who had come with the group crawled up next to Justus. They laid their hands on the top of one of the large rocks in the side of the gully and began to pull. After a few seconds of struggle, the stone loosened, and the men rolled it out from its place, revealing the entrance to the tunnel. The hole was about twenty inches high and fifteen inches wide. A large iron ring had been drilled or screwed into the concealed portion of the rock, undoubtedly to be used for resetting the stone.

As soon as the opening was clear, Justus nodded to one of the young men. He let go of the rock, placed both hands on opposite sides of the hole, and began lowering himself down feetfirst into the darkness. Then he quickly pulled his hands from the sides of the opening, lifting them over his head as he slid abruptly out of sight. In a second, he was gone. The middle-aged woman then lowered herself into the hole, followed by one of the older men.

Justus then motioned to the children to go down. Ariel went first. Following the others' example, she lowered herself down into the opening feetfirst. She could feel that the tunnel sloped steeply downward, dropping away into what felt like nothing. She held her breath and quickly released herself. Her heart stopped for a moment as she slid down the dirt slide. A moment or two later, her feet touched down on a solid dirt floor. She came to a stop still leaning against the narrow wall of the dirt slide.

It was pitch-black in the tunnel; Ariel could not see her hand in front of her face. While she was still trying to reorient herself, a hand reached out and pulled her gently but firmly farther into the tunnel. A few seconds later, there was another abrupt sliding noise and a gentle thud as Anthony descended into the tunnel.

One by one, the remaining members of the group slid down the pit and into the tunnel. Justus was the last to enter. Although he was not a large man, his strength proved exceptional. He maneuvered his way into the opening, seized the ring with both hands, heaved the stone into position above the opening, and then let himself slide downward while still clinging to the ring. His body weight pulled the stone back to its original position, concealing the tunnel's entrance. Justus then released his grip and slid down to the bottom of the tunnel.

After a moment of silence, the children heard Justus's voice, ever so softly.

"The stone is in place; light the torch," he whispered.

The young man who had been the first to enter the tunnel ignited a small torch stuck in the wall of the passage. He did this with the aid of a flint stone tied to the handle of the torch. The torch was small, and it did not give very much light, but it was enough for everyone to see each other and the outline of the tunnel. The passage was a little over six feet high and two and a half feet wide. The walls showed that the surrounding terrain consisted of mainly dirt and small rocks. The children could see that some additional support beams and shoring planks had been built into the walls and ceiling to protect against a cave-in.

"Ready, sir?" the young man whispered to Justus in the rear of the group.

"Yes," responded Justus, "let's go."

The man turned and began walking deeper into the tunnel toward the city. The others followed, walking in single file. Everyone was totally silent, as they had been instructed. The young man in the lead took care to walk as softly as possible; the other members followed his example. The children listened for any sound from above but could hear nothing.

After they had walked about one hundred yards, the tunnel began to slope further downward and get smaller in area. They now had to bend over to keep walking. They continued in this fashion for a few minutes. Then, finally, the young man carrying the torch stopped somewhat abruptly and fell softly to his knees. He lowered the torch in front of him, and the children could see that the ceiling dropped steeply downward and then leveled off, leaving less than a yard of space between the floor and ceiling of the tunnel. They would now have to crawl.

Keeping the torch a safe distance from his face, the young man lay down on his left side and began crawling forward using his left arm and right leg to move himself along. He kept the torch in his right hand extended in front of him to light his path. One of the middle-aged men and the woman knelt down and crawled on their hands and knees, following the light of the torch. The two children followed, keeping as close to the person in front of them as possible.

Among the dirt of the tunnel's floor, the children could feel some gravel and small rocks. They saw that the builders had taken extra precautions to protect this section of the passage from collapse. This was one of the most vulnerable parts of the passage, and they could not risk it being breached. The group crawled their way forward, placing their arms as gently as possible to prevent them from being cut and scratched by the small rocks. The tunnel went on in this manner for a little over twenty yards; then, it began to open up, gradually getting larger.

After about two minutes, they were able to stand up and walk again. However, they noticed that the lead man had slowed his pace and that everyone was keeping to the left side of the tunnel as they walked. The children followed his example. Then the lead man stopped, turned around and faced the group, and extended the torch past the person behind him. He seemed to be counting, ensuring that no one had fallen behind. Once satisfied, he raised his finger to his lips and motioned with his hands, telling everyone that they must be extremely quiet and walk very softly.

The Final Message to Rome

The young man turned and walked on, not on his tiptoes, but stepping very lightly and transferring the weight on his feet slowly as he took another step, making his movements almost completely inaudible. Everyone followed his example, as before. The pace of the group slowed, no one fell behind, and even the sound of breathing grew faint. The tunnel was beginning to lead upward, and it dawned on everyone that they had passed under the city walls. Just a fathom or so above them, there were people; asleep or awake, it didn't matter. The slightest sound could give them away. The suspense grew with every step they took; time seemed to slow down.

They proceeded in this manner for close to five minutes, but it seemed to them like a half hour. The tunnel kept leading upward by degrees. The lead man came to a halt for a brief moment and pointed with his left hand while he raised the torch with his right. The people behind him saw that, just ahead, the tunnel widened considerably, making it look like a small room. The cavern was circular in shape, measuring approximately nine feet in diameter and eight feet in height.

The young man ventured into the open space, still taking care to watch his steps, and turned to his left. There, up against the wall, was a ladder, leading upward into what looked like a narrow shaft or chimney.

Reaching the foot of the ladder, the man handed the torch to Justus, who had taken his position there. Justus raised the torch as high in the shaft as he could while keeping it away from the ladder, ceiling, and walls of the passage.

With the shaft illuminated, the young man ascended the ladder. Watching from below, the children could see that about eighteen feet up, there appeared to be a large stone or brick covering the top of the shaft. Gently, the man reached up with a fist and began tapping on the stone. He knocked for a few seconds and then listened. Nothing happened. After about thirty seconds, he tapped a few times and waited again. This procedure went on for several minutes with no response. Then, just as the man raised his hand to tap again, he suddenly lowered it and raised his head, turning his ear upward against the stone, listening intently. After a few seconds, he tapped twice more and stopped. The children heard a faint knocking come in reply. The young man smiled, nodded to the people watching from below. Then he placed both hands on the stone and pushed.

The stone did not move at first; then it began to groan and budge slightly. A few moments after, one end of the stone came up, and a glimmer of light appeared. The young man heaved once more on the stone, clearing it completely from the top of the shaft. A hand reached down from above and grasped his hand firmly, then hoisted him up into the light and out of sight.

"Next," Justus said in a low voice.

The woman was next in line. She climbed the ladder to the top of the shaft and disappeared from sight as the young man had before her.

Justus reached out and laid his hand on Ariel's shoulder. "Your turn," he said.

Ariel climbed up the ladder as the others had and saw that the shaft ran up to an opening leading into a well-lit room. Standing around the hole were two men. When she reached the top of the ladder, one of the men reached down to her. Ariel reached up and grasped the man's hand. Clasping hers with a solid grip, the man drew her up through the hole and into the room above.

Ariel scrambled to her feet and looked around her. The room appeared to be part of a small stone house. There was very little furniture in the room, but it was clean, dry, and well organized.

Just as Ariel was about to step away from the hole, the two men told her to brush the dirt and dust that had accumulated as she was crawling through the smaller section of the tunnel off her clothes. Finishing this, she stepped away from the hole into the corner of the room where the man and woman who had ascended the ladder before her were standing.

One by one, each person in the group ascended the ladder and was lifted into the house. Justus was the last to come out of the tunnel. After reaching the top of the ladder, he handed the torch to one of the men standing beside the hole. The man took the torch from him and passed it on to the woman who was standing next to the opening. The two drew Justus up through the hole, and the three of them picked up the stone and returned it to its place in the floor.

The woman and the two men in the house gave the children a warm welcome. The children had only a minute or two to tell the people who they were and what had happened to them before Justus and the other believers were ready to move on.

"We have to check the streets first," one of the men said. "Then you can leave."

The two men exited by the front door, one at a time, a minute apart. Nobody looked out after them. The men split up and surveyed the streets and buildings to ensure that the house was not being watched. They returned a few minutes later and reported that all was clear.

Apparently, the five other believers who had come with Justus knew this part of town quite well or had often used the tunnel to sneak into the city before. One of the older men accompanied the woman as she left the house, but all the others left the house alone, heading in different directions. Justus noticed that the children seemed a bit puzzled by this.

"We never leave as one group," he said, leaning over toward the children. "Even though some of them live in the same area, they each take a different route back. It helps to avoid suspicion and makes the house more difficult to find. It took several years to build the tunnel, and we had to conceal it as best we could, so we built this house around it. It's been a couple years, and no one suspects anything. We'll wait a few more minutes, and then I'll take you back to the senator's house."

"Where are we?" Anthony asked.

"We are on the southeast side of the city, just inside the walls. All we have to do is head north till we hit the highway you came out on after escaping the thieves. From there we'll take another route to the senator's house that doesn't use the main roads."

"Wait," said Ariel. "Where do you live, Justus, or where and when could we meet you again? We have to keep meeting with others just to keep heart. It takes so long to get out to the catacombs someone may realize we are gone. Is there another place in the city, close to the senator's house, where we can meet with you or other believers?"

"This house is probably the closest place to where you can meet with other believers right now. So many of them have lost their homes or had to move with their masters. A large number of our fellowship here in Rome are slaves. Sometimes we find a place in the city to meet together, but it's very dangerous, and from what you have found out, it's only going to get worse. Still, I'll try to find other believers in this area that can help you. Until then, you can come back to this house, but not too often, and you must make sure that no one sees you come or go from here. I am afraid that's the best I can do for now."

Both the children pressed their lips together, slightly disappointed, but understandingly smiled and nodded. "Thank you. Thank you, Justus."

Justus nodded in reply.

"Now we must go," he said. "Follow me."

Opening the door, Justus led them out into the street. There were no lights, only the moon and stars, but that would be more than sufficient for them to follow him without stumbling or losing each other. Justus led them along several roads, pointing out a few landmarks and describing the location of the streets so the children could find their way back to the house. Justus led the way navigating through a series of passages and back alleys taking care to stay off any of the main roads. He moved along at a brisk pace all the while pointing out landmarks that would help the children find their way if they ever had to travel alone.

"Follow this route," Justus said, "and it will take you straight to the road where the Senator's house is located. It's about a quarter of a mile from the secret house."

The directions were fairly simple, and the distance was relatively short, so both the children felt they would have no trouble finding their way back.

The journey back to the senator's house seemed to pass much quicker than the children's trip out of the city. Justus led the way at a spry pace, still taking care to stay in the shadows.

As they went, the children reminded Justus about the difficulty that they had had getting past this intersection, and their adventure in the alley.

"The soldiers that you saw were probably there guarding the city gates," Justus responded. "This road and the one the senator's house is on, connect just inside the city walls. Beyond those crossroads, there is another gate that will take you out of the city heading east.

"We can't stay on the road with those soldiers on guard, so we'll have to use the alleyways that you used. I know the alleyways fairly well; hopefully we won't encounter any thieves or ruffians this time. It is dangerous, but right now, it's the best way to get around the crossroads without being seen."

The two children shrugged their shoulders.

"Very well," Anthony said.

Justus was walking in the front with Ariel behind him and Anthony following along. The two children felt a bit more secure with him leading the way, but they were both very apprehensive about what might happen or who they might meet in those alleyways. They kept on walking, too worried to say anything to Justus or each other. After a minute or two, it dawned on both of them. They had a problem, and neither of them had the answer for it, but someone else did.

As they walked along the road, observing the buildings that they had passed before, they remembered how they, or rather how God, had protected them and led them out of the city and now back in. They remembered the ruffians in the alleyway and the guards at the city gates, what obstacles God had already overcome. Obstacles that, to them, were impossible, but to God, they were as easy as anything else that he did. He had done a miracle in getting them through the city gates without being seen.

He was working out his will for both of them. He had allowed them to be captured by the slave traders and sold into the senator's house together. They could have been separated, but he had kept them together. Anthony remembered the fear that he had felt in that dark room on the night they were kidnapped and how confused he had been working in gardens. If they had been separated, it would have been much easier for them to lose hope. God had kept them together so that they might be an encouragement to each other, and from what they had heard, they would certainly need it.

The Lord had not simply allowed them to be enslaved. He had purposely brought them to the senator's house so that they would learn of the danger and warn the other followers of Jesus. They were doing his will. He had brought them this far. He had answered their prayers before; he could do it again. As each of them remembered all that Jesus had already done for them, the worry seemed to fade away. He still loved them, and he would take care of them as they continued to trust him.

They had been too scared to talk about it to each other when they should have been talking to God. Both silently whispered a prayer, thanking Jesus for protecting them, using them to deliver a warning, shielding them from many dangers that night, and now guiding them back to where they needed to be. They affirmed their trust in his love and that he would never leave or forsake them. They praised him as the god who rules over everything, everything that happens in the world.

Jesus, Ariel prayed silently, *no matter what happens, I will love you and praise you. I will not be afraid.*

"Here we are," Justus whispered over his shoulder. "This is where we get off the road and into the alleys."

His voice came as such a surprise to the children. Each of them had been lost in their thoughts and prayers; the time had passed so quickly. *Well,* Anthony reflected, *now is our chance to do what we said we would do. This is the test, if we believe that God will do what he said he would do.*

"All right," said Ariel, "lead the way."

Justus reached down and took Ariel by the hand. "Join hands," he said. "It's dark in the alleys, and we mustn't get separated."

Ariel reached behind her and grasped Anthony's hand with a firm hold. Leading the way, Justus moved off toward a narrow passage between two buildings, then paused for a moment before entering, looking in with an intense gaze. Turning his head, he nodded and entered into the passageway with the children following.

The children noticed almost at once that this passage was different from the one that they had traveled. They could see that this alley was far more illuminated than the other. The light enabled them to move quickly without stumbling or tripping. All three of them kept their eyes and ears open, but there was nothing to be heard, and the alley was deserted.

Leading the way, Justus was keeping his attention fixed on the buildings that they were passing. After a few minutes' walk, he stopped. They had been traveling northwest; now Justus turned and pointed toward another passage leading due north.

"Take a good look around you, and try to remember this area," he whispered. "This is where we change alleys. That one over there"—he motioned toward another passage much narrower than the one they had come out of—"will lead up to the street the senator's house is on."

Although it was still very dark, the children were able to pick out a few distinguishing features of the path and surrounding buildings. Feeling confident that they had seen enough to identify the area again, they followed Justus to the next passage. The three still held hands and kept a consistent pace.

Their focus shifted when they saw a small ray of light ahead of them in the passage. This could be the end of the alley. The shadows of the buildings were gradually fading, and the faint but distinctive appearance of light ahead was increasing. In half a minute, they could see the outline of buildings silhouetted against the star-filled sky. Anthony and Ariel breathed a long sigh of relief; they had finally reached the end of their long night adventure—well, almost.

Justus knelt down at the corner and looked both ways before the three ventured out of the alley. "Now," he said, turning to the children, "remember where this alleyway comes out on this road so you can find it again."

Then, changing the subject, he asked, "Can either of you tell how far we are from the senator's house?"

The children looked both ways. To their right, they could see the crossroads they had navigated around. On their left, the street seemed much as it had before, dark, silent and empty, but nothing stood out as to where they were or the house they were looking for.

Finally, after studying the street for almost a minute, Anthony spoke up. "I'd say the house is probably off to our left. I don't know how far, but it should be pretty close."

"Let's see," whispered Justus.

They crept along, scanning the buildings across the road, hoping they had not missed the house. They had gone only thirty yards or so when Ariel placed her left hand on Justus's shoulder and pointed down the road with her other hand.

"There it is," she exclaimed, keeping her voice as low as she could, "just a stone's throw away."

Anthony gazed where she was pointing. "I believe you're right, Ariel."

They walked on up the road, keeping a steady gaze on the house until it was directly across from them. It was indeed the senator's house. After looking the road over one last time, the three scurried across as fast as they dared. Following the small alley running alongside the house, they found the door they had exited by. Ariel pulled the key out of her pouch and quietly unlocked the door. She breathed a sigh of relief, then turned and threw her arms around Justus in a warm embrace. This came as a bit of a surprise to Justus.

Ariel turned her head, looking up into Justus's rather surprised gaze. She was about a foot and a half shorter than him.

"Thank you, Justus," she said. "Thank you for everything."

Gently, Justus placed one of his hands on her shoulder and smiled. "You're welcome," he said. "I was glad to do it."

With a smile, Ariel released Justus from her embrace and stepped back. Anthony stepped forward and grasped Justus's hand in a firm hold while extending his other around Justus's shoulder. The two clasped each other in a solid hold. This was good-bye for who knew how long.

The two released each other, but Anthony kept his arm on Justus's shoulder, with their hands clasped firmly together. "Thank you for all of your help, Justus," he said. "I hope we will meet again soon."

Justus nodded in reply. Anthony felt his throat and voice start to crack as he and Justus let go of each other. Justus shifted his gaze between the two children and spoke again, his voice filled with a strong and calm resonance.

"Be strong," he said. "Strengthen each other, and keep praying for the rest of the church and for our enemies."

The children nodded. "We will," they promised.

"Now I must go," said Justus. "Until we meet again."

He smiled, and strode off down the alley back toward the road. He turned round at the end of the alley, his figure lighted by the moon and stars. He raised his hand and waved a last farewell, and the children did the same. Justus turned his face toward the street and in another moment was out of sight.

The children eased the door open; the hinges began to squeal, and they stopped. There was enough room for one to pass through at a time. They stepped through one at a time, then closed the door and carefully locked it.

Both exhaled a sigh of relief and glanced at each other for a moment, musing over the events of the evening. It seemed like they had left the house days ago. So much had happened the last few hours, it was almost hilarious to think about it all. They smiled at each other and covered their mouths to keep from laughing. Ariel was the first to speak.

"We can talk about everything later, Anthony," she said. "Now we have to get to bed."

Anthony nodded with a smile, and the two made their way back to the servants' quarters after changing their clothes. They lay down and slept till morning, waking up at the usual time with all the other servants. Remarkably, they did not feel any of the tiredness that one would expect after staying up so late at night. They continued their household duties, and no one ever suspected what they had been up to that night. This was the first of many night excursions for Anthony and Ariel.

Chapter 6

A New Assignment

The next few days flew by in an absolute blur of activity for the two children. The duties in the house seemed to increase, and by the time the day was over, the children were completely exhausted. They had just enough strength to drag themselves to bed and, with the other servants, fell silently into a deep and dreamless sleep. The children had intended to meet secretly at night and discuss their midnight adventure, but all the busyness of the house prevented them. As the days passed, both began to feel a bit lonely and isolated.

By now, both children had gotten into the habit of praying silently to God as they worked. The opportunity to draw away from the daily activities and people to converse with God were becoming rare. Finding a quiet place in the house where one could be alone was next to impossible. Following the example of the brethren who had cared for them, both children spoke to God briefly when they arose in the morning and when they retired for the night. They also gave thanks to God for his many blessings before each meal. The brethren had always done the same when they broke bread together, but the children had to be sure that no one would see them.

On the morning of the third day, the children woke up and proceeded with their daily duties as usual. Anthony went to work in the gardens, and Ariel proceeded to wait upon the senator's daughters. The two women almost invariably ate their morning meal in the garden, and today was no exception. Whenever they came into the garden, Anthony was very careful to stay out of the way and out of sight so as not to interrupt their serenity. The garden was approximately twenty yards in length and ten yards wide. The two ladies were seated at one end of the garden, with Ariel standing behind their couches, out of sight but within call. Today, the morning was especially cool, and the two ladies had not requested that Ariel fan for them. Anthony had concealed himself behind some bushes about halfway across the garden, on the right side. He had just finished pruning some shrubs and was about to move on to some other plants, when Claudio appeared on the other end of the garden, opposite the ladies, and called out Anthony's name.

Responding with his usual attentiveness and enthusiasm, Anthony sprang out from behind the bushes and answered with a strong and cheerful tone, "I am here, sir."

"Come with me," said Claudio, beckoning to him, "at once."

Hastily brushing the dirt and leaves off his clothes, Anthony scurried across the landscape and followed Claudio out of the garden and into the main house.

Hearing the sound of Anthony's name, Ariel peered out from behind the hedge where she was standing, anxious to see what would happen. She saw Anthony emerge from behind the bushes and rush off after Claudio. She stood still for a moment, puzzled, and then quickly drew herself back behind the hedge. Both children had agreed that it would be best if no one in the house knew they were close friends. Ariel wondered what Claudio wanted with Anthony, but she could not be seen showing interest in the matter. Pondering what to do, she decided that it would be best for her not to bring up the subject with anyone, not even the other servants.

The day continued on as any other day at Senator Marcus's house. Ariel did her best to stay focused on her responsibilities and not worry about what could happen to Anthony. They could be moving him to other duties in the house. Or maybe they suspected him of some wrongdoing. Worse still, they may have concluded that he was not necessary in the house and decided to sell him. Then, of course, there was always the possibility that someone had seen them sneak out of the house in the night.

Stop, Ariel said to herself. *It won't help any to worry. God sees what's happening. He knows if Anthony is in any danger. He cares about what happens to Anthony more than anyone else, and he is fully able to protect him.*

Lord, Ariel prayed silently, *I don't know what is happening to Anthony or even what lies ahead for each of us, but you do. So, I give all these fears and worries to you. Before you returned to heaven, you promised that you would always be with us, no matter what happens. I will trust your promise and rest in your love. I love you, Jesus.*

As the day progressed, Ariel found it necessary to constantly remind herself of the Lord's promise and love as the worries continued to come. The day dragged on slowly for her with this on her mind, and she couldn't wait to help the other servants prepare supper.

The evening tasks were routine, as no dinner guests were expected. While carrying a large vessel of wine to the kitchen, Ariel, who was feeling exhausted from the day's activities, neglected to watch her path and collided with another maidservant. The collision was not with great force, but the shock of it caused Ariel to lose her balance and drop the vessel of wine to regain herself. Both girls shrieked as the vessel descended to the floor, and then gasped as a pair of hands reached out and caught the vessel just before it crashed on the pavement. The two girls breathed a sigh of relief as their hearts began to beat again.

"That was close," a voice said.

Ariel's head spun, and she looked twice at the face before contenting herself that it was indeed Anthony, but not Anthony as she remembered him. When she had last seen him, he was dressed in humble servants' attire covered with dirt from working in the garden. Now he was wearing a bright and ornate tunic suitable for servants waiting upon royalty. Anthony's tall stature and strong build fit well with the clothes, as did his black hair and brown eyes. The other girl was equally surprised and interested in the change. Anthony smiled at Ariel's surprise and amazement as he handed the vessel back to her.

"Where have you been all day, Anthony," the other girl asked, "and why are you wearing those fancy clothes?"

"I received a new assignment," he replied. "Senator Marcus wanted one of the servants to accompany and wait on him while he was at the Senate. Claudio thought that I would be the best choice. They needed me to wear some clothes that would be more presentable than the ones I use for working in the garden."

"So you were at court today. What was it like?" she asked.

"I was kept busy waiting on Senator Marcus," Anthony replied, "and we should get back to preparing the hall."

With a nod, Ariel continued on toward the kitchen, carrying the vessel of wine that she had almost lost. Anthony walked back to the dining area with the other girl following, still talking. Ariel was relieved to know where Anthony had gone and that he was not in any danger.

The senator and his family shared a rather quiet evening over their meal and then left the hall, going their separate ways. Some retired for the night, and some went to further enjoy the evening in the quiet of the garden.

After everyone had left the hall, Ariel and the other servants began their usual cleanup. Both the children were exhausted from the day's activities. They went to bed at the usual time and slept all through the night.

The days continued on in the senator's house. Ariel continued to wait upon the senator's daughters, and Anthony acted as Senator Marcus's page when he was at court or worked at the house when Senator Marcus was not going out. A week had passed since their visit to the catacombs, and they had been unable to meet in the garden. That evening, something happened that drastically changed the attitude and perspective of both children.

All the servants had set to preparing the evening meal for the usual time when Senator Marcus was expected to return. Anthony had gone with the senator, as he was usually accustomed. Claudio was directing the work of all the servants, and Ariel was occupied with arranging the hall. On this particular evening, the senator returned much later than was his custom. In addition, Ariel noticed a change in Anthony's behavior. In the past when he had returned with the senator, he would immediately set to helping the other servants prepare for the festivities of the evening, but tonight he didn't. On her return from the kitchen, she was a surprised to see Anthony approach Claudio, exchange a few words, and then stride off at a swift pace. Following this brief encounter, Claudio stopped directing the meal preparations and addressed all the servants with a loud and commanding voice, as he had never done before.

"Listen, listen to me, all of you," he announced. "Senator Marcus has just returned from the Senate with some very important news. He has requested that all members of his household be assembled here in the hall to hear what he has to say. Go, call everyone in the house, and tell them to come here immediately."

At once, everyone laid aside his or her load and dispersed through the house to summon everyone to hear what was about to be said. Ariel went immediately to inform Julia and the senator's daughters, whom she had just left a few minutes before in their private chambers. Just as she was approaching the door and raising her hand to knock, another hand reached out from behind and took hers in a gentle grasp. Despite the surprise of the action, the hand was so gentle and calming that Ariel did not start or scream.

"Wait, Ariel," came Anthony's voice from behind. "Before you knock, I must tell you something."

Ariel turned softly to face Anthony.

Releasing his hold on her arm, Anthony whispered with a graveness and urgency that Ariel had heard in only a few dire cases. "What the senator is about to announce is the action the emperor intends to take concerning the followers of Jesus. I have been keeping my eyes and ears open while I was at court with Senator Marcus. The report you heard at the banquet a week ago may be even more serious than we thought. We have to meet in the garden again, tonight. What we are about to hear from Senator Marcus is only part of what is about to happen."

"All right, Anthony, I'll be there," Ariel replied, excited at the chance to talk to each other again.

With a smile, Anthony turned swiftly and strode away. As soon as he was out of sight, Ariel knocked on the door and, after being admitted, informed the three women of Senator Marcus's wishes.

It took only a few minutes for everyone to assemble in the hall. Ariel and Anthony had taken care to position themselves toward the front of the crowd, where they could see and hear everything. Senator Marcus was standing on a small platform, elevated above the crowd, watching as the household gathered. He was holding a scroll in his hand, and his face was drawn tight with a serious and despondent look unlike anything Ariel had ever seen in him. Claudio mounted the platform and scanned the crowd, counting the servants. Having satisfied himself that everyone was present, he informed the senator and stepped off the platform.

With a deep breath, Marcus cleared his throat and addressed the company. "As all you must know, about eight months ago, the city of Rome suffered untold destruction from the great fire in which many people lost their lives. Even the emperor's own house was destroyed. Both the Senate and the emperor have been doing everything in their power to restore the city and care for the victims of the fire. Emperor Nero himself joined with the search parties in rescuing people from the rubble. He has ordered in stores of food and water from neighboring towns and opened public buildings to shelter the victims of the fire, including his own gardens.

"In addition to ensuring the recovery of Rome and its people, he has also been making a thorough inquiry into the cause of the fire. He has come to the grave conclusion that the fire was not an accident but the conspired work of a sect of seditionists. Here in Rome, we know them as Christians. The emperor has pledged to take swift and decisive action. He has issued a new edict to apprehend and punish them for this heinous and treacherous act."

At this, Marcus unrolled the scroll in his hand and read it aloud to the assembly. The document was written fairly simply, and none of the servants had trouble comprehending it. It had been carefully worded to convey as much care and concern for the protection of Rome and its citizens as possible. It declared that the fire had been the seditionist work of Christians, and it denounced them as enemies, enemies not just of Rome and the state in particular but also of human society and general order. As such, these dangerous conspirators were to be pursued and apprehended, wherever they may be found, and delivered to their just punishment. The document stated that the emperor would not rest until he had thoroughly purged the empire of all members of this treasonous faction.

When Senator Marcus finished reading, he closed the scroll and looked gravely among the faces of the servants.

"It is well-known that this sect of conspirators is overwhelmingly comprised of slaves. You would all be wise to carefully evaluate the integrity and motives of those who you associate and serve with. If you should become aware of anyone's involvement with, or association with, these Christians, it is your duty to report them immediately. Take heed, the emperor is very serious in his intentions to put an end to these seditionists. Not one of them will be spared. Remember this warning, and take heed to yourselves for all our sakes. That is all. You may return to your duties."

Senator Marcus stepped down from the platform, and everyone returned to his or her assigned tasks. Ariel and Anthony assisted the other servants in preparing and serving the meal and cleaning the hall when the meal was over. The senator's announcement affected not only the servants' mood but also those of the senator and his family. There were no smiles around the table that night. Supper was eaten quietly, at a slow pace, and everyone's appetite seemed to have been greatly reduced.

Ariel was glad when the room was cleared and the servants were permitted to retire for the night. She, of course, remembered what Anthony had said, that they needed to meet in the garden after everyone else was asleep. The servants wasted no time in making their way to their beds and falling asleep. Ariel stayed in her place till she was sure that all the servants were asleep and no one else would be moving about in the house. Then she crept down to the garden, taking care to make no noise and stay out of sight. Moving along the stone wall surrounding the garden, Ariel worked her way toward the center of the garden. Then she knelt down, crawled into the bushes next to the path, and lay there, looking to her right and then to her left. Her position gave her a perfect view of both sides of the garden, while the bushes she was lying under made her practically invisible to anyone walking by.

The minutes trickled by slowly, and Ariel was finding it difficult to stay awake. She hoped that Anthony had not fallen asleep while waiting for everyone else to. A glance to her left, and a movement in the shadow of the archway to the garden, told her she was wrong. She saw a figure—though she was unable to confirm its identity—crouch down beside the arch and crawl across the stone-paved path, and into the bushes. At this, Ariel lost sight of it.

After backing out from the bushes she was lying under, Ariel crept along the stone path running along the side of the garden, toward where she had last seen the figure, still keeping in the shadow of the bushes as much as she could.

I might be better concealed crawling among the bushes, she thought to herself, *but I'd make more noise rustling the branches. If I see anyone else, I'll slip back into them.*

As Ariel neared the far end of the garden, she slowed her crawl and listened more intently. Hearing something several strides to her right, she lay down and began looking among the bushes. There he was, Anthony, crawling on his hands and knees among the bushes, in the opposite direction, just a few arm's lengths to the right of where she was lying.

Deciding that it would be best not to call out, Ariel waited until Anthony was almost right on top of her. She expected him to see her and so remained still. To her surprise, Anthony did not check his pace but crawled right by her. Ariel smiled to herself. He had completely missed her. Feeling a bit playful, she maneuvered her way around and crawled along the path just parallel to Anthony and then into the bushes next to and a few feet behind him. They had crawled next to each other a few paces with Anthony still completely oblivious to her presence. Deciding that the charade had gone on long enough, Ariel reached out and gently patted him on his lower leg. Anthony froze.

Ariel crawled up next to him and whispered, "It's all right, Anthony. I'm here."

Anthony sank down to the ground, on his face, and breathed a sigh of relief. "I'm glad you're here," he said.

Ariel crawled around in front of him so that they were looking directly at each other. "Well, let's waste no time," she said softly. "What have you learned?"

"As you know," Anthony began, "the senator has requested that I accompany him to the Senate, wait on him, and deliver messages for him while he is there. The Senate and the emperor have been very busy trying to restore Rome since the fire. I can't ask a lot of questions, but I have been watching and listening carefully to everything that is happening at the Senate. I have especially been keeping my eye on the emperor himself.

"Ariel, he's gone mad. There's just no other way to say it. He was away from Rome, in Antium, when the fire broke out. By the time he returned, the fire was approaching his own house. They tried to save it, but it was no use. The house and everything around it were reduced to ashes. Three of the city districts were completely wiped out by the fire; there's nothing left of them but ashes.

"Then somewhere, somehow, a rumor was started that the emperor was responsible for setting the fire. It has spread all over the city, and the people believe it. No one knows whether the report is true or even where it got started, but several things happened during the fire that have made the people very suspicious. The fire burned for five days before it was put out, and then it broke out again. During that time, a lot of citizens tried to put the fire out, but they were always stopped. Nobody knows who was doing this, but there were people who claimed that they were acting under someone's authority, and they forbade anyone from extinguishing the fire. They said they had orders that no one was to even try to stop the fire. It's possible they were just criminals who wanted to do their robbing without anyone stopping them. I may be wrong, but I can't blame the people for being a little suspicious. No one has any idea who these people were, and the emperor seems to have no interest in finding them.

"After the fire was put out and they started to rebuild the city, Nero took over the land that was burned out and started building a most grand and opulent palace for himself. He set the palace and the grounds in between the three hills—Palatine, Caelian, and Esquiline—right where the fire did most of its damage. Nero has been known for going to extremes when it comes to luxury, but this palace is beyond anything he has concocted. Seeing the elegance of this palace, the people suspected that Nero set the fire just so he could clear out land to build this palace for himself. Everyone knows he has no scruples when it comes to something he wants.

"When the fire was finally put out, the emperor became benevolence itself. He called in stores of food and water from nearby towns, opened public buildings, built temporary shelters and opened his own gardens. He even helped rescue people who were trapped in the rubble. Whether he was doing this because he cared about the people or was just trying to gain popularity, we don't know, but it would seem the people were not impressed. The rumor that he started the fire only grew stronger. Finally, Nero decided that he was going to put an end to this rumor no matter what it took. As best as I can make out, he is not doing this because he genuinely hates the Christians; he's trying to gain political power and popularity for himself. His deeds as emperor have turned so many people against him, and if it continues, he could be overthrown. He'll do anything now, even something drastic, like what you overheard at the banquet a week ago. Everything you heard was true, and the specifics of his plan are even uglier than we thought.

"For some time now, the emperor has been pushing and pushing to gain the support of the Senate. I've seen him myself at the Senate for these past few days. He has been ranting and raving like a madman. He has decided that Christians started the fire, and he won't consider or even hear any other explanation. He has given the Senate no proof of this, only said that the Christians are guilty, and that's the end of it. Now he is demanding that they support him in his noble venture to stamp out all remembrance of these foul and treacherous enemies. Some of the senators have risen up and questioned or challenged him, but he will not be deterred. He has issued the order that the senator read to us tonight. So many of the senators are afraid of him. He has been unscrupulous his entire reign. He has killed anyone he considered to be a challenge to him, even his own mother. The senators know that he will not spare them if they get in his way. Even if they hate what he is doing, there's no stopping him.

"Unfortunately, that's just what I have learned from watching the Senate; there's more. Just this evening, after the emperor finished drawing up his order and all the Senate members had been dismissed, Senator Marcus told me to wait for him at the door of the house. He said that he had a private matter to attend to, so I went. I was standing next to the door, on the right side, beside a large pillar, when I heard footsteps from a passage on the left side of the room coming toward the door. For some reason—I don't know why—I hid behind the pillar. I couldn't see who was talking until they left the room. It was two high-ranking soldiers. They entered the room and walked straight over to the pillar I was standing behind. I heard every word.

"Nero gave them orders to begin apprehending the believers, even before he gained approval from the senate. Of course, he knew that he could get their support with a little intimidation and the citizens of Rome won't question him. Nero plans to have all of us tortured and killed in the cruelest fashion ever. Even though the Emperor is not very popular with the people, they have a greater hatred for us. Besides, it will give them some entertainment; they enjoy seeing a good kill.

"According to the soldiers, Nero is planning yet another ruse to convince the citizens that we set the fire, false confessions. He intends to apprehend some of the believers and demand that they confess to starting the fire. He doesn't care if they are innocent or guilty. He will also force them to confess where other believers may be found. If they don't comply, they will be tortured without mercy until they do confess and as soon as they do, he will have them killed. He's going to have it done secretly, so no one will be able to tell the truth about how he got the confessions. If anyone ever lived to tell about it, it would mean the worse for him. Once they are all dead, Nero will publish their confessions all over the city and use it to silence any questions. Also as an excuse to justify all the evil things that he is planning.

The soldiers heard someone coming so they moved on.

"Once they were gone, I peeked out from behind the pillar to make sure that no one else would see that I had been hiding there," Anthony continued. "The room was empty, so I came out and stood in front of the pillar as I had before, and just in time too.

"A few seconds later, a group came into the hall, heading toward the front door. It was a group of senators along with one or two attendants. Senator Marcus was at the head of the group, carrying a scroll in his hand, the same scroll that he read to us tonight.

"The group stopped in front of the doors, and the senators gave each other their farewells for the evening. I kept my eye on Senator Marcus but still kept at a good distance. As they were saying their good-byes, two soldiers clad in very ornate armor stepped out from the small hallway on the left side of the room. I could tell that they were members of the Praetorian Guard, an elite unit of soldiers that reports directly to the Emperor himself. The older one must have been a general or commanded some position of prominence."

"The same ones you overheard?" Ariel interrupted with a gasp.

"I couldn't tell them by sight, but once they started speaking, I knew it was them," replied Anthony. "They, too, gave the senators their regards and wished them a good night."

"They didn't suspect you had heard them, did they?" questioned Ariel.

Anthony's voice and expression turned decidedly grim. "Maybe," he said. "As they passed through the room, going down the hall on my side of the room, they walked right by me. They younger one glanced at me rather suspiciously. They paused on steps going down into the hallway, and I faintly heard them exchange a few words. The younger one was a bit suspicious as to where I had come from; he hadn't seen me before. Fortunately, the older soldier had seen me working as an attendant to Senator Marcus. Once the younger one heard that he didn't seem suspicious anymore.

"Senator Marcus gave his last regards to the other senators, then hurried back, along with his two attending guards and me. Right after we came in, he told us to gather everyone in the house to the banquet hall; he said he had an important announcement to make. Immediately, I knew it couldn't be anything else. That's why I asked you to meet me here.

"This is what truly awaits us," Anthony said. "Nero will stop at nothing to save his reputation. He's going to find or forge some kind of evidence to show that the Christians are guilty. He's already made up his mind and refuses to hear of anything else. Once he has them arrested, he'll demand that they confess to setting the fire, and torture them until they do. He will also force them to tell where other Christians may be found. Once they confess, he will undoubtedly have them executed. He's not going to take any chances of the people finding out about this. As I said, he's gone mad, or worse."

Ariel exhaled a long breath. "Well, what should we do?" she asked. "Do you think we need to sneak back out again?"

"No, not right now," said Anthony. "They already know what the emperor is planning from our last warning. It's not urgent that they hear about this immediately, and it doesn't warrant the risk of braving the thieves at night. I'll keep listening whenever I am with the senator, and you stay alert around the house. We'll pass on what we learn to the brethren as soon as we can. Still, we should sneak back out again soon, just to be with the believers."

"Why?" questioned Ariel? "You just said the news was not so urgent."

"It's not because of the news," said Anthony. "There is something even more important than what Rome is plotting."

"What's that?" asked Ariel.

"Meeting with God and his followers," Anthony replied. "This whole week has been so busy with working around the house that we have had so little time to pray to God. Do you remember when we were living out in the catacombs? I always felt very strong and close to God. I was able to spend more time talking to him and with the other believers, but here it is so different and dangerous. Here, we can't tell anyone that we believe in Jesus, and it's harder to meet with him. We didn't have to keep our faith a secret before, but now we do. If anyone finds out, they'll have us killed, but there is another danger I have been thinking about: getting separated from Jesus.

"We both know that Jesus brought us here for a reason. He allowed us to be kidnapped and sold as slaves, but he had a reason for it, so that we could warn the others what is coming. He had Senator Marcus bring me with him to the Senate so I could find out more information. Still, as we are being careful not to be discovered, we can't let that keep us from staying close to him and the others. It's risky to sneak out of the house, but becoming too busy to be with Jesus or losing our bond with the brethren is even worse.

"Emperor Nero is planning some fearful things for us, but the only way we can hope to overcome them and overcome fear itself is by hanging on to Jesus. If we don't hang on to him, when the trials come, we will not be able to withstand them. We can't let the fear of being discovered keep us from worshiping him as we should."

Both children were silent for a few moments. Ariel thought hard on what Anthony had said. She had been feeling many of the same things in a different way.

She nodded. "You're right, Anthony. The real danger is that we would lose our faith. I've really missed everyone back at the catacombs, and this week has made it even worse. Not being able to be with them has made me feel very discouraged. I never knew how important they were or how important Jesus was, until now. You and I have to keep meeting with the other believers in the city and also with each other.

"It's already dangerous, and it's only going to get worse, but the only way we'll get through it is by holding on to Jesus and each other. God is the only one who can truly protect us. My parents taught me the story of the prophet Daniel. He was kidnapped, made a eunuch, and forced to serve in pagan lands just like we are. He kept his faith strong by praying to God three times a day every day. He also kept a strong bond with three Hebrew friends who also feared God. They were all tested, but they knew that pleasing God was more important than being safe. They risked their lives to stay faithful to him, and he honored them for it. They faced some very scary things, but the Lord always protected them, no matter how hopeless things got.

"Let's not forget, as we think about our faith in Jesus, that we need to share it with others. Jesus commanded us to spread his good news through the whole world no matter how dangerous it may be. He warned us that it would be dangerous and that we had to be wise, but we are much safer pleasing him than trying to protect ourselves."

Anthony nodded, then reached out and grasped Ariel's hand firmly in his own. "Thanks, Ariel," he said. "I needed to hear that."

Ariel smiled back. "So did I. Where and when should we meet again?"

"We'll try to meet the night after tomorrow. Let me know if anything changes. I'll do the same," Anthony replied.

Crawling alongside the path, hidden by the bushes, the two slipped back to where they had made their entrances into the garden. Before each returned to their part of the house, they whispered a brief prayer to the Lord.

"Dear Father, we commit ourselves into your hands. Keep us faithful despite the dangers, and devoted despite the fears and distractions. We will hold on to what you have told us and trust you to defend us no matter what may happen to us. Amen."

Without another word, the two snuck back to their sleeping quarters and didn't awake till the chirping of the birds announced the coming of dawn.

Chapter 7

The Nightmare Begins

ANTHONY'S REPORT PROVED fatally true. The emperor's order was officially announced two weeks later. Emperor Nero and several other heads of state publicly proclaimed that the seditionist Christians had set the fire in Rome deliberately. Expressing themselves with an exceptional display of concern for the lives of all Roman citizens, they adamantly declared that undeniable proof had been found confirming the Christians' guilt. Nero, with his other heads of state, swore a fierce oath to find and punish the conspirators behind the burning of Rome. It was quite a performance they put on.

The order which the children had heard from Senator Marcus was now read aloud and posted all throughout the city—in the public square, the marketplace, the temples, and everywhere else. It denounced all Christians as enemies of the state, Rome, and all of humankind, to be sought out and punished accordingly, wherever they may be found. Nero himself promised to lead by example in Rome and thoroughly purge the city of these wicked and dangerous criminals.

Anthony and Ariel were very pained to hear such things said about their friends. Accusations that they knew were not true. It hurt even more that people believed them. These Christians were the people that had saved their lives and nursed them back to health, given them a family, a home. Best of all, they had showed them what made life worth living, loving Jesus. The children constantly had to restrain themselves from speaking. They were always hearing someone say something false or vengeful against the believers both in the house and outside the house. It was hard enough for both of them having to keep silence even apart from being believers. Both had been members of upper class families where they were free to speak their minds. Now they were slaves. Ariel especially had been very accustomed to speaking her mind around her family, with respect of course.

Some of the accusations the children remembered hearing before they had become followers of Jesus. These false claims had gained widespread acceptance all throughout the city. Although there was no verifying evidence, the Romans suspected the Christians of such crimes as incest, child murder, and cannibalism. They looked down on the believers because they abstained from the theaters, banquets, and shows at the circus and amphitheaters. They also hated the Christians for their refusal to acknowledge the Roman gods while maintaining the existence and supremacy of only one god, Jesus Christ. The Romans were incensed that the believers would dare to declare all but one god false, inferior, and nonexistent. The Romans believed in many gods and many paths to an eternal reward, if they even believed in an afterlife at all. Considering these presuppositions, it was not surprising that the Romans did not question the emperor's campaign to exterminate the Christians.

Over the evening meals when guests were present the children would hear about all the latest news and gossip from around the city. Personally, Ariel considered the news to be about as reliable as the gossip. They would often hear of some public spectacle where captured believers were executed. It broke their hearts to listen; yet they knew they had to if they were to learn anything that could save the lives of their friends. The timing of their previous warning could not have come at a better time, for as soon as the edict was announced, enforcement began immediately.

Nero's soldiers and spies had already been at work before the edict was announced, searching out and learning of any place where Christians may be found. No sooner had the edict been made public than the raids and arrests began. The houses in which the believers lived, or simply met to pray and worship, were stormed, and anyone found in them arrested. The enterprise had not gone on long before the emperor announced that some of the Christians had been apprehended and had confessed to their crime. He assured the citizens that they would be justly punished.

Both the children knew full well what this really meant. He had found some believers and tortured them till they succumbed to his demands to confess. Now that he had their confessions, he would silence them forever while using their confessions to justify his mad rampage and convince the citizens of the Christians' guilt. Using the fire and these fraudulent confessions as excuses, he went on to implement the cruelest, most horrendous, bloodthirsty, and terrifying punishments Rome had ever seen.

On the occasions when the children were able to meet with the brethren, they heard about the persecution from those on the receiving end. Of the believers that were seized, many were never seen or heard from again. One could only guess that they had died in prison, whether by starvation, disease, secret execution, or torture to the very end. However, Emperor Nero seemed to be making a specific effort to make a public example of the Christians. It was in this that his cruelty was clearly seen by all.

In the amphitheaters of Rome, large groups were herded into the area for the entertainment of the citizens and the emperor. The spectators would look on as lions, leopards, bulls, and other wild beasts were released upon them, tearing, goring, trampling, and devouring them in a most horrifying and merciless fashion. Others died in the streets or in their own homes at the hands of Roman soldiers. To discourage others from joining with these criminals, Nero ordered them to be publicly scourged or even crucified. Crucifixion was a punishment specifically reserved for slaves or those who did not enjoy the rights of Roman citizenship. In the past, the Romans had made a public example of their enemies by crucifying them outside the city, all along the highways that ran in and out of Rome, and leaving them there long after they had expired. Everyone traveling on the roads would see that the emperor was fiercely devoted to the annihilation of these seditionists—and what awaited them should they decide to join them.

Emperor Nero already had a tradition of hosting feasts in his gardens for citizens and friends. He could not resist the chance to use even these as an opportunity to make a spectacle of the believers. Crosses, like those used for crucifixion, were erected throughout the garden. The innocent believers were nailed or bound to these crosses and then smeared with pitch or dressed in stiff shirts of wax. When night came, Nero ordered them burned on the crosses to provide lighting for the evening festivities.

Many a time when the children would retire for the night they would cry themselves to sleep. They did their best not to, for fear of being discovered, but sometimes the pain was just too much to hold in. Both of them possessed a very tender heart. Almost every night they entreated God on behalf of their brethren. Yet, even as they prayed that their Father would deliver them from evil, they were also careful to pray for grace to endure the trials. Their friends out in the catacombs had asked them to pray that God would strengthen their faith through the persecution and by their example he would be glorified. Ariel and Anthony knew this; it was just hard to remember that the real danger was not that they would lose life, but that they would lose faith.

At the beginning of the emperor's warfare against the believers, the inhabitants of Rome already held the Christians in disdain and distrust. The Romans themselves had ascribed this name, Christian, to the followers of Jesus as a mark of humiliation, shame, and enmity. The emperor went out of his way to glamorize the torture and execution of the Christians. Throughout his entire reign, the emperor had possessed an incessant desire for pleasure, a desire so foul and twisted that it was sickening. This became clear to the people seeing the emperor's war on the Christians. Though they believed the Christians were guilty as charged, they could also see that the emperor's actions were not motivated by his care for the people or a desire for justice but by his insatiable thirst for cruelty. Emperor Nero took such pleasure in seeing the Christians die in agony, and the people of Rome quickly saw this too. To him it was entertainment, indulgence for his foul and depraved self.

The Final Message to Rome

The church had never faced such cruel opposition. Yet, as their affliction and oppression dragged on, the perception of the citizens and their feelings toward the Christians shifted. Instead of viewing them with reproach, the citizens came to regard them with empathy. Though they may still have believed them to be enemies of humanity, the motivation of the emperor made them detest the whole business.

Often Ariel was called to accompany Gloria and Floriana to the public bathhouses where the Senator's daughters would bathe and relax along with friends and extended family. Many of these ladies had witnessed the demise of Christians in the amphitheaters and were puzzled that the Christians were not moved by their tragic fate. The stories that these ladies told of the Christians were very inspiring to Anthony and Ariel.

In spite of the horrendous ordeal they faced, the Christians behaved themselves with the utmost devotion and faithfulness to their God, and an unsurpassed love and forgiveness for their persecutors. When they were driven into the arena to be eaten by the lions, they would not quake or weep for fear of death. Instead, they would gather together, encouraging each other and offering songs of praise to God and prayers of compassion for their enemies. Unarmed and defenseless, they faced the lions with unflinching courage. Their faces seemed to glow with a shining light that came out of nowhere.

The effect that they had on those around them was also beyond comprehension. At times, when they were imprisoned before execution, they would be placed in the company of thieves, murderers, and other violent and hardened offenders who were soon to be executed. Whether these criminals died alone or in the company of the Christians, those watching witnessed an unmistakable change in many of them. Instead of perishing with fear and despair, as criminals so often did, they died with an air of hope and joyfulness that no one could understand. In the emperor's gardens, as the believers were bound to the crosses on which they would soon be burned, they did not shout out words of hatred or curses to the people watching them perish. They remained serenely silent with a display of peace and love on their faces. If they did speak, it was to pray to God for courage and strength, and to entreat those watching to repent and embrace faith in Jesus Christ. If they prayed for mercy, it was not for themselves but for their persecutors.

Witnessing the courage and love of their brethren filled Anthony and Ariel's hearts with more joy and hope than anything else. They were so proud of their friends. They prayed that when the time came for them to be tested that they would respond in a way that would bring as much glory to God as their brothers and sisters had.

The Romans watching knew not what to make of these Christians. They could not understand them and wondered what it was that enabled them to stand firm and endure in the face of such cruelty and destruction. This strength, peace, or whatever it could be that enabled men to live and face death in such a way baffled the minds of the tormentors and roused the curiosity of the spectators. This was despite the fact that the Romans were captivated and entertained by the spectacle of blood and violence. This was especially evident in their obsession with watching gladiators fight and slaughter each other in the amphitheaters.

The Roman citizens were not the only ones awed by the sacrifice of the Christians. The slaves of Rome were intrigued by the stand of the Christians, particularly because a vast majority of those that died were slaves. These slaves lived their lives under a crushing and repressive yoke of bondage. This was true not just in the city of Rome but all throughout the empire. Sentenced to a life of hardship, servitude, and abasement, they lived with no purpose but the pleasure and opulence of their masters and, of course, Rome. To see people like them stand against the will of an empire that was, to their minds, all-powerful was more than just an unprecedented phenomenon. It gave them hope, hope and purpose for their lives and even the hope of a better, an eternal life. Their lives were barren of true satisfaction and genuine gladness. They had little to live for but to survive with a few necessities. To see life lived out with a reason greater than mere survival captivated the hearts and minds of the slaves in Rome. They were eager to understand more of this way of life.

Distressed over the many failures and atrocities of their leaders, the Roman citizens themselves had fallen into resignation and despaired of the hope of eternal salvation and the ultimate triumph of good over

The Final Message to Rome

evil. Life on Earth was all they could hope for: to survive for a while and eventually die as all men were destined to. The believers had given them back the hope of a divine king, who did rule the world and would deliver true justice.

Though some may have perceived the believers as incognizant or indifferent to their situation, the believers were very troubled over the persecution that they saw around them. Forced to exercise the utmost caution and secrecy as they lived out their faith, the church went into hiding. Their activities had always been as secretive as possible, as Jesus had instructed, but now they were not hiding to escape the praise of men but to escape torture and death. The emperor's soldiers and spies were everywhere. If they were overheard or discovered, even by ordinary citizens or slaves, they could be reported and arrested. In spite of the many dangers, the believers would not be deterred from their commission to preach the gospel. Multitudes of believers were forced to flee the city and take refuge in the catacombs. Others, like Anthony and Ariel, who were bound to their masters, remained in the city, keeping their faith as guarded as possible. The underground network of tunnels and caves in the catacombs proved a reliable safe haven from the Romans. Not only because they were well concealed but also because they were where the believers buried their departed brethren. The Romans knew this to and were loathe to enter the catacombs to apprehend the Christians. There was a Roman custom to not bury the dead within the city; cremation was the more standard procedure for the disposal of a corpse in Rome. Although, a few Non-Christians were buried in cave networks adjacent to the Christian catacombs. Whether out of sacred reverence or superstition, the Romans chose not to pursue the believers hiding in the catacombs.

Although they were temporarily shielded from their pursuers, the Christians did not remain hidden in the catacombs. They ventured out into the city to continue the work they had started. Though behaving with the utmost vigilance and discretion, they were ever bold and unashamed of the message they delivered and the works they did. The poor, the widows, and the orphans of Rome benefited immensely from the service of the believers. Meanwhile, other believers were busy inside the city, constructing tunnels, secret passages, and houses to meet in, anything at all that would enable them to continue in the Master's grand design while still remaining undiscovered. Numerous Christian families could take up residence in a single house and meet to worship and encourage each other while attracting little attention from the outside or their landlord.

The fact that a considerable portion of the city had been reduced to ashes gave the Christians a decided advantage. In addition to his persecution of the Christians, Emperor Nero was rebuilding the city that had been lost in the fire, along with palaces for himself. The reconstruction of Rome was the perfect alibi for the believers as they constructed a new secret network of houses and tunnels throughout the city. The network proved crucial in the years that followed.

Senator Marcus often entrusted Anthony with delivering messages to the other senators. Sometimes these messages were delivered while they were at the Senate; others Anthony had to deliver directly to the home of the receiving senator. Anthony used this to expand his knowledge of Rome, navigating the streets and buildings. He still kept his ears open for anything that could be useful to the believers. He listened to the senators to learn the overall plans of the government, and he listened to the soldiers for specific methods and tactics they used for finding the Christians. As time passed, Anthony sensed that there was a shift in the feelings of the Romans toward the Christians. This was not only in the Senate. All over the city, people everywhere, officials, citizens, even the soldiers and executioners themselves, were beginning to sympathize with the Christians.

The two children continued to meet secretly in the garden at night to pray and encourage each other. The days flew by as they poured themselves into their work at the house and at the Senate. Both the children had been brought up in families where they were taught the importance of hard work. While in the catacombs, they had witnessed the other believers working with such energy and joy as they would for Jesus himself. Following this example, they distinguished themselves as some of the most reliable servants in the house. Their initiative, diligence, responsibility, and enthusiasm gained them the favor and praise of their masters and of other people.

Anthony overheard several senators' comment to Senator Marcus on the fine performance of his new servant. Some even asked if he would consider selling him to them. Claudio gave Anthony a special word of commendation after a long day at court with the senator. Anthony responded with the utmost humility, voicing his gladness in serving the senator.

As Claudio walked away, Anthony heard him mutter to himself, "Where do they find slaves like him?"

A chill passed through Anthony's body. *This could be dangerous,* he thought to himself. *You live your life to please Jesus, and in no time, they figure out that something is different about you. Next thing you know they find out that you are a Christian.*

He was walking back to the servants' sleeping quarters, feeling a bit worried over where the situation could potentially lead, when he remembered that Jesus had indeed called him to a life of danger. With this thought, a feeling of lightheartedness so overtook him that he almost broke out in laughter.

As he lay down to sleep that night, he whispered a prayer to the Lord.

"Jesus, Master," Anthony prayed, "you told us not to do good deeds before men to receive their praise, but with you living out of me, I just can't escape notice."

To think about this seemed perfectly hilarious to Anthony, but his mood changed at the thought of what would happen if they found out he was a Christian.

"Lord," he continued, "I am living the way you want me to, and it could lead me into trouble or even death, but it's what you want me to do. So, I trust that as I am obeying and pleasing you, you will take care of me."

Ariel served Gloria and Floriana with such sweetness that the two of them actually started thanking her for fulfilling a service, something they did not often do with the other servants. They started to look forward to Ariel greeting them with a smile each morning, as bright and refreshing as the dawn. Ariel was exceedingly grateful to God for giving her the opportunity to serve and please these ladies, as he would have done.

One night as she lay down to sleep, she prayed, "Dear Jesus, shine through me. Let your spirit rest on me, and may your love flow through me to Gloria and Floriana. Speak to them, Lord; prepare them to hear your good news. Touch their hearts and heal them. Keep using me to be a blessing to them. I want you to be praised. I love you, Jesus."

To reward the two children for their hard work, their overseers allowed them a small amount of time to be relieved of their duties around the house, certain that they would not run away. The children used this precious time to return to the house that Justus had showed them. Miraculously, the overseers were not the least suspicious of their activities outside the house; the children seemed so innocent. In addition, the children also received some small wages. This was not uncommon, for slaves to receive some payment from their masters, though it was not required.

After meeting with Justus again, he led them to another house where the believers frequently met to break bread, encourage one another, and pray for each other and for those who did not understand faith in Jesus. This was typically where the children would go to meet with other believers. They were always very careful passing through the streets of Rome. Being out in the day was not as dangerous as being out at night, but in the daylight, it was much easier for them to be followed. To avoid this, the children would alter the route that they took to the house, keep a distance between themselves as they walked, and stop now and then to make sure they were not being followed. Only on rare occasions did they split up. Nero's soldiers and spies were everywhere. They knew the danger was great, but the danger that they would lose their faith was even greater. There was also a danger of spies infiltrating a group of believers. The believers had learned to watch for false believers just as they had learned to watch for false teachers who taught a different gospel.

The Final Message to Rome

The children took care to ensure that they were not being followed to the house and that the house was not being watched before they entered. They were equally cautious when they left. Nearly every time the children would return to the house, they would notice that somewhere there was an empty chair; someone was missing. The believers were continually being discovered and sentenced to death, but despite these losses, their numbers did not decline but only increased. For every place left by their fallen brethren, there was always another or two to take his place. Though they grieved the loss of their friends, they took courage and hope in knowing that it was Jesus who was protecting them and keeping them alive. As they were doing his will, he would not suffer anyone to touch them until their work was done. Anthony and Ariel continued to meet in the garden at night to pray for and encourage each other. Though always sober and cautious, they had no need or reason to be afraid.

Chapter 8

A Plot Discovered

Time passed on in Rome, and the carnage only got worse. Nothing was beneath Nero, and everyone knew this, especially the Christians. His cruelty and oppression tested the believers like never before, but their faith could not be shaken by hardship. Instead, it grew stronger. They became even more bold and daring. They did not dwindle in numbers but multiplied, growing faster than Nero could kill them. Frustrated at his failure to save his name, and humiliated at his defeat by the Christians, Nero's madness only grew worse. He had hoped that the fake confessions and his fury in punishing these "heinous criminals" would convince the people that he was only doing what was best for Rome. He was wrong. The love and forgiveness displayed by the Christians as they met their fate made it obvious who the real villain was. Instead, the people of Rome grew even more suspicious of the emperor. They pitied the estate of the Christians and concluded that the emperor was merely trying to glut his own lust for blood and cruelty.

Nero was outraged. He had failed to win back the worship of Rome, and now he was seen for the man he was. He was also being made to look weak. He who was emperor, all-powerful, could not stamp out a people that were so small, yet from their hearts displayed more courage and strength than he ever could.

He had failed. Still, all he could think to do was to kill and torture even more. To add insult to injury, the Christians were becoming even bolder as they spoke out for Jesus. The apostle Peter, who had always been very resolute, was drawing more and more attention as he spoke out for Jesus Christ as Lord, and against Caesar, who was not Lord.

Nero was filled with hatred and a desire for vengeance. He could not let Peter go unpunished, and he swore to himself and to the Roman gods that he would make a public example of Peter. This could be just what he needed to stop the growth of the Christians. Peter was probably the most prominent and respected leader among the Christians in Rome, if not the world.

If I can make an example of him, Nero thought, *kill the leader and his followers will scatter.* And so it was that Nero committed himself, his soldiers, his spies, and all the resources he could muster to finding this man, Simon Peter.

Though the precise date of these events may be debatable, it was at this time that the real drama in the story of Anthony and Ariel unfolded.

It was a day much like all the other days in the senator's house. Ariel was busy waiting on the senator's daughters, and Anthony was with the senator at court. Senator Marcus returned home at the usual time, showing no signs of anything out of the ordinary. Supper proceeded in its routine fashion, and all members of the house retired to bed. The two children had planned to meet in the garden that night. It had been four days since their last meeting, as the last few had been exceptionally tiring.

Following their usual plan, Ariel waited for a while in her bed, acting as though she were asleep, until she was sure no one would hear or see her leave. She snuck through the house, in her usual cautious fashion, and into the garden. While slipping across the path into some bushes, she heard Anthony's voice calling to her softly from behind the hedge growth. The children took care never to meet in the same area of the garden twice in a row. Anyone walking about the garden in the day would surely see the pattern of disruption in the landscape and grow suspicious.

The Final Message to Rome

Ariel slipped behind the hedge quietly, and the two embraced each other as a brother and sister.

Before Ariel could say anything, Anthony began speaking with a deep sense of urgency.

"Ariel, there is something that I have to tell you," he said with a grave and solemn expression on his face. "I had to sneak out to the catacombs two nights ago. Peter is leaving. He's going to leave Rome, if he hasn't left already."

Ariel was speechless. She did not know what to say or even what to think of such shocking news. Finally, she regained herself and asked with a slow stammer, "Why? What happened?"

Anthony now related to Ariel the events of his latest adventure that had taken place two days previous. He recounted the events as best as his memory served. As to the exact details of what had happened, they are as follows.

Anthony was called to accompany Senator Marcus and wait upon him at the senate, as was his usual custom. At first, the day proceeded in a fairly normal fashion, but shortly after the noon hours, the emperor himself came to the assembly. He was there because the Senate had been asking him questions about the progress of his campaign against the Christians. The emperor spoke briefly on how he has been working very hard to remove these villains from Rome and said they are capturing and killing more than ever before. One of the senators, a rather bold fellow, spoke up after the emperor finished.

"And where is the progress you are making?' he challenged. 'The entire city can see that you are killing these Christians like never before, but what positive effect is all this having? Anyone with eyes can see that the Christians aren't getting smaller in number; they're only getting bigger. All your efforts in killing and torturing them have not reduced their numbers; it has only increased them. Besides all this, the people of Rome are becoming sympathetic toward the Christians, and it is making us look bad. The people are losing respect for you and us. What are you going to do about this? If you truly want to get rid of these Christians, you had better come up with a better way than killing and torturing them. Your plan isn't working.'

Nero became furious. He flew into a violent rage and railed on everyone that they would even question his judgment, him, the emperor, the only man alive with revelation and power from the gods. Yea, even God himself. He ranted and raved for quite a long time. When he finally ran out of things to say, he exhaled a long breath and got a very smug expression on his face. He then scoffed at the senators, calling them fools for even considering the possibility that he had made a mistake.

"'But,' Nero said, 'just to prove to you that I know what I am doing, I will tell you what I am going to do next. I am aware of the large growth among these Christians, and I know why it is happening' it is because of their leaders. An army cannot fight without a king to lead them, nor can these Christians survive without someone to lead them. Without their leaders, they will fall apart, and their memory will disappear. Kill the leaders, and the followers will scatter. This is what will keep them from multiplying. In a few days, my generals, soldiers, and spies will all be focused on apprehending and making an example of the men who are leading this sect. We are especially interested in one man; they call him Simon Peter. This particular sect of conspirators began about thirty years ago in Judea. Their leader was a carpenter, a man called Jesus. He is the one the Christians all follow and worship as the Son of God, for so he claimed himself to be. Though he was crucified and buried, his disciples, as they were called, refused to accept reality. They somehow managed to steal his body from its grave and have propagated the lie that he rose from the dead. As crazy as it is, people actually believe this fable.'

"Nero laughed before the whole Senate, hoping they would find it as amusing as he did. The senators were not impressed. Nero coughed and pretended to be clearing his throat to hide his laughter. He went on.

"'This man Peter is looked up to by the Christians as one of the few who were very close friends with this Jesus. His disciples have scattered all throughout the world. However, we know for certain that Peter is here in Rome. It is his influence that is enabling them to hold out despite all our best efforts. If we can find him—no, we will find him, and we will make an example of him. We will make an end of him, the same way we made an end of their leader, Jesus. We Romans know that nothing sends a message like crucifixion. This is how we will rid ourselves of him and how we will begin to make an end of these conspirators.'

"Nero was very persuasive; no other senator challenged him or asked him any more questions. Several even applauded and cheered after he finished speaking. Right then, Anthony knew that he had to make it back to the catacombs and tell them what Nero was planning. He tried to tell Ariel about what had happened that night, but both of them had been very busy that day and were quite exhausted. They had planned to meet in the garden several nights later, and because of all the other servants that were about Anthony could not have spoken to Ariel without being noticed. Weighing the possible risks against the danger if he did not act, Anthony decided to sneak out of the city on his own.

Navigating the streets at night was nothing new to the children. They both could tell if someone was following them and with their knowledge of the streets evading a pursuer was no trouble at all. There were not too many patrols that night, but Anthony still had to walk softly, stay in the shadows and keep his eyes open for thieves.

He had made it safely to the house where Justus had brought him and Ariel. He walked past the house and farther down the street to make sure no one was about. Then he circled around and came up behind the house, by way of a back alley, as an extra precaution. Justus was inside praying with several other men. When Anthony told them what he had found out, everyone immediately agreed to help Anthony get out of the city. As it happened, Justus knew exactly where Peter was that night. He was at the catacombs, leading a group of believers as they, prayed, sang, and broke bread.

Justus addressed the small group present. "Friends, we have to get Anthony out there, now. Many of the brethren have been entreating Peter over the danger in the city. They have been pleading with him, for his own sake, that it may be best for him to leave Rome. Peter is not convinced that he should leave just yet. He needs to hear this from Anthony himself."

"Look out into the street," Justus advised, turning to the lady of the house. "Is there anyone coming or watching the house?"

"It was deserted when I came," Anthony offered.

The woman parted the curtains and looked out as casually as ever. No one outside would have guessed that she might be hiding something.

"It still is," she said with a smile.

"Open the tunnel. Make haste," Justus commanded, looking at the men standing by. "We have to get out there as fast as we can. It's already late. Once the meeting is over, Peter will likely go somewhere else. There no telling where he might be found after that."

The men pushed the table aside and, with the help of some levers, drew up the large tile in the stone floor. The woman handed a torch to Justus, and he stepped down into the hole and onto the ladder. None of the men moved to follow him as he descended into the vault below. Justus had left the torch unlit so it would be easier to climb with. Once he had reached the bottom, he drew a strip of steel and a flint stone from a small pouch that hung on his belt. Striking a light, he lit the torch and held it up to provide light for the others as they made their descent.

As soon as the light of the torch appeared from below, the men motioned for Anthony to climb down. One after another, the group descended into the tunnel, and the stone was replaced. Then they made their way out, walking and crawling through the tunnel as it grew bigger and smaller. Justus led the way, followed by three men, Anthony, and another behind him. Once they made it to the end of the tunnel, Justus put out the torch and crawled up the dirt slide with another man beside him. The two behind them supported their feet as they ascended the steep incline. Reaching the top, they heaved on the stone and dislodged it. Justus crawled out first with some help from the man beside him. Then he pulled the other man out. The second man had brought a rope with him, coiled around his waist. Once out, they sent one end of the rope down into the tunnel and hauled the rest of the group out one by one. A man would crawl up the slide, supported by the man behind him, using the rope to help him climb, and then be pulled out of the hole by the men above. When the last man was out, they reset the stone and moved on. Anthony noticed that Justus was moving faster than he had ever seen him and that he was taking a different route than the one he had used on the children's last visit. He led the group to one of the caves that neither of the children had visited.

The Final Message to Rome

"Where are we?" Anthony inquired.

"You've probably never been to this part of the catacombs," Justus said. "These caves were only recently built. They are where many of our dead have been buried. We have had to build more since the emperor declared war on us."

A large boulder was laid over the door, like a gravestone. Justus picked up a rock from beside the path and hammered on the stone several times, then stopped. As soon as the stone began to move, everyone offered their strength to push it aside.

Once inside with the opening sealed, they were led to the large chamber of the cave where everyone had gathered. They were just in time. The meal had ended, and Peter was blessing them all in prayer as they prepared to leave. As soon as he finished, Justus spoke up.

"Brethren, wait," he proclaimed. "Please don't leave. We have received some very important news from this young man here." Justus motioned to Anthony. "He is a fellow believer, who is a servant in the house of a Roman senator. He has been called upon to serve his master at the Roman Senate, where he has been vigilant to learn anything that may be of use to us. Today, he overheard the emperor disclosing some of his new plans against us, and Simon Peter in particular. He snuck out of his master's house to inform me, and we brought him here as fast as we could. You must hear him; it is of the utmost importance."

Justus paused for a moment to see if the people would give him audience. Looking here and there among each other for a few moments, the believers took their seats in silence with their gaze fixed on Anthony. One of the elderly men standing close to Peter addressed Anthony.

"What is your name, young man?" the elder asked.

"My name is Anthony," Anthony responded.

"Then please, Anthony," the man said, "tell us what you have learned."

Stepping forward into the midst of the crowd to be clearly seen, Anthony recounted everything that he had seen and heard that day at the Senate, leaving out no detail.

When he finished, the room was silent; the slightest sound could be heard. The suspense of the room was so great; everyone was all but holding their breath. For a long time, no one knew what to say.

Finally, another elder standing beside Peter broke the silence. "Thank you, Anthony. This warning may have come just at the right moment." Then, turning to Simon Peter, he asked, "Well, what are you going to do? Do you still think that you should remain here in Rome?"

Peter was silent, with a strange calmness on his face. He didn't seem to be moved at all by the report Anthony had brought.

Then he spoke. "Our Lord Jesus warned us of the dangers that we would face for his name. The very first time he sent the twelve of us out, he said, 'I send you forth as sheep in the midst of wolves, so be as wise as a serpent, yet as harmless as a dove.' He told us that we would be brought before councils and scourged in the very synagogues. 'All men will hate you for my name's sake, but if you endure to the end, you will be saved.'"

At this, a second elder rose from the table as Peter paused in his oration. "We know this all too well, Peter, and we have not forgotten your own words, 'Do not think it strange concerning the fiery trial that is to try you as though some strange thing happened unto you.' We know that you have told us to rejoice that we are partakers of Christ's sufferings and to commit the keeping of our souls to the Lord who is our faithful Creator. But, do you remember that Jesus also told you at the same time he sent you out, 'When they persecute you in one city, flee into another'? Your very presence here in Rome was because you were forced to flee from Jerusalem. Do you remember Saul of Tarsus, who by the grace of God is now called Paul? There are times when we must flee."

The elder had seemed a bit agitated as he spoke to Peter, but Peter remained as calm as he had been before. Now he answered.

"Well said," Peter replied, "and you are right, Jesus told us that there are times to flee. Jesus fled himself at times, and so have we his disciples, but never out of fear. 'Fear not them which kill the body but are not able to kill the soul, but rather fear him which is able to destroy both soul and body in hell.' You and I who belong to Jesus have nothing

The Final Message to Rome

to fear. He does not forget the welfare of sparrows, and he has assured us that we are more precious to him than many sparrows. We should not be afraid to confess him before men anywhere. He came to Earth to do the work of his Father; part of that work included starting a war.

"He left us here to carry on that war, and that war will be with those of our own household. As he said, 'He who loves his father or mother more than me is not worthy of me. He who does not take up his cross, whatever that cross may be, to the death, he is not worthy of me.'"

As Peter said this, he fixed his gaze upon Anthony. It seemed that he intended these words specifically for him. Anthony wondered what Peter was trying to communicate, but Peter went on.

"'He who tries to save his life shall lose it, but he who loses his life for my sake shall find it life.'"

Now Peter paused and studied the faces of the people throughout the room. Although Anthony may not have been able to see it, there was fear and confusion, but there was also assurance and hope. The room was quiet, quieter than ever. The drop of a pebble could have been heard when Peter finished speaking; the sound of everyone's breathing could be heard, if they were breathing at all. This calm must have lasted for at least a minute, but as time went on, each of the brethren, one by one, silently bowed their heads and began to pray silently. How long this lasted no one knew. To some it seemed short; to others it seemed long.

At last, a third elder rose to his feet and addressed Peter. "Peter, we know you are not afraid to die. We all know how many times you have risked your life for Jesus. We're not asking you to flee because of the danger, but we are asking you to consider that God may be trying to send you a message. God has moved you all throughout the world, Peter. He brought you from Jerusalem to Rome, and he has used you, but he has also called you to serve him in other places. He used Saul of Tarsus and his cruelty to push you and the other disciples out of Jerusalem to spread the gospel throughout the world. It is not the fear for your own life that we ask you to consider, but that God may have use for you elsewhere. You may be more useful to him just now in another city than you are here in Rome. Jesus used every one of his disciples"—he paused, and his gaze turned downward as he spoke in a low voice—"even Judas Iscariot, and he continues to use you, as you listen and follow him. Peter, please consider. Could this be the Lord leading you to serve him in another place?"

With a murmur of low voices, all the believers standing or sitting about the room nodded in agreement, and Peter clasped his hands in front of him and lowered his gaze in silence. A minute passed, and he raised his head.

"Yes," he said, "yes, perhaps it is. Perhaps this is God leading me on to somewhere else. Many of you have been entreating me to leave Rome for some time, and this report may be the final confirmation. It would be foolish for me not to at least consider your counsel. Your concerns are well intended and reasonably sound. My heart aches every time this happens, every time I must leave the people that I have grown to love, but our Lord has told me to do it before, and even Jesus himself had to leave us many years ago."

Peter paused again and was silent for several moments.

"Very well," he said, "I will. I will leave Rome."

Peter's voice affected everyone in an unusual way. One by one, the believers rose from their places and approached Peter to embrace him and say their last farewells. These people had all entreated him to leave, and for his own sake, they were glad to see him do so. Still, he could see in their faces and hear from their voices that they were all very sorry to see him go. They all assured him that he would be in their thoughts and prayers and that they would carry on where he had left off. Anthony, too, said good-bye to Peter, wishing that Ariel could have been there. The group dispersed after saying good-bye, and Justus led Anthony and the others back into the city.

The journey back was very quiet and even a bit somber. No one said anything to each other; they were too overcome, either with grief or shock. Nobody had thought that this would all happen so fast. Justus found the tunnel entrance, and the group crawled back through the tunnel to the house where they had come from. They didn't stay long; it was now very late, and everyone had to sneak back. The lady checked the street to make sure the coast was clear. The street was as silent as

The Final Message to Rome

ever. Then they all went out two at a time, walking together for a few minutes, then disappearing from each other into the shadows. Anthony stayed under cover all the way back to the senator's house, escaping all detection.

"I'm really sorry, Ariel," Anthony said as he finished his report. "I wish you could have been with me. I know you really would have wanted to say good-bye."

He paused to let Ariel absorb everything that he had said. She was silent, lost in her thoughts and feelings. A minute or so passed before she replied.

"Yes, I'm sorry, too, but you did the right thing. You had to get that message out to them as soon as possible." She smiled a little bit. "Who knows, you may have even saved Peter's life. I sure am going to miss him."

Anthony nodded; he had never thought of his message as saving Peter's life.

"What do you think will happen now to everyone in Rome with Peter gone?" Ariel asked. "Do you think we'll be able to carry on without him?"

Anthony shrugged. "I guess we'll have to."

"What should we do?" Ariel asked.

"We'll keep doing what we have been doing. You and I really need to find someone we can tell about Jesus, someone who won't turn us in, if we can."

Ariel reached out her hand. "Let's pray," she said, "and then we should get back to bed."

With a smile, Anthony nodded.

"Dear Jesus, thank you for your servant Peter, for everything he has meant to us, all he has done here in Rome. Keep using him, Lord, wherever you lead him; give him courage and boldness no matter what he may face. Protect him, and give him wisdom to hear your voice and see your plan. For those of us who are left here in Rome, keep us strong, protect us from our enemies, and we trust you for the grace to love our enemies. We love you, Jesus. We will speak out and tell someone about you. Amen."

The two children embraced, then slipped out of the garden and back to their sleeping quarters.

In the days that followed, the children continued meet in the garden, but it was a while before they were able to sneak out of the house again and connect with the other believers. Still, they pressed on with new strength, keeping a cheerful attitude and doing their work heartily as unto the Lord. The overseers took notice of their hard work, commending them and promising to reward them. The situation in Rome continued as it had before. Nero was still hunting for Christians in the city and having them executed. So many were dying, in scores like never before, yet new believers always arose to take their place. How long, how long would this go on, and what would be the outcome? Everywhere in Rome, the Christians wondered; any day could be their last.

Chapter 9

Rescue and Tragedy

A week or so after Anthony had reported that Peter had made his departure from Rome; the duties in the senator's house began to slow. The children were grateful that things were subsiding, hoping that soon they would be able to sneak out again and meet with their friends. Their hopes were rewarded when each of them was separately called in to speak with their overseers, Claudio and Julia. Senator Marcus, his wife, and his two daughters were leaving Rome to take a few days of vacation in the countryside along the Tiber River.

This was quite common for upper-class Roman families who owned considerable land. In addition to their house in the city, wealthy families were known for having one if not several homes in the country. Senator Marcus had a rather large estate in the country that was managed by more of his slaves. He and his family retreated there quite often to get away from the city life. Conditions in the country were much simpler, and while it lacked the modern conveniences of the city, life there was pure and delightful. The children's presence was not requested, which meant that their duties would be only a few light tasks. They would be allowed the better part of the afternoon and the evening off, but they would have to be ready to serve the family upon their return. Whenever the senator's family left the city that was the time for the children to sneak out and meet with the other believers.

On children's last midnight excursion, Justus had told them that a large number of believers would be coming to meet at another house a few city blocks away. The children had been to this house several times in the previous months. As God would have it, they would be meeting on the very same night that the senator and his family were going out. Seeing their opportunity to sneak out, the two children finished their daily responsibilities earlier than usual, in the midafternoon. Claudio permitted the servants to take an early supper and gave them leave to do as they pleased that evening. Anthony and Ariel discussed their plan secretly behind the hedge in the garden. They would wait till the activity in the house died down, then change into their street clothes, rendezvous in the garden, and sneak out of the house.

The plan worked to perfection. They left by the side door nearly an hour before sunset. Ariel still had the key. They locked the door behind them and headed out into the street. Ariel kept the key in her pouch. Both felt it would be safer than leaving the side door unlocked and risking a break-in, besides if a break-in did happen, it would likely be discovered that the side door had been left unlocked. The trail would lead back to them, and their association with the Christians would be discovered. No one saw the two children leave the house.

Both the children had become quite adept at navigating through Rome, and they did it best at night. Following a series of back passageways and dark alleys, the children arrived at the house after about a twenty-minute walk without any trouble.

The house was located on a small street toward the middle section of the road, among numerous other houses. The only entrance was the front door, which faced the street. The house was fairly large in area and had three floors. Two were equipped with rooms, and the third was a large balcony, which covered most of the roof of the building.

What made this house so special was the fact that the believers had built a tunnel underneath it to use for a quick escape in the case of emergency. This tunnel was a great secret, even to many of the believers. The entrance was hidden under a large stone in the floor of the front room. The tunnel was about one hundred yards long. It came up under a haystack in a small stable next to another house behind the first one. This second house was off the main road and only accessible through several alleyways. If the street outside was being patrolled or someone was watching the house, the Christians could crawl through the tunnel and leave one by one, heading in different directions.

Arriving at the house with the usual caution, the children found the street deserted. There were no soldiers about, and the people in the surrounding houses were returning to their homes for the evening meal. The two decided to double-check the alleyway that ran behind the house before entering. It, too, was empty and silent. Feeling relieved, the children approached the door, acting as nonchalant as ever. They knocked and were promptly admitted.

Both of them were exuberant to see their friends again, to hear what had been happening to them and how God had been at work in their lives. All the believers greeted them with a warm embrace and were equally excited to hear what had been happening to them. Most of the believers had heard the news that Peter had left the city. They were all very sorry to see him go; his presence and leadership would be sorely missed. There were between twenty and thirty people in the house. The children were grieved to hear the news that some of their friends had been captured and were almost certainly dead by now. This happened almost every time they met with the other believers.

On this evening, Justus stood up and began reading from a copy of a letter that had been sent to the church in Rome by the apostle Paul some years previous. Several sections of the letter spoke strongly to the heart of the believers as they thought of their current situation. Paul exhorted them to rejoice in hope, be patient in tribulation, persevere in prayer, and to bless those who persecuted them. He urged them further, as his dearly beloved, not to avenge themselves. For true vengeance was God's alone, and they had his promise that he would repay. They were not to lose faith and allow themselves to be crushed into renouncing their Lord, nor were they to become weary and return evil to their enemies. Instead, they were to demonstrate the love that they had seen in Jesus, return love for hatred, trust God to strengthen them and ultimately change the hearts of their enemies. After Justus finished reading, he laid the book aside and began simply to speak from his heart on what this meant to him. The people listening joined in with comments or questions; others shared personal experiences that they had lived through or were still living.

When the discussion of the letter ended, Justus stood up and delivered some news and requests for prayer from around the city. A few other people present offered a few others. Then, with Justus leading, everyone knelt and joined together in prayer. They asked for Peter's safety, for the grace to press on and rejoice, also that God would deliver them from their enemies and that their persecutors would find the love and forgiveness of Jesus Christ. The requests were accompanied with praise and thanksgiving to the Lord. An hour or two passed, but to everyone present, it seemed like no time at all. By the time the prayers had ended, everyone's heart was overflowing with a joy that was almost hilarious. A few of the believers broke forth in song, and everyone else joined in. They almost forgot that their voices could be overheard outside.

Both the children were once again overcome with joy, and then they realized that they would soon have to return to the senator's house. So without any further delay, they said farewell to their friends, until they should meet again, and made for the front door. Anthony unbolted the door and stepped out with Ariel following.

Suddenly, he stopped dead in his tracks just outside the door; Ariel bumped into him as she was trying to close it.

"Anthony, are you all right?" she said.

He didn't move. He was looking down the road to his left.

"Quiet," Anthony said. "I hear something."

Ariel could tell from his tone of voice that his state of mind had drastically changed. She looked about her and listened, trying to discern what Anthony had heard that so concerned him. Before she could detect anything out of the ordinary, Anthony turned swiftly. An expression of urgency and peril covered his face, and his eyes were larger than she had ever seen them.

"Back inside," he said.

Ariel did not hesitate or ask any questions. The two slipped back inside, and Anthony hastily locked the door.

"Justus," Anthony exclaimed with urgency, "horses are coming. It could be soldiers. Please, open the tunnel, just in case."

Justus nodded to the two men who were sitting at the table on top of the stone that covered the tunnel's entrance. They immediately rose to their feet, pulled the table aside, and began to pry up the stone with a pair of levers sitting nearby. Anthony did not wait for the stone to be removed. He maneuvered his way through the crowd as fast as he could and bounded up the stairs with Ariel and Justus close behind.

He ran up to the third floor and knelt down behind the small wall overlooking the road, just above the front door. Looking down into the street, the three saw a group of seven Roman soldiers ride into view and stop a few houses down. They looked about themselves, studying the houses along the road. One of them pointed toward the house that the believers were meeting in.

Anthony turned to Justus. "Tell them to bar the door, close any windows, and get into the tunnel as fast as they can."

Justus nodded and ran for the stairs.

The troop trotted up the street and halted several houses down. For about a minute or so, they stayed there exchanging words and glances.

The two children knelt there, spellbound, looking down the road at the soldiers. There was no back door, and there were too many people inside. There would not be enough time to escape before the soldiers broke down the door.

We're trapped, they thought to themselves, and they both knew what would follow once the soldiers got into the house.

Anthony looked over his shoulder, across the balcony. His mouth dropped open for a moment, and then he sprang back from the wall, pulling Ariel with him.

"I know what to do," he said. "Go back down, and tell them I need four men up here, now!"

"What are you going to do?" she pleaded, frightened and confused.

"I'm going to keep them outside as long as I can. If they get inside, we're all dead. Now hurry," Anthony urged. "Tell the others to keep the door from being broken in. Bring me an oil lamp and a torch, but don't light the torch."

Ariel rushed downstairs as fast as she could and relayed Anthony's request.

Anthony watched as the soldiers rode on, a bit slower, reined their horses directly across the street, and dismounted. Two of the soldiers stayed behind, holding the reins of the horses, while the rest of the group ventured across the street, heading for the house, two soldiers leading the way with torches.

Four men rushed upstairs to the balcony as Ariel found an oil lamp sitting on the table in the front room. One of the other people in house retrieved a torch from the storeroom. By the time she made it back to the roof, Anthony and the men had moved three clay jars over to the wall above the street, along with several bundles of flax and straw that had been lying around on the balcony. Ariel handed the lamp and torch to Anthony just in time to hear a loud knock on the door below.

"Open the door," came a strong and stern voice from below. "In the name of Caesar, open this door!"

Anthony crouched down against the wall, holding the lamp in one hand and the torch in the other. On his left, directly above the door, one of the men knelt in front of the wall with a few small bricks and an empty clay jar. To his left, another man crouched holding a large jar filled with oil. Behind the three kneeling against the wall were two other men on either side of a large stack of flax and straw. The other two jars and the rest of the straw and flax were pushed a little off to the side.

"Remember," Anthony said in a low voice, turning to the men beside and behind him, "we drop the bricks first, then the jar. Don't hit them; just drop them close enough so they will back away from the door. Then throw the flax down. Make sure you drop it right in front of the door. As soon as it lands, pour the oil on, and I'll drop the torch. Everybody understand?"

The men nodded silently. Anthony smiled in return and went back to listening to what was happening at the door.

"Open this door, I say, now!" shouted the soldier below, pounding much harder.

Several of the men were holding their breath, and Ariel could see that Anthony was shaking. They were all very scared.

"Get ready," Anthony whispered.

For a moment or two, the door was trembling on its hinges, though still closed. The knocking suddenly stopped. For several moments, nothing was heard from below.

"Very well, break it down," came the order.

Instantly, Anthony sprang to his feet. "Now!" he yelled at the top of his lungs.

The man kneeling above the door leapt up and began hurling down the small pile of projectiles lying at his feet. The plan worked even better than Anthony had hoped. After hearing Anthony shout, the soldiers turned their faces to the wall above them, and as soon as the storm of missiles descended on them, they jumped back, dropping their torches in front of the door as they put up their hands to protect their heads. The empty jar descended to the pavement with a crash, sending projectiles flying in every direction. The soldiers retreated several yards and then spun around, looking up with scowls of hatred at the shadowy figures on the roof.

One of the band, the apparent leader, unsheathed his sword and shouted to the two waiting with the horses, "Sound the alarm!"

Seizing a metal horn that hung from the saddle of his horse, the soldier blew a resounding blast. Long and loud it came, then more, one after another. The loud blasts of the horn awakened the occupants of the neighboring houses. Cries of shock and surprise were heard from inside the house that had just seconds ago been resting as peacefully as ever. Doors and windows were thrown open. Residents looked out, wide-eyed and breathless. The light of torches and lamps sprang from the inside of the houses and increased as people rushed out into the streets.

All of this drew little attention from Anthony and his comrades. It was the soldiers before them, and the others soon to arrive that presented their real danger. As soon as the soldiers had retreated from the door, the man who had thrown down the bricks and rocks moved swiftly to his right, toward Anthony, clearing the way for the two waiting behind him with the flax. Immediately, the two picked up the stack of flax, one at each end, stepped to the wall, and hauled it down into street below. As intended, the flax landed directly in front of the door and was ignited by the torches abandoned there by the soldiers just seconds before. This had not been part of Anthony's original plan, but he saw at once the advantage it gave them. Using a strip of steel and a flint stone he had found on the rooftop, he lit the torch and threw it down, igniting more of the barricade below.

Meanwhile, the soldiers below had regained their composure. Two ventured forward to retrieve their torches but were stopped when the flax was thrown down. They reached for their swords to push flax away from the door, but they had scarcely removed them from their sheaths when the flames shot up higher and hotter as the oil was poured down from the balcony. They leaped back, startled. At the sight of the ignition, the horses across the street reared up, neighing and snorting. Overwhelmed with panic, the two horses tossed both their riders from their saddles, and the whole group of horses sped off down the road at full gallop.

Anthony now assisted the other Christians in tossing down more flax, straw, and a few bundles of sticks. The flames grew larger and hotter, forcing the soldiers to abandon their hope of moving the fire away from the door with their swords. Now the five of them encircled the house, trying to find another entrance. Fortunately, there was no other door to the house, and the windows were too high and small for a man to crawl through.

Ariel raced downstairs to see how many people were left in the house. Only seven remained. She felt a surge of hope and relief wash over her. Perhaps they would all escape safely after all. She dashed back upstairs as fast as she could and reported to Anthony and the others.

Anthony and the four men hurled down anything they could find on the roof that would burn. When they had nothing left, Anthony sent three of them down to escape through the tunnel. The flames were still burning fiercely, putting out large billows of smoke. For a minute or two, the fire had been large and hot enough to keep back the soldiers by itself, but the fire quickly devoured the straw and flax. Now

Anthony and the last of the four men stood over the wall, each with a jar of oil. Anytime the soldiers approached to thrust the burning brush aside from the door, Anthony or the other man would cast down some oil onto the fire, forcing the soldiers to fall back. Both were careful to control how much oil was thrown and when. Their objective was not to injure the Romans but to keep them at bay. This went on for nearly two minutes. Then, just as Anthony started to worry that they might run out of oil before everyone could escape, he heard Justus's voice beside him.

"Well done, Anthony," Justus cheered him, placing one of his strong hands on Anthony's shoulder. "Everyone is out but us four."

"Just in time too," said the remaining man. "Look."

He pointed down the road in the direction the mounted soldiers had come. Another band of soldiers was fast approaching. These were on foot, carrying spears and shields and far greater in number than the first party.

"They'll be able to clear away the fire with those spears, then they'll force the door." Anthony exclaimed. "Give your jar to Justus," he said to the man beside him. "You and Ariel run for the tunnel. Justus and I will follow as soon as we can."

Whirling around, Ariel flew across the roof, down the stairs, and into the tunnel as fast as she could, with the man close behind.

She lowered herself into the opening, climbed down a few rungs and then leapt off the ladder, falling away into the darkness. It was a drop of eight or ten feet. Ariel landed feetfirst, but lost her balance and fell onto her back. Quickly, she rolled over and began crawling. She heard a soft thud as the man behind her descended into the tunnel.

She crawled as fast as she could in the dark, stumbling at times but crawling faster than she had ever done. The light at the other end of the tunnel came as a welcome relief. Leaping to her feet, she scaled the ladder and crawled out into the stable where the tunnel came up, and there waited for Anthony and Justus.

Back on the roof, Anthony paused momentarily, assessing the situation. The approaching soldiers were now just seventy yards away. He saw that the embers of the fire were only a yard from the front door. Justus interrupted Anthony's thoughts.

"What are we going to do, Anthony?" Justus pleaded urgently.

"We're going to set the door on fire; they won't be able to force it without a battering ram," Anthony responded. "Stand right here." He pointed to a spot just above the door and slightly to the right. Anthony stood just above and to the left of the door. "I'm going to pour my oil down to lead the fire to the door; then I want you to pour all your oil at the base of the door."

Anthony leaned over the wall, holding his jar out away from the wall. He poured a tiny stream of oil onto the side of the fire closest to the door. As soon as the oil ignited, he leaned out even farther over the wall, pouring down more oil, directing it in a stream leading toward the door. The fire followed the path of the oil across the pavement and onto the door.

"Now!" Anthony yelled, emptying the last of his oil onto the doorstep.

Immediately, Justus leaned out and threw down all his oil onto the door below. An enormous blast of flames erupted. Justus quickly pulled himself back from the wall, tossing the empty jar down into the street as the door was engulfed in flames. Anthony now hurled his jar over the wall, and it crashed on the pavement below, just in front of the wall of fire.

Anthony scanned the roof of the house and the street below one last time. There was no more oil left on the roof, and the soldiers had covered nearly half the distance to the house. There was nothing more they could do to keep them outside, but it would take the soldiers some time to remove the burning debris and break down the door. Hopefully, it would be long enough for them to escape and close the tunnel.

Anthony returned Justus's urgent waiting gaze with a nod of approval. "To the tunnel," he cried with a smile of satisfaction. The two turned swiftly and dashed across the roof to the stairs, with Justus leading the way. Suddenly, an overwhelming sense of danger and uncertainty swept over the two as time was brought to a standstill.

Justus heard a sharp hissing noise; but before he had time even to guess what it was, Anthony let out an intense cry of agony. The shock of the moment caused Justus to immediately check his pace. He skidded for a few feet before regaining his balance and wheeling round.

Anthony had fallen behind a few paces, his mouth open, gasping for breath, and his eyes nearly closed. Off balance, he staggered forward a pace or two and then crumpled to the ground facedown, an arrow in his back.

Justus flew to Anthony's side and turned him over into a sitting pose. Supporting him around the back with his left arm, Justus slapped Anthony on the cheek, hoping he was still alive.

"Anthony! Anthony!" he pleaded.

No response. Anthony's head fell limp onto his chest.

Shaking his head with sorrow, Justus gently let Anthony's body roll back to its original position. Gathering his wits about him, Justus rose up quickly and bolted for the stairs. He would have to grieve later.

Outside, the new band of soldiers rushed in and began thrusting the burning debris aside with their spears. In barely a minute, they had cleared the way to the door. Seeing that they could not throw their shoulders against the flaming door, two stood on either side and began pounding on it with the shaft end of their spears.

Justus bounded down the stairs as fast as he dared, hoping the burning door would delay the soldiers long enough for him to close the tunnel. Arriving in the front room, he grabbed the large stone that would conceal the entrance and began maneuvering it as best as one man could over to the hole. Adrenaline flowing, his heart skipped a beat as he heard the sound of the spears thudding against the front door. A shadow of fear and doubt flashed across his mind. What if he didn't make it?

Casting the fear aside, Justus heaved once again on the stone, harder than before. It inched across the floor with a grinding scrape as Justus lifted and pulled. The pounding on the door grew louder. Once again, time seemed to slow down.

Straining with every muscle he had, Justus set the stone down, leaving half of the hole exposed, just enough for him to slip through. Hastily, he lowered himself down to the top rung of the ladder in the tunnel shaft. Once on, he climbed down a rung or two so that his head was just below the floor of the house, then turned around on the ladder, bracing his back firmly against the wall of the shaft. He lifted and pulled again. It was harder to move the stone in this position, and the door could give way at any second. Justus kept heaving with all that he had. With still a few more inches of the hole left to cover, he was surprised and confused when he heard the pounding on the door halt.

Still heaving on the stone, Justus mused on why soldiers had ceased their attempts to force the door. He would soon have the stone in place and be able to crawl away to safety, but just as he reached to set the stone in its final place, a loud thud on the door caused Justus to jump.

Now they have a battering ram, he thought to himself. *It's now or never.*

Frantically, Justus pushed up on the stone again, heaving with more strength than he knew he had. Taking care not to lose his balance, he negotiated the stone into its exact niche in the floor and let it down with a soft thump. Another crash on the front door softly reached Justus's ears as he turned on the ladder and made his way down into the shaft. Then came another. Justus breathed a sigh of relief; the door was still holding. They hadn't seen him close the tunnel, but once inside, they would almost certainly find it. He couldn't think about that now. He had to make it to the other end of the tunnel and get away from this part of town as fast as he dared. While crawling, he considered the layout of the streets and buildings, pondering how best to escape without being spotted

Chapter 10

Surprise for Ariel

MEANWHILE, ARIEL WAS still waiting at the other end of the tunnel. She a few of the other men who had been on the roof emerge as she looked on. They ran to the door, glanced about to make sure no one would see them, then dashed out in different directions. Ariel's heart was pounding, and her palms were sweating. She looked out the door, into the street; the coast was still clear. The seconds dragged by, seeming more like minutes. She paced back and forth wondering what was taking so long then decided to look down into the hole herself. Gazing down, she caught a deep breath and her heart leapt up with relief and joy as she saw a figure climbing up the ladder. Though it was still in the darkness, Ariel planted herself beside the hole. Bending over slightly, she squatted down and extended her hand as the figure came into the light; it was Justus. He reached up and took a firm hold on her hand. Pulling with all her might, Ariel drew him swiftly up and out of the hole. Justus scrambled to his feet from his knees once he was out of the hole.

Ariel looked down into the hole again expecting to see another figure, Anthony, climbing up. Her heart froze; the tunnel was empty.

"Where's Anthony?" she gasped, holding her breath.

"He didn't make it," Justus said, hurriedly seizing the floorboards that were used to cover the entrance. "He was hit by an arrow. I'm afraid he's dead."

Ariel's whole body went numb; she could not believe what she had just heard. How could it be? Her dearest friend since both of them had lost their parents. She had just seen and talked to him a few minutes ago. Now he was dead, gone forever.

Justus spread some straw over the floorboards and placed a large jar on top of it. Ariel was still standing by, looking down, as still as a statue.

"Ariel," urged Justus, rising swiftly to his feet, "we have to leave, now."

Ariel was still confused and lost in her mind. How could she leave Anthony?

Seizing her by the arm, Justus rushed her to the door.

"What am I to do?" Ariel asked, talking, it seemed, to herself.

"I'll take you back to the senator's house, unless you'd rather go back to the catacombs?" Justus offered.

"No, I'll go back to the senator's house," Ariel said, still not quite herself or fully knowing what she was saying.

"Then off with us," declared Justus.

Taking her by the arm again, Justus led Ariel out of the stable. He let go of her for a moment and secured the door behind them. They raced across the street and disappeared into a dark alleyway. Ariel gathered herself together as best she could and managed to keep up with Justus as they darted up one alley and down another. Justus's knowledge of Rome proved sure. No one saw them as they left the area, and they made it back to the senator's house faster than Ariel had expected.

It's good that I was carrying the key to the house and not Anthony, Ariel thought to herself, *or else I would not be able to get back in.*

Justus led her to the side door, but as she was reaching for the key to unlock it, Justus stopped her.

"Before you go back, Ariel," he said, "tell me, how are you feeling?"

Ariel was quiet for a moment. Then, shaking her head with her lip quivering, she raised her hands palms up, and then let them drop to her sides. "I don't know."

Then, covering her face with her hands, she burst into tears. Justus wrapped his arms around her.

The Final Message to Rome

"It's all right, Ariel. Go ahead and cry, but do it out here, not inside," Justus whispered.

At this, Justus, too, began to weep, and the two of them cried together for who knew how long. When Ariel seemed to run out of tears, at least for the moment, Justus took the key from her and opened the door.

As he handed the key back to her, he said, "I wish I could do more for you, but I will pray that God will comfort and heal you. You know where to find me, so if you ever need anything, anytime, just come."

"Thank you, Justus." Ariel choked between sobs. "I will."

"Good-bye, Ariel, dear sister."

With soft footsteps, Justus slipped back into the street and was lost in the night. Before going back to her sleeping quarters, Ariel returned the key that they had borrowed to its original place. Then, sneaking back to the sleeping quarters, she lay down and tried to calm her mind enough to get to sleep, but what an impossible thing to do. Her mind ran wild thinking back over the events of the night. This went on for some time; then she began to pray, asking God questions, hoping to make sense of it all.

"Why, God? Why did you let this happen? Why did Anthony have to die? And why now, at the same time when Peter is leaving, when we need him most?"

After tossing and turning through most of the night, Ariel finally fell asleep.

As she awoke that morning, she prayed, "Jesus, please keep me cheerful so no one will see that I am grieving."

THE HOUSE OVERSEER, Claudio, immediately took notice that Anthony was missing and questioned all of the male servants when they arose early that morning. Since both the children had operated with such stealth and caution, no one had even the slightest idea of where he could be. All of the male servants testified that Anthony had been given leave for the evening and none of them knew where he had gone. They knew only that he had not retired with the other servants at the usual time.

Claudio ordered the whole house searched immediately. When they could not find him, he ordered the storerooms examined, fearing that something may have been stolen. He himself examined the senator's private treasury and found that nothing had been taken. At this, Claudio contented himself.

When Senator Marcus and his family returned from their visit to the country three days later, Claudio reported to the senator that the slave Anthony had run away. The senator took the news rather hard, sorry to lose such a reliable servant. Marcus had tried not to treat him as a common slave, knowing that he was legally a Roman citizen, though still young.

Waiting on Gloria and Floriana was hard, but Ariel managed to keep a smile on and work as best she could. No one asked her if anything was wrong. It was just another day in the senator's house. Grieving the loss of Anthony seemed as difficult for Ariel as losing her parents. She continued on, serving as best she could while grieving out of sight.

Both the children had succeeded in hiding their close friendship from the people in the house. Julia announced to the ladies under her oversight that the servant boy Anthony, who had been the senator's page at court, had escaped and asked if anyone knew anything about it.

He didn't run away, Ariel thought to herself. *He would never do that. He could have run away a long time ago. He stayed because he felt this was where God wanted him.*

Ariel said nothing, and Julia chose not to push the issue any further.

The night after the senator returned, Ariel was making her way upstairs to her sleeping quarters, when she overheard voices coming from a room along the hallway. The door was partially open, and Ariel somewhat absentmindedly stepped closer to hear what was being said. She recognized the voices immediately. It was Claudio and Senator Marcus.

"Well, sir," said Claudio, "have you decided what you are going to do? Are you going to report this matter to the authorities?"

"No, I am not," Senator Marcus replied. "In the first place, the boy was not a slave. He was the son of a Roman family that we believe tragically perished in the fire. No, let him go. By law, he is entitled to his freedom. I only wish I could have talked to him before; he might have chosen to stay. I knew a few things about his family, and there was a small possibility that his parents may have survived. I have been searching for them these past few months. I didn't want to mention it to him until I was sure. I kept him here not as a slave, not really. I treated him as best I could. That's why I brought him to court.

"Oh well," Marcus sighed. "We'll let the matter rest; I won't report him as a runaway slave. Keep this between you and me; don't say anything more about this, especially not to the servants. That is all."

"Yes, sir," Claudio responded, and made for the door.

Ariel leapt back from the door and dashed swiftly around the corner of the hallway, out of sight, just in time to avoid being seen. She made her way back to the sleeping quarters acting as though nothing had happened and fell asleep without any difficulty. It was a small comfort to her knowing that the senator had showed even a little concern for Anthony, even though she knew he was dead.

She continued to think over the whole matter in the days that followed. It still seemed very strange to Ariel that Anthony was gone; she had difficulty believing it herself. The world seemed so empty without him. A deep feeling of loneliness crept into her heart. Now there was no one she could pray with or talk to freely. With no one else to go to, she poured herself out even more before God, still wondering why he had allowed this to happen, praying and hoping that somehow the pain would be eased, that somehow everything would be all right. Dare she even hope for such a thing? She did, and her answer came four days later.

It was late in the afternoon as the servants were preparing for the evening meal. The Roman Senate had not convened to do their usual business that day, and the senator and his family had decided to spend the day at one of the amphitheaters and public baths. The senator returned home ahead of his wife and two daughters shortly before dusk. Ariel stood by the front door, awaiting the arrival of Gloria and Floriana. Senator Marcus was standing only a few yards away giving some instructions to Claudio when they were suddenly interrupted by a knock at the door. Ariel immediately moved to answer it, assuming it to be the rest of the family. She was startled to see a uniformed soldier carrying a scroll. The shining splendor of his uniform and armor revealed him to be an officer of significant stature.

"Yes, can I help you?" Ariel greeted the soldier.

"I am looking for Senator Marcus," the soldier replied. "I need to speak with him on a matter of the utmost importance."

Overhearing what was said, Senator Marcus immediately stepped to the front door.

"I am Senator Marcus," he said.

"Senator, for the past few weeks on your visits to the Senate, a young servant boy has accompanied and waited upon you. In the last four days that you have been at the Senate, he has not accompanied you. Roughly a week ago, a boy was arrested on the south side of the city. The arresting soldiers believe that he is the same one who has been waiting on you at the Senate. He is being held in the fortress dungeon."

At this, the officer handed the scroll to Senator Marcus.

"This is an order requesting that you come immediately to the fortress and identify the boy, whether he is your servant or no."

Ariel's heart gave a leap of joy. This meant that Anthony was still alive.

"What is the boy charged with?" Marcus asked.

"Conspiracy, espionage, resisting arrest, and treason against the state," the officer answered.

Marcus's forehead wrinkled and his eyebrows dropped in confusion. He could not believe what he had just heard.

"Excuse me?" he said. "A young boy charged with those crimes?"

"He was found to be in league with the Christians," the officer replied.

The senator's eyes widened in disbelief, while others listening gasped. After a few moments of silence, Marcus raised his bowed head and cleared his throat.

"Very well," said Marcus, "I will come and identify him."

"Thank you, Senator," the soldier answered. He snapped to attention, respectfully bowed, and strode off.

The Final Message to Rome

Turning to Claudio, Marcus told him to tell his wife and daughters that he had been called out on some urgent business and to proceed with the evening meal even if he had not returned.

"Do not tell them specifically why I have been called," Marcus warned Claudio. "It must remain a secret. Call two guards to go with me to the prison."

"Yes, Senator." Claudio nodded and hurried off.

The senator and his escort were off in no time. Ariel continued waiting at the door to receive the rest of the family.

Standing there, she considered the news they had just received. Obviously, Anthony was still alive, but as he was in prison, there was almost no hope of his survival. Once Senator Marcus identified him, he would be executed, but one thing puzzled her. Since they had found him with the Christians, why had they kept him alive for the past eight days, and why was it important that they identify him as Senator Marcus's servant? Unless...

Oh well, it really didn't matter for Anthony. He was still in prison, and since they knew he was a Christian, they would kill him even if Senator Marcus did not identify him. Ariel's thoughts were interrupted by a knock at the door; the senator's wife and daughters had returned.

Later in the evening, while serving at supper, Ariel saw the senator return from his visit to the prison. He looked very despondent, even more than he had when he left. His wife and daughters asked him what had sent him out so late, but he refused to tell them. After completing her normal evening duties, Ariel retired for the night feeling very distraught and somber.

As she lay on the floor, trying to go to sleep, she whispered a prayer to the Lord.

"Dear Jesus, I'm so sad. Anthony is in prison, and they will most certainly kill him. I'm so lonely; he's the only close friend I've had since my parents died. Oh Lord Jesus, please help him. Please don't let them kill him. Rescue him; save his life. What is happening here, Lord, and why? Please help me. Please get me through this."

This was all Ariel managed to say. She was overcome by a flood of emotions and began sobbing softly yet uncontrollably. For the past few days, she had been very careful not to let anyone see how sad she was, but now there was no holding it back. Fortunately, all the other servants in the room were fast asleep and were not awakened by her cries.

Ariel didn't know how long she cried or when she fell asleep, only that sometime during the night, she was suddenly awakened and sat up with a start. She didn't know what had roused her. The room was quiet, and everyone was still sleeping. Just then, a thought occurred to her. Anthony was still alive.

The soldiers could have killed him, but they didn't. If he is still alive, then God could deliver him from being killed, couldn't he?

Immediately her mind flashed back to the stories that she and Anthony had been told while they were recovering from their wounds at the catacombs. Peter had been there one night and had told them a story of how he himself had almost lost his life.

When the church was still very young, Peter was preaching in the land Judea. Due to the persecution of Saul, the cruelest of the Pharisees, the believers had been driven out of Jerusalem and had scattered all throughout the world. They fled the area, hoping to find a better and safer place to live while still speaking out for Jesus, but things did not get better; they only got worse. The king of the Judean providence, Herod, had been trying to gain favor with the Jews there for some time. While still the emissary of Caesar, Herod was a native of the land of Palestine. Ruling Judea was a complicated balancing act between convincing Rome of his loyalty on the one hand and gaining popularity with the Jews on the other. Since both the Jews and Rome had an interest in eliminating the Christians, Herod saw the situation as a win-win for him, an opportunity to score on both sides. Herod ordered one of the Christian leaders, James, to be arrested and executed.

This James had been one of the three disciples Jesus was closest to. The other two were James's brother, John, and then Simon Peter. These three knew certain things about Jesus that no one else did. One incident they witnessed was so earth shattering that Jesus warned them not to reveal it to anyone, even to the other disciples, until after his resurrection.

It was a severe blow to all the believers in Jerusalem to lose someone they loved so much and who had known Jesus so well, but the nightmare went on. When Herod saw the approval and popularity he had gained from the Jews by executing James, he saw his chance to push it even further. Peter was still preaching in Judea. Herod ordered him arrested and imprisoned until a convenient time when he could bring him out to be tried before the Jews. Everyone in the church knew what would happen next, an exact replay of the trial of Jesus or Stephen, the first Christian martyr.

Stephen had been a deacon in the church of Jerusalem just after Jesus had returned to heaven. He was not a church leader, but members of the synagogue had a personal vendetta against him for defeating them in public debate. In rage they brought false accusations against him, rigged the trial, and incited the people to kill him by stoning. A form of execution that was strictly forbidden under Roman law and only the Roman authorities could administer capital punishment. In spite of this they got away with killing Stephen, no one did anything.

The religious leaders hated Peter and all the believers. With the influence the leaders had with the Romans and the Jews, as well as their ability to produce false witnesses or bribe the authorities, ensuring Peter's conviction and execution would be no trouble at all.

In the midst of this terrible tragedy, the believers united in prayer, pleading with God to spare Peter's life. To the very end, they kept on praying. Then, just when all hope seemed lost, the night before Herod was to bring him to trial, something happened inside the prison. Peter had gone to sleep that night chained between two soldiers. Herod was taking no chances that Peter might escape. Peter and his associates had pulled this kind of stunt before, escaping from prison without leaving a trace, but he fully expected that he would die the next day. That night an angel awakened him and told him to get up and follow him. The chains that bound him fell off his hands. Peter got up, dressed himself, and followed the angel, who led him out of the cell, past all of the guards, and out of the prison. When they reached the gates of the fortress, which led into the city, they opened completely on their own. This whole time, Peter couldn't tell if he was dreaming or if all this was really happening.

The angel led Peter into the city and down one street; then he disappeared. It wasn't until after the angel was gone that Peter realized this was no dream.

Overwhelmed with joy, he went to the home of one of the believers to tell them what had happened. What he didn't know was that a large group of believers were at that very same house praying for his deliverance. A servant girl named Rhoda heard him knocking at the door. When she recognized his voice, she was so excited she ran to tell the people in the house, and she completely forgot to let Peter in. When she told the others that Peter was knocking on the front door, they couldn't believe it themselves. They thought she had lost her mind, but she assured them that she was not crazy and that Peter was outside. They then concluded that she must have heard Peter's ghost, thinking he was already dead. The prison that Peter was being held in was impossible to escape from.

Meanwhile, Peter kept on knocking at the front door. It must have been the longest wait he had ever endured. When the people inside finally heard the knocking and decided to answer the door, they couldn't believe their eyes. They had come to pray for his deliverance, and now he suddenly had showed up at their front door. Peter told them what had happened, and then he left. No one knew where he went, and it was best that they didn't.

The prison was in complete pandemonium and confusion the next morning when they found that their number one prisoner was missing. When Herod learned of his escape, he had the prison guards executed for letting such a valuable prisoner escape. Now Herod could not gain the popularity from the Jews he had hoped. Instead, he looked like a fool. What he had planned out as the best political move of his career turned out to be the most embarrassing and humiliating experience of his life.

The Lord heard the prayers of his people, and he answered them. He achieved what even they thought would have been impossible. Jesus himself had told his disciples, "With God all things are possible."

These words seemed to speak directly to Ariel's heart. Anthony was in prison, and he would certainly be killed very soon. With God that

The Final Message to Rome

didn't matter, nothing did. Regardless of the situation Anthony was in, God could still get him out of it. He had already done more than would be expected. Normally, the soldiers would have killed Anthony as soon as they found him in his wounded state, but they hadn't. As she thought of this, a sense of hope seemed to engulf her and fill her heart.

What if he does die? Ariel thought to herself. *What then?*

Thinking on this, her mind raced back to another story from the life of Jesus.

When Jesus lived on Earth, he, too, had lost a dear friend, a man named Lazarus. He had fallen ill, and his sisters had asked Jesus to come and heal him, but he delayed coming for two days. When he did come, he knew even before he arrived that Lazarus was dead. On his arrival, Lazarus's family and friends did not know what to make of his coming. His sister Martha was frustrated that he had not come to heal her brother, though she still believed that he was, at the very least, a messenger sent from God. Jesus declared himself to be even more, the hope of a life after death.

To prove his point, he went to Lazarus's tomb, weeping for his friend. Then, when they came to his grave, he had the tomb opened and called to him to come out. The people thought he must have been forgotten that Lazarus was dead and could not hear him, let alone respond. Many had been amazed at his ability to cure diseases, but to bring the dead back to life, that was something totally different. They were totally dumbfounded when they saw Lazarus walk out of the tomb as alive as ever. He was dressed in the same graveclothes they had bound him in four days ago. Lazarus lived on as if nothing had happened to him. Many of the people who witnessed this miracle believed that Jesus was who he had always been claiming to be, the Son of God, but others still refused.

Even if Anthony did die, as so many of the other believers in Rome had, he still had the hope of living again. God could even bring him back to life if he chose to. Either way she had the hope of seeing him again.

Raising herself up, Ariel knelt, looking up at the ceiling. With tears of both sorrow and hope streaming down her face, she prayed.

"Dear Lord, Anthony is your child, your son. He is in your hands, as he has always been, even now as he is facing death. Take care of him. Give him courage to be faithful to you and to speak out for you. Oh Father, I beg you, please save his life. Let me see him again safe and alive. I know that, even now, you can rescue him. If not, I know I will see him again. I will still love you and trust you, no matter what happens."

Lying down again, Ariel thanked God for sending those two stories to comfort her and give her hope. She fell asleep and awoke the next morning to fulfill her usual tasks. She continued to pray for Anthony's deliverance and release, convinced that this was how God would have her pray. The days passed by, some of them easy and some hard, as she clung to the hope that she had in Jesus. Then, quite unexpectedly, the situation took yet another turn.

Almost two weeks passed since the senator had been called to identify Anthony, and nothing new reached Ariel as to the progress of his state. The activities of the day had been quite routine and the whole household had retired for the night. Ariel had gone to bed with the other servants, fully expecting tomorrow to be another day at the senator's house. She was seriously mistaken.

While relaxing in deep sleep, Ariel was awakened by someone gently shaking her and whispering her name. It had been only an hour or two since she had lain down.

It was too dark for her to see, but she recognized the voices; it was Gloria and Floriana. What were they doing here in the servants' quarters, and why would mistresses so secretly wake up their maid in the middle of the night? Something was wrong, very wrong.

Chapter 11

IN THE DUNGEON

AFTER JUSTUS MANAGED to seal the tunnel's entrance and escape, the soldiers crashed in the burning door with a battering ram. Thrusting the burning debris aside, the soldiers surged in to apprehend or slay anyone who might be inside. They had suffered no casualties, or even injuries, but were infuriated at having their efforts frustrated in such an ingenious manner. They had never encountered resistance of this kind before.

Never suspecting that the house was equipped with a tunnel, they stormed in, with swords drawn, fully expecting the house to be filled with people. No one knew how they had discovered that the Christians would be meeting there that night. Clearing the first room, they raced on to the next, then another, and another, finding them all deserted. By the time the soldiers reached the top floor, they were completely bewildered. How was this possible? The house had been full of people only a few minutes ago; now it was deserted. Where had these Christians gone? They mounted the stairs and emerged onto the balcony, completely dumbfounded to find nothing but Anthony's body lying on the floor, motionless, with one of their shafts in his back.

The commanding officer couldn't believe his ears when he received the report. "Search it again," he said, "thoroughly, and look for special hiding places or a secret passage for escape."

The Romans had surrounded the house and were certain that no one had leapt from the walls or windows, and there was only one door. They searched the whole house twice over, suspecting there may be a secret hiding place in or under the house. They especially searched the rooms on the ground floor, expecting to find a tunnel. Nothing was unearthed. The Romans were both infuriated and perplexed. How could they manage to disappear like this, vanish into thin air? These Christians were even more dangerous than they thought.

The leading officer ascended the stairs to the roof one more time accompanied by another soldier carrying a torch. A few other soldiers remained on the roof. Up until now, the force and pain from the arrow shot had left Anthony completely senseless. Now, at last, he began to regain himself. Still lying facedown, he let out a low moan of agony. The soldiers turned their heads and saw Anthony move his arm. Realizing that he was still alive, one of the soldiers unsheathed his sword and stepped forward to finish him off. His blade was descending to sever Anthony's head from his shoulders, when the commanding officer reached out and seized his arm with a firm grasp, checking the blow.

"Hold, not yet," he ordered. "Bring the torch."

Giving Anthony's body a small push with his foot, the commander rolled it over to its side and knelt down to look at his face with the light of the torch. The soldier's eyes widened, and he drew closer to see more clearly. Exhaling a long breath, the soldier stood up, shaking his head in disbelief.

"Wait here," he said to the soldiers standing by. "I'll be back."

The officer returned a few minutes later accompanied by another officer, older and even more superior in rank than he was.

"Is it him?" the younger officer asked.

"Yes. Yes, it is," the older one replied gravely.

"What shall we do with him, sir?" another soldier inquired.

"Put him on one of the horses, and take him back to the fortress. See that you do not harm him in any way. I want him alive. Have a physician remove the arrow and dress his wound. Then put him in a cell, but keep him apart from the other Christians we are holding there. Keep a close watch on him, and let me know when he is well enough to be questioned. This boy may be useful to us."

"Yes, sir," the soldiers responded.

One of the soldiers hoisted Anthony onto his shoulder and carried him downstairs. Being as careful as they could, they laid him across one of the horses and lashed his body to the saddle. Concluding their search, the commanding officer ordered three men to stay behind in the house. The other soldiers departed on their horses, bringing Anthony with them. They brought him to the prison in the city where so many other Christians were being held before their execution.

Anthony awoke delirious the next morning to find himself lying facedown on a small bed of straw in a prison cell. He could remember nothing of what had happened to him since he had been shot on the rooftop.

The wound on his back had been bandaged, and his body felt very stiff. Anthony lay there all through the day and night, too weak to move. On the second day, about midmorning, a physician came into his cell, changed the bandage, and applied some special salve to his wound. Slowly, Anthony began to recover from his injury. After a week or so, he was able to stand up and walk about. The guards watching him gave a report of his progress to the officer who had brought him in.

On the evening of the eighth day, Anthony was seated on his bed, looking up at ceiling, wondering why the Romans were keeping him alive and what they would do next, when he heard footsteps coming down the corridor. He rose to his feet, still very weak. There was a clank and squeak as two soldiers unbarred the door.

"Come with us," they said.

After binding his hands behind his back, they led him out of the cell and to another section of the prison. Both the soldiers supported him by the shoulders, as he was still very weak to walk. Anthony surmised that he must have been in a cell situated deep underground, as he was led up several flights of stairs. Passing through the halls and rooms, he saw more and more soldiers here and there. The two guards led him up to a heavy wooden door with two sentries standing guard on either side.

"Who do you bring?" one of the sentries questioned.

"A young boy, no one knows his name," one of his escorts replied. "The centurion told us to bring him up immediately. He is expecting us."

One of the sentries knocked on the door and listened for a reply. After being granted admittance, he entered and shut the door behind him. He emerged again less than a minute later.

"You may go in," he said.

The two guards escorted Anthony inside and barred the door behind them. Glancing briefly about the room, Anthony saw at once that it was the post of a very revered officer, but almost at once, his attention shifted as he saw who was present. There, seated before him at a table, were three officers, judging from their appearance, officers of significant authority and responsibility. To their left stood the two officers that he had seen at the Senate, the ones he had overheard discussing the emperor's plans to eradicate the Christians. To the right of the table stood Senator Marcus himself. The senator's eyes widened and his mouth gradually opened in disbelief as he saw Anthony ushered into the room.

Anthony's heart sank. *They must know who I am now. It's over for me.*

His thoughts now rushed to concealing anything that could expose the other believers. With Senator Marcus here, Ariel could be in danger. He must choose his words very carefully.

The soldier present took notice to Senator Marcus's reaction.

The center officer seated at the table turned to him and asked, "I take it this is your missing servant, the one who has been accompanying you to the Senate?"

Releasing a long breath, Marcus replied, "Yes, this is him."

"Thank you," said the officer, turning his gaze back to the men holding Anthony. "You may take him away."

Leading him from the room by the shoulders, the guards escorted Anthony back down into the prison and returned him to his cell. Anthony was relieved that they had not asked him any questions.

Exhausted by the walk up to the interview, and still very weak from his wounds, Anthony fell upon the bed and in a few minutes was asleep.

The Final Message to Rome

He awoke, unable to tell what time it was, but as the prison was still very quiet, he guessed that morning had not yet come. A day passed. He felt much stronger and was able to walk about the room without losing his balance or tiring quickly.

Seating himself back on the bed, his thoughts drifted, wondering what would come next. How much did they know? Well, they knew that he was a Christian, Senator Marcus's aide in the Senate. What else? Had any of the other believers been captured? Had the tunnel been discovered? Why had the Romans taken the trouble to be sure of who he was by having Senator Marcus identify him? Then there were the two officers from the Roman Senate. They must have identified him as Marcus's page. It would certainly be a very serious matter to them, having a Christian, a spy, listening in on the emperor's plans. No one at the Senate knew that he was a believer. Judging from Marcus's shock at seeing him, he hadn't suspected that Anthony was a Christian either. He would certainly tell everything that he knew about him, but what did Marcus know? Not much. He was a new slave, a hard worker, but nothing else. Except, Anthony now recalled that when he was brought into the senator's house, Claudio had asked him his name. He had given his full name and that of his family, who were likely dead.

So what do they know? Anthony thought to himself. *I am a Roman boy, an orphan, who has become a slave, who has now become a Christian and a spy. What will they do to me? Being a Christian alone is an act of treason, but for a Roman citizen, it is far worse. To act as a spy for seditionists against one's own people is the epitome of being a traitor. This will make them furious. By law, they cannot punish a Roman citizen without a trial, but after this, who knows? They may not even grant me a trial, even if I am of age, but does it matter? They will have no trouble proving that I was helping the Christians, and I cannot deny my faith and loyalty to Jesus. If they do give me a trial, it will be to make a public spectacle of me.*

Now Anthony's thoughts shifted. *They haven't killed me because they think I am more useful to them alive than dead. I'm not one of the leaders. They must want some kind of information from me, but what?*

At this, Anthony fell to his knees. *Oh Lord, what must I say? I don't want to betray you or endanger any of the other believers. Guard my mouth. Keep me strong so I do not break.*

At this, there came flashing into Anthony's mind the words of Jesus that Peter had relayed. *"But when they lead you, and deliver you up, take no thought beforehand what you will say, neither premeditate: but whatever shall be given you in that hour, that you shall speak: for it is not you that speak, but the Holy Ghost."*

Anthony breathed a sigh of relief. "Very well, Lord, Holy Ghost, you speak."

Rising to his feet, Anthony began to walk about the cell; thinking and praying for the believers that he knew were still in hiding, and especially for Ariel. A soldier passing by his cell looked in and saw him walking about with relative ease. He reported this to the officers who had called Anthony to be identified the day before. Hearing this, they decided that he was well enough to be questioned but hopefully not strong enough to resist interrogation.

It must have been two days later when the soldiers came and brought him back up to the room where they had taken him to be identified. The same three soldiers he had seen were seated at the table. Anthony's hands were bound behind his back, and he was placed in a chair before the three officers. Now was the time, if any, for them to extract some information from him.

"What is your name, boy?" one of the soldiers asked.

"My name is Anthony, Lucius Valerius Anthony," he said, giving his full Roman name.

The soldiers were not a bit astonished to hear that he was a member of a Roman household. When asked for more details, Anthony explained to them much of his life's history and his parents'.

"Tell me, Anthony," one of the soldiers said. "We understand that you are in the service of Senator Marcus and have been acting as his personal attendant at the Senate and you are a servant in his house. How do you, the son of a wealthy Roman emissary, become the slave of a Roman senator?"

The Final Message to Rome

Anthony was silent for a moment, thinking how to effectively, yet truthfully, answer this question without jeopardizing anyone, especially Ariel. Briefly, Anthony explained how he had been injured in the great fire, lost his parents, and almost died himself. He recounted that the Christians had rescued him and helped him recover. Shortly thereafter, he was kidnapped and sold as a slave into Senator Marcus's house. He left out the details that Ariel had been with him when he was captured. He did not even mention her name or anything about her. Anything he said could get her arrested and killed. He recounted the basic details of how he had served in the senator's house and later been brought to the Senate.

Now the soldiers began asking for specific details of what he and his Christian conspirators were planning. Anthony answered that he knew of no coordinated strategy of the believers that was under way. He also affirmed that neither he nor any of his friends were involved in any acts of treason against the state. The officers continued to press the question, trying to extract some confession of guilt from him. Anthony remembered that these Romans had likely used torture to extract confessions from other Christians and then executed them. He still confirmed that neither he nor anyone he knew was plotting against Rome.

"Who and where are your friends?" they demanded.

Anthony was silent. Now was the crucial moment. If he revealed anything of what he knew, his friends would be put at risk.

Choosing his words very carefully, he answered, "I will answer all your questions truthfully, but I answer for myself. I will accuse no one and say to you that neither I nor any Christian that I know has ever committed any act of treason against the state. I will not deliver up anyone simply because they are a Christian."

"How did your friends escape from the house where you were taken?" the officer pressed.

Anthony's mind raced. Why would they be asking how the others had escaped, unless...unless they had been unable to find the tunnel. The tunnel was not hard to find. Perhaps God had somehow prevented them from finding it. As long as it remained undiscovered, the tunnel was still of use to the Christians. If he said anything of where the tunnel was and where it came up, other people would be put at risk.

"To answer your question would be to accuse the innocent. I cannot help you, sir."

The soldier slammed his fist down on the table. "Now you hear me, boy," he shouted. "You will tell us who and where your Christian friends are, or we will make you tell us."

"No," Anthony said as firmly as he could.

At this, one of the other officers broke in with another question. "Anthony, as a page, you saw and heard many of the things that took place in the Senate, including the emperor's latest campaign. Did you or did you not tell any of what you heard to any other Christians in Rome?"

Anthony paused for a moment. "I will answer for myself. Yes, I did. Anything I learned of the emperor's plans against the Christians, I reported to my fellow believers."

The expressions of the officers turned even graver than before.

"Do not be so disrespectful, boy," the first officer said sternly. "Consider well what you are doing. You are the son of a respected Roman ambassador, and you have joined with a dangerous group of seditionists and conspirators. You should know by now the fate of those who plot against Rome, and if you do not want to share in their fate, you would be wise to answer us. Now I ask you again, who and where are your Christian friends? How did they escape from the house where you were taken? There is some passage or tunnel in that house. Where is it?"

At this, the second officer seated before him interjected, in a much calmer tone, "Anthony, be wary in your answering. Do not be rash here. You are only a boy. You have your whole life to live. Do not be so quick to throw it away. You may not understand the true seriousness of the conspirators that you have fallen in with. They are not going to come and rescue you, and if you do not comply, you will die.

"We are appealing to you. You would not be talking to us here were it not for the efforts of Senator Marcus. He has taken it upon himself to search for your parents, and he has spoken on your behalf to the emperor. We are here asking you these questions informally. If you will

The Final Message to Rome

be reasonable, the matter will rest here with us. Tell us what you have done to assist these Christians, renounce your partnership with them, and tell us who they are. Give your allegiance and loyalty back to the emperor, your emperor, Lucius Valerius Anthony. If you will do this, you will be released and receive a full pardon for whatever you may have done for these Christians. Now, will you help us?"

Anthony was silent, as were the soldiers. So many thoughts darted into his mind, he could not think clearly.

He shook his head and said, "No, no."

"Do not be hasty in your decision, Anthony. This is a very generous offer we are making, and you may not have it again. If you refuse this offer, you will face trial as a Christian and an enemy of Rome. I will give you time to think it over. It is now close to noon. You have till the end of the day to make your decision. If you refuse again, we will have no choice but to deliver you up for trial. This may be your last chance, Anthony. Don't throw it away."

The officer now nodded to the soldiers standing behind Anthony. They stepped forward and led Anthony from the room. Just as they were going out the door, the officer called out to him again.

"Anthony," he said.

The soldiers stopped and released their hold on Anthony as he turned to face the officers.

The officer continued, "You said that you lost your parents in the fire, that you believe they are dead. I would venture to say that the Christians told you that. It's a lie. Your parents are not dead. They survived the fire, but they left Rome, thinking you were dead too. They have returned. Senator Marcus managed to find them. It is on their behalf that we are making you this offer. Think of them and what your decision will do to them. Open your eyes, Anthony; the Christians have lied to you. They have been using you this whole time for their own purposes. They are not going to come and rescue you. They never have; they never will. You are not betraying them; they have betrayed you. Consider this well as you make your decision."

Behind the table on the right-hand side of the room, there was a door with a sentry standing beside it.

The officer turned to the sentry and said, "Bring them in."

The sentry opened the door, and who should come through but Anthony's mother and father. The sight was almost too much for Anthony to bear; he almost fainted. His father was looking very despondent, and his mother was in tears. Anthony hadn't noticed that there was a small porthole in the wall of the room, through which his parents had witnessed the entire interview.

Wiping the tears from her face, his mother spoke first. "Anthony, please, we beg you. Be reasonable. Accept the mercy they are offering you. We love you, Anthony; we miss you. Please don't do this to yourself. Don't throw your life away. Tell them what you know, and we will take you home."

The soldiers escorting him waited for his response. Anthony stood frozen in his tracks for a long time. Tears clouded his vision. The excitement at seeing his parents alive was almost too much for him.

No, no, he thought to himself, *this isn't right.* He hung his head, not wanting to see his parents' reaction as he shook it. He felt so sorry that he had to cause them this pain, but he didn't see how he could help it.

The soldiers escorted Anthony from the room and returned him to his cell. It was midafternoon by now, and Anthony would sit on his bed in utter silence the entire afternoon, wondering what to do.

As it stood now, his life was not completely lost, as he had thought. If he complied with the Romans' demands, he would live. Just then, the thought occurred to him.

Their entire offer could be a lie to get information out of me. As soon as I tell them what I know, they may kill me right here. Still, if I help them, I may have a chance, and it's better than no chance at all. If I don't help them, I will be thrown to the lions, burned to death, or killed in some other horrible way.

Anthony had never felt this way before. The end of his life seemed just a few days or maybe even hours away.

The thought of being tortured and dying terrified him. He was so young. Was this all there was to life?

Why did I even get involved with these Christians? Anthony thought to himself.

His thoughts now turned to his parents. A day hadn't gone by that he didn't think about them. He really missed them, and now they were interceding on his behalf to get him out of prison and save his life. The thought of having his family back really excited Anthony, and all he had to do was tell them everything he knew about the Christians. When he thought of this, the pain was too great. He laid himself facedown on his bed and cried like a small child until at last he fell asleep, but he could not sleep for long. He awoke an hour or two later to a cold sweat and a severe headache. He sat on his bed trying to sort everything out.

At this, the painful thought of what would happen to his friends—and yes, they had been the most loyal friends he had ever had—the thought of what would befall them if he helped the Romans stung like a slap to the face.

"What am I thinking, helping them?" he said to himself. "What will happen if I tell them what I know? Do I even have to ask that question? They will be arrested, tortured, and killed." He tried to push these thoughts aside, remembering his fate. "I must not think about what will happen if I help the Romans. I must just do it."

As soon as he said this, his mind raced back to something that Jesus had said. This had been a favorite saying of Peter's, one that he had lived by: "Whosoever shall save his life shall lose it, but whosoever shall lose his life for my sake and the gospel's, the same shall save it."

This saying gave Anthony conviction.

"All right, Lord," he said, "tell me what you would have me do."

His mind slowed, and he began to think back on everything that had happened to him since the great fire. He remembered the love with which the Christians had cared for him when they had brought him in half dead, the stories they had told him of Jesus, and the loyalty that they had for each other.

Informing on the Christians would mean betraying all those people who rescued me, cared for me, gave me a home and a family. It would mean turning on Ariel.

With everything that had been happening, he hadn't thought much about what might be happening to her. She had lost her family, too, and she was the closest friend he had had since being enslaved. How could he send her to her death? How could he live the rest of his life knowing that he had betrayed people that truly loved him, and that he loved, all just to save his own skin?

What about Jesus? A friend had betrayed him. He had given up his life so others could keep theirs. He had died in Anthony's place. How could he betray someone who had died for him just to save his own life? What kind of life would that be? That wouldn't be saving his life at all.

Now he remembered Peter and what he had said before he left Rome, the words of Jesus: "He that endureth to the end shall be saved; what shall it profit a man if he shall gain the whole world and lose his own soul? Whosoever shall be ashamed of me and my words in this adulterous and sinful generation, him shall the Son of Man be ashamed of when he cometh in the glory of his Father with the holy angels."

"No, Lord," Anthony said out loud, talking to himself and to God, "a thousand times no, this is not what I want. I'll never give up, not on you or any of the others."

The words of Jesus now came flashing into his mind: *"I am with you always, even unto the end of the world. No greater love than this, that a man lay down his life for his friends."*

To be like Jesus, to die in someone's place, a high honor, Anthony reflected.

Falling to his knees beside the bed, he looked up at the ceiling with tears in his eyes.

"Oh Lord Jesus, please hear me. I miss my mother and father, and I fear to be tortured and killed, but I don't want to live as a coward. I don't want to turn on you or on the others. I cannot do it myself. So help me, Lord. I'll hang on to you. I will not denounce the other believers, and I trust you for strength to see me through this. So do with me what you will, Lord. I am ready to live or to die. I belong to you."

It didn't matter anymore. Whatever happened was no longer important. All that mattered to Anthony was that he stayed true to Jesus. A great burden of care and anxiety eased off his mind and heart.

"What should I do now?" Anthony said, thinking out loud. "Of course. He leapt to his feet with a smile on his face. "I should praise him." He recalled a story of two believers named Paul and Silas.

The Final Message to Rome

They had been arrested in the city of Philippi for freeing a girl who was enslaved. She was tormented and abused first by a foul spirit of divination, and second by her masters, who saw her sorrowful plight as a chance to get rich quick. Touched by the anguish and enslavement of this girl's soul, Paul confronted the demon and commanded it to leave her.

The girl was free from this torturing spirit, but her lords were furious that their moneymaking scheme had been spoiled. Under a false charge, they had Paul and Silas arrested, whipped, and thrown into prison, all without a trial. Despite their situation, Paul and Silas were not discouraged. With their backs torn open and bleeding, their feet bound in stocks, they began to sing songs of praise to the Lord.

That night, the prison was rocked by an earthquake, which broke the prisoners' chains and ripped the doors from their hinges. When the jailer saw all the prison doors thrown open, he immediately assumed that all the prisoners had escaped. Knowing that death was the penalty for letting a prisoner escape, he drew his sword and would have killed himself, but Paul stopped him. That jailer, who had most cruelly treated Paul and Silas, believed in Jesus and was baptized along with his entire house.

Anthony began to sing the songs that he had learned, first softly; then as his heart began to spring forth with joy, he sang even louder. He was so overcome with joy and a feeling of God's presence he could not stand still. He began to leap and whirl about the cell as nimbly and gracefully as the dancers he had seen perform at the Roman feasts. At length, there was a knock on the cell door. Anthony rose up and walked across to the portal as the soldiers on the outside unbarred it.

The door squealed open to disclose two soldiers, one a regular legionnaire, holding a torch, and the other a centurion.

"Well, Anthony," the centurion said, "the day is gone. What is your decision? Will you renounce your association with the Christians and assist in apprehending them or not?"

Anthony was surprised, almost shocked, at how quickly the day had passed. It had seemed like only an hour or two to him, but now was the time to choose. For Anthony, he did not even need to give it a second thought; his decision had already been made.

With a smile on his face, he shook his head. "No, I will not renounce my faith in Jesus, and I will not turn on my fellow believers."

The centurion frowned and slammed the heavy door with a clank. Anthony heard the faint sound of their footsteps fading away in the passage. Anthony sat down on his bed wondering what would happen next. He had done all he could do. He could not turn on Jesus or his friends, no matter what happened. He had made the right choice to please his Lord. His future was in God's hands now.

Chapter 12

On Trial

THE NIGHT PASSED without event for Anthony, as did the next day. A week passed, and still nothing happened. Anthony began to wonder when he would be taken to trial or if he would even be given a trial. Early on the morning of the eleventh day, just as the sun was beginning to rise, Anthony awoke to the sound of the door being unbarred. He stood up to meet the soldiers as they entered.

Two of the regular prison guards were there along with two others he had seen before in the prison. As they entered the cell, Anthony noticed that they were carrying a small chain with shackles.

So today, I go to trial, Anthony thought to himself.

"Your hands, prisoner, front," one of the soldiers ordered.

Anthony extended his hands in front of him, and one of the soldiers locked them in the shackles. The second guard clapped a second set of chains round his ankles. Having safely secured him, they led him out of the cell. As before, he was made to climb the stairs up to the ground floor of the prison. They halted at the gates of the dungeon, where a few other prisoners, also bound, were waiting. Three or four more prisoners were brought up from other places in the fortress. At this, the group of about fifteen people were bound together with a lighter chain and led out under the guard of five soldiers on horseback.

Marching through the city of Rome, Anthony did his best to ascertain exactly where he was, but all to no avail. After about ten minutes of brisk walking, they reached the judgment hall, where all matters of civil or criminal justice were decided. This was well known to the Romans, and the citizens frequently watched as judgment was dealt out to the criminals who were brought before the judges. While waiting for the court to assemble, the accused were held in a secure room under guard until their names were called.

It was during this time that many of the other prisoners began to converse with each other, and especially with Anthony, who was certainly out of place in the group. Most of the men were in their twenties or thirties in terms of age, while Anthony was only in his mid-teens. Most of the prisoners were facing charges for murder, robbery, and other standard offenses. When Anthony told them that he was facing charges as a conspirator against the state, a Christian, at first they laughed at him, thinking he was joking. These men had heard some rumors about the Christians. They had imagined them as cannibals of human flesh, atheists who would not worship the many Roman gods and who rejected the divine lordship and authority of the emperor.

Smiling, Anthony recounted his story of how he had been injured in the fire and rescued by the Christians, how he had been drawn by the love of Jesus to commit his whole life to bringing him glory. He then answered some of the questions regarding exactly what the Christians believed and why. Some of the men smiled and laughed as he spoke, while others remained silent.

"What will happen to you today?" one asked in a taunting manner.

"I will almost certainly be found guilty and be executed," Anthony sighed, shrugging his shoulders.

The man's eyes narrowed. "And that doesn't cause you any fear or concern?"

"No," said Anthony. "Though I loathe the agony that will come with death, I do not fear death itself."

"How can you say that?" the man wondered. "Your life is about to end, and you are so young."

"No, sir," Anthony replied, "my life is not about to end. It is only just beginning. When Jesus died and rose from the grave, he conquered death, for all time. Death has no power over me to end my life. Instead, my Lord has chosen to use even this monster to bring me from this life, which is so short, to a newer and better one that will go on forever. As for what I must suffer, Jesus has promised that he will be with me to the very end, even in the arena."

The men were silenced, unable to answer or ask him anything else.

Looking about the room at the faces of the men, Anthony took the initiative.

"As you face trial for your crimes, consider that you must also give account of yourselves before the true and living God, not some idol fashioned or sculpted by the hands of men. You would be wise to consider your own sins and the pardon that Jesus offers you if you will repent and believe in him as Son of God, the hope of eternal life."

Just then the door opened; the prisoners rose to their feet.

"You, boy, come out," an officer ordered.

Two soldiers came in and unlocked Anthony from the chain that bound him to the other prisoners. Anthony strode out of the room, still shackled hand and foot, glancing one last time over his shoulder to give the prisoners a smile of encouragement.

Passing through a series of hallways and passages, they at last brought him into the judgment hall. The room roughly resembled a rectangle, nearly one hundred feet in in length, forty feet in width. The two long sides of the room were lined with a seating gallery reserved for Roman citizens and other court officials. The rows of seating pyramided up to the walls of the building, much like the seating of the Colosseum or the Circus Maximus. The gallery was elevated approximately two yards off the ground, with a wall separating them from the judgment hall floor. The seating on both sides of the room was filled to its full capacity. At the far end of the hall stood a small platform with stairs leading up to it. On the platform, a throne was set with two seats on either side. Seated on the throne was Nero himself. On either side of him sat two other officials of significant stature and influence. Several soldiers stood behind the throne and on either side of the platform.

The soldiers led Anthony, still bound, to a seat toward the center of the room, where the accused was to be tried. After he had been seated and the escorting soldiers had withdrawn, two soldiers on the platform raised trumpets to their mouths and blew a loud blast. The muffled talking among the onlookers was hushed, and all gazes were fixed on the emperor. Glancing along the public galleries on either side, Anthony was startled to see his mother and father only twenty feet from where he sat, in the front row of the public gallery off to his left. So many emotions filled his heart as he looked his parents in the face. He was enthralled with joy at seeing them again. He felt sorry for them, seeing the pain on their faces and knowing the concern that they must be feeling having their son on trial, facing death. Almost choking up, he smiled gently to them as a tear streamed down his cheek.

The soldiers lowered their trumpets, and another standing by declared, "The judgment hall will now come to order. All rise. Hail Caesar." He raised his right hand. "The emperor Nero presiding."

All present, soldier and citizen alike stood to their feet, raising their right hands. "Hail Caesar!" they all shouted.

Nero now took the floor. With his right hand raised, he gestured gently about the room, glancing from side to side with a look of command and satisfaction.

"Senators, Romans, friends, be seated," he said.

All present took their seats.

Turning his gaze toward Anthony with a look of smug contempt, he said, "The accused will stand."

Anthony had risen a few moments before when the rest of the room had hailed the emperor, but he had not joined in the salute. Though the believers did reverence civil authorities as ministers of God, to hail the emperor as Caesar, Lord and God, was an act of idolatry. He rose to his feet, facing the emperor.

"Your will be done, Lord," he whispered.

"Are you Lucius Valerius Anthony, son of Lucius Valerius Regulus, present, and servant to Senator Flavius Aurelius Marcus, also present?"

"I am," Anthony replied.

Nero now unrolled a scroll and read aloud, "You stand before this assembly accused of the following charges: treason against the state, being in league with a group of seditionists known as Christians, betrayal and treachery of your Roman nationality, acting as a spy in the Roman Senate, resisting arrest and assisting the escape of other seditionists, and refusal to give information for the capture of your criminal associates."

Turning his head to the right side of the room, where a several soldiers were seated, Nero called out, "The court now calls upon the soldiers who witnessed this boy at the Senate and arrested him three weeks prior."

One of the soldiers seated on a bench at floor level, below the seating gallery for regular citizens, stood up and walked to the foot of the platform. He turned so as to keep Anthony in his view to his right while respectfully giving the judges on the left his full attention.

"Tell us your name and rank, Soldier," Nero requested.

"Titus Horatius Triarus, centurion of the Praetorian Guard," the soldier responded.

"Please tell us what you saw of this boy," Nero requested.

"I first witnessed this boy waiting at the front door of the house of the Senate. His presence looked a bit unusual, so I mentioned it to my consul. I was fairly new to my duties in the Senate, and the consul told me that the boy waited upon Senator Marcus as a page. I have since seen him numerous other times in the Senate, performing his said duties for Senator Marcus. It was through this that I learned his identity and face.

"Some nights ago, I was called to ride with a detachment of men to conduct a search of a certain house on the south side of the city. We rode up to the house, dismounted, and approached the door. We could hear voices inside and see moving shadows. There must have been at least ten people inside. After knocking several times on the door, demanding admittance, which we were denied, we attempted to break down the door. At that moment, several bricks and pottery were thrown down from the roof. We had no shields to cover our heads, so we jumped back from the door. At first, we couldn't see who or how many people were on the roof, but they threw down several stacks of flax, straw, and small sticks in front of the door. They dumped oil down onto the straw and then dropped a torch, which set everything on fire.

"The fire blazed up. We tried to get closer to remove the burning brush, but all we had to remove it was our swords, and the fire was too big and too hot for us to do it. Whenever we got close, they poured down oil and made the fire blaze up, forcing us to fall back."

At this, Nero stopped him for a moment. "Were you or any of your men injured by all of this?"

"No, sire," the centurion replied. "None of us were hit by the falling bricks, and none of us were burned by the fire."

"Pray continue then," Nero said.

"There was no other entrance to the house, so we blew a horn, calling for more men. We surrounded the house and then waited for reinforcements. They arrived a few minutes later. These regular soldiers were armed with spears and shields, so they were able to clear away the brush without being burned. The men on the rooftop poured down a last bit of oil just before we started clearing a path. They threw down more fuel on the door and set it on fire.

"At last we made a path to the door, but it was still burning. Fortunately, the reinforcements were carrying a battering ram. We used this to break down the door and get inside. The whole house was empty except for this one boy here today. We found him on the roof with an arrow in his back. We tried to find a secret passage or some explanation for how so many people could have disappeared from the house, but we could find nothing. One of the soldiers was about to kill this boy, when I thought I recognized him from the Senate, so I stopped him. I took a better look at him and felt sure that it was him, so I told the consul. The consul was commanding the reinforcements that helped us, and he agreed that it was the same boy from the Senate. The consul ordered him to be taken to the prison, given care from a physician, and then questioned."

"And are you certain that this is the same boy from the Senate and the one you arrested?" Nero asked.

"I am, sire," the centurion answered.

"You may step down," Nero said. "Next witness."

The consul the centurion had mentioned in his testimony now came forward. He related his account of seeing Anthony at the Senate as Marcus's page and again at the raid on the believers' house. The consul, who had seen even more of Anthony at the Senate, confirmed that he had been present when the emperor first announced his campaign, many of his secret plans, and also his intention to seize and make an example of the apostle Peter.

The other witnesses that were called to testify included the Roman soldiers who had questioned him while he was in prison. They recounted how Anthony had been questioned and how he had refused to supply them with any information. Last of all, Senator Marcus and Claudio were called to testify on what they knew about Anthony, how he had come into their house as a slave, and his activities in the house and the Senate.

Both were asked directly if either of them ever had any suspicion that Anthony may have been a Christian. Both resoundingly affirmed they had never suspected anything foul or dangerous.

After the witnesses had finished giving their testimony, Nero addressed Anthony. "You have heard the testimony that has been given against you. How do you plead? Do you affirm or deny it to be true?"

Even though he knew it could be dangerous to him, Anthony decided that it would be better not to deny what he knew was true, in the hope of confusing the court. His safety was in God's hands now.

Clearing his throat, he drew a long breath and said, "The statements made here by these witnesses are all true. I do not deny any of them."

"Then you confess that you are guilty of the charges brought against you?" Nero asked judiciously.

"I will answer to each of the charges separately, and I pledge to answer truthfully before my God and the authorities and witnesses present. To the charge of treason in joining a seditionist sect known as Christians, I do indeed affirm that I am a Christian, a believer in Jesus as the Son of God. However, I deny that I, or any other believers that I have known, have ever said or done anything to rebel against the state or overthrow the governing authorities.

"To the charge of betrayal of my Roman nationality and heritage, I did not betray anyone or anything in giving my allegiance and fidelity to Jesus Christ. I remain a loyal subject and citizen of Rome. I am not a traitor because I worship Jesus Christ as the one true Son of God. I am a Roman and will always be one.

"As to the charge of treachery by acting as a spy in the Roman Senate, ever since I entered the Senate, I was alert to hear of anything that could endanger the lives of the believers in Rome, and I reported my findings to my friends. I attest that I have never reported anything that would have jeopardized the lives or security of anyone in Rome, the state included. I reported only what I knew would be essential to protect and save the lives of my fellow believers.

"As to the charge of resisting arrest and assisting in the escape of other seditionists, I say that it is because I knew that my friends and I were innocent that I defended them so that they might escape. I was ever careful in what I did not to harm any of the soldiers who came to the house to arrest us. I did indeed assist them in escaping from the soldiers, yet I attest that there was not a single seditionist among them.

"And as to my refusal to supply information for the capture of my associates, to do so would be to accuse the innocent. If there were any among the Christians that were engaged in rebellion or insurrection against the state, I would give whatever information I could without hesitation. Yet, I avow that there is not one among those that I have had the honor and pleasure of knowing. I am a Christian, I am a loyal Roman, and proud to be both. This is my defense."

The judgment hall was silent. Anthony shifted his gaze from one side of the room to the other. Nero and the judges on the platform whispered back and forth to each other.

Nero sat still staring at him. A smirk crossed his face; he glanced back and forth at the judges on either side of him and then out to the audience. Rising to his feet, he raised his arms and sighed.

"Romans, please, do we have to go through this old routine again? How many times have we heard this? How many times have the Christians contested their guilt? Even assuming that this boy has never actually tried to overthrow the state, as a Christian, he challenges the position and authority of the gods and me, the emperor. How many

The Final Message to Rome

times have we heard these conspirators shout in the arena, 'Jesus is Lord!' We all know this is a lie. They declare that this Jesus, a mere Jewish carpenter, also a criminal, declared himself to be the Son of God. This madman's followers have spread all across the world, stirring up trouble. Even if they are not rioting or committing such crimes as we have seen here in Rome, they are subverting the authority of the emperor and denouncing the gods. They claim that there is no other god but their own. They are denying the majestic works of the gods as only a fool or a rebel would do. Who could look at such wonders as the sun, the planets, heroes of war, love, or even me, the emperor? I put it to you, Romans, who else could deny the existence of the gods but a madman, or a total rebel, and a rebel who recognizes no person, god, or position of authority but himself and what he imagines for himself. Tell me, Romans," Nero shouted. "Who?"

The crowd listening began to nod in agreement, give shouts of acclamation, applause in support of the emperor's oration. When the shouting finally died down, Nero again addressed the audience.

"Then I put it to you again, Romans. Tell me, is this boy merely a misguided fool, or is he a true enemy of the state? There can be no other alternative."

The crowd again began to erupt. Some shouted, "Rebel!" or "Criminal!" but then other voices broke in with "He is but a boy!"

"Order. Order. Silence, all of you," Nero said, projecting his voice. Then he turned his attention to Anthony. "Does the accused have anything further to say in relation to this charge?"

"Sire, if I have broken the law in any way, show me the law and how I have broken it. I still maintain that I have not become an enemy of Rome through my loyalty to Jesus, nor shall I ever do. As to what has been said regarding my denial of the gods, I am not mad, nor am I in rebellion to deny the many idols worshiped here in Rome, which I myself worshiped as a child for many years. I am not blind to the many wonders and spectacles of the world and life, yet I do not see each of them as a god. Rather, I see their wonder as proof of the existence of the one who created them for his pleasure and ours. I worship the Creator, not the creation, and in this, I do not rebel against the state."

Anthony guessed that his response may meet with the approval of a few in the audience, but he could see that Nero was really becoming annoyed.

"And what of me, the emperor, do you deny my divinity?" Nero challenged.

Knowing that his answer could seal his doom, Anthony chose his words very carefully. "As a Christian, I am persuaded that the governing authorities are to be respected as ordained of God but not to be worshiped as a god."

"Aha!" cried Nero, leaping to his feet with a shout of triumph. "Then you do deny my divinity."

"Your divinity, sire?" questioned Anthony, pausing for a moment. "And did you always possess this divinity, or did you receive it when you assumed the position of emperor?"

Nero was silent, unable to answer.

Anthony smiled at him and went on. "This divinity came to you only when you became the emperor. It is not you that is worshiped as God, but the position of authority. Is this position truly God or merely an object of worship in the minds of people?"

The whole room was silent, some in awe; others, like Nero, were too furious to find words.

At last, Nero took the floor again.

"Your have heard him deny the divinity of the emperor and the gods." Glancing at the judges seated beside him, he demanded, "How do you find him, guilty or innocent?"

At first the judges were silent, but Nero's stare proved very effective in loosening their tongues.

"Guilty," they all said, one after the other.

"Having already confessed to being a Christian," Nero continued, "do you have anything further to say to the charge of betraying your Roman heritage and nationality?"

"Only as I have said before," Anthony replied, "that I have not betrayed Rome in being a follower of Jesus. As a follower of Jesus, I know that the offices of civil authorities are ordained by God and as such should be respected, but not worshiped in the place of God. Nevertheless, I am a Roman, and a Roman I remain."

Rolling his eyes slightly, Nero glanced to the judges seated beside him. Anthony could tell that he was really becoming annoyed listening to him.

"How do you find him?" Nero inquired with a sigh of annoyance.

The judges nodded. "Guilty," they both said.

"And now," said Nero, addressing Anthony, "as to the charge of acting as a spy in the Roman Senate, you have already said that you reported anything that could protect the lives of your fellow Christians. What information did you pass on to them?"

This is the time when anything I say may be used against my friends, Anthony thought to himself. *I must be careful not to say anything that could lead them to my friends. If I refuse to answer, they will only become angrier. As long as I do not expose anyone else, I can answer.*

"These are the messages that I overheard and passed on to my Christian brothers: first, that the Christians were to be blamed for the fire in Rome; then the emperor's new campaign to hunt down the Christians and have them tortured and killed; also that the confessions of the Christians' guilt in setting fire to Rome were extracted from captured members by means of torture, after which, those who confessed were executed."

As Anthony said this, he could see Nero's eyes widen and his face tighten as he began to shift and squirm in his seat. A low murmur of voices was heard in the audience, but Anthony went on.

"Any specific plans to capture them, any knowledge of their whereabouts, any- and everything that could protect or save the lives of my friends."

Nero took the floor immediately. Anthony could hear that his voice was cracking a bit.

"Since you confess to disclosing the secret plans of the Senate to its enemies, we find you guilty on this charge also. Moving on to the third charge of assisting other Christians in escaping arrest," Nero continued, "what did you do to help them escape, and how did everyone but you disappear from the house where you were taken?"

Nero is trying to get away from how he obtained his confessions by torture. He knows what will happen if he asks too many questions, Anthony thought to himself. *They still don't know how we escaped from the house. God wants me to keep it a secret.*

Anthony answered, "You may ask the soldiers who arrested us what we did. I have already told you that I helped them escape because I knew they were innocent. As to how the other believers made their escape, what does it matter? Is it truly relevant to whether I am guilty or innocent?"

"How did your Christian friends escape?" Nero demanded.

"Our escape was of the simplest nature, but I can see that you have not been able to discover it. It is our Lord Jesus who has blinded your eyes and baffled your minds. He has opened the eyes of the blind, and he has made seeing eyes blind. He would not want me to reveal this secret to you."

"You defy me, boy," shouted Nero, rising to his feet. "Answer the question."

"Sire, I have answered the question," Anthony countered. "You have charged me with resisting arrest and assisting the escape of fellow Christians. I have answered you truthfully. I have told you everything that I did to help them escape. The means by which they escaped has no bearing on whether I am innocent or guilty of this charge."

"So we find you guilty of this charge also," Nero fumed, seating himself once again.

"And now to the final charge, refusing to give information of your fellow seditionists. I do not have to remind you that in spite of your crimes, you are still a Roman. As such, it is your duty to assist your nation and your emperor in eliminating her enemies. Think well on how you answer, Anthony. While in prison, you were offered a full pardon for your crimes if you would but renounce your allegiance to these seditionists and this dead Jesus they call a god. Tell us everything you know of these Christians, and your life will be spared. You rejected this generous offer once already, but we here are, still willing to be merciful. We offer you this proposition yet one more time. Consider well what you are about to do. Don't throw away your life for these criminals and a dead Jew. They will not save you. Be reasonable, for your own sake and the sake of your parents, who are here"—Nero pointed to the gallery where Anthony's parents sat—"who still love you and care for your life. We ask you again, Anthony. Release yourself from these Christians, and tell us who they are. Think of yourself and your parents."

Hearing a tearful cry, Anthony turned his head toward the gallery where his parents sat. His mother was in tears.

"Please, Anthony," his mother begged, extending her hands over the wall of the gallery toward him, with tear-filled eyes.

Looking his parents in the eye, Anthony's heart began to ache, as it never had before. He missed seeing and being with them, now more than ever. He felt his throat tightening up and his lip beginning to quiver. Realizing what was happening, he tried to pull himself together, but it was to no avail. His head dropped and his hands came up to come his face as he began to sob uncontrollably. He was standing at first, but as the tears continued to come, his whole body began to feel very weak, and he was no longer able to keep his feet. He sank back down upon the small place where he had been sitting and cried his heart out like a little child. How long this went on, Anthony could not remember, but he cried until something enabled him to regain himself. The many tears had moistened his clothes, and his face was red as he wiped the tears away and began breathing to regain his composure.

Any noise in the judgment hall had been suppressed upon seeing Anthony's reaction. Nero, the judges, and the citizens sat staring at Anthony and his parents, who were also weeping, though not as profusely as Anthony, wondering to see how much he loved his parents but still refused to recant. It seemed a great puzzle to them. What could possess such a boy to give up his dear parents and even his own life, or would he? Perhaps he would be reasonable and yield to the desire of the court and the emperor. Nearly everyone present was earnestly hopping and anticipating that he would comply and they would be able to see him joyfully reunited with his parents. How horrible these Christians were, deceiving, indoctrinating, and abusing this young boy for their own purposes. Tearing him away from his mother and father, who loved him, and sending him to his death for a worthless cause.

Anthony, too, had his thoughts, more than one could write. For the longest time he sat there, motionless before the court.

Becoming a bit impatient, one of the judges, seated to Nero's left, spoke out to him. "Well, what is your decision, Anthony?"

Nero reached out and touched the judge on the arm. "Patience," he said quietly. "Give him space to think."

It was all confusion at first for Anthony, but then his mind cleared, and he was able to reflect clearly. He wanted so much to be with his parents again, but that came with such a high cost. He would be betraying his friends, people he loved deeply, Ariel included. The other believers loved him; they believed in him as a loyal Christian. That night when he had been wounded and arrested, he had done it all to save them. He had risked his life to save theirs. Should he now betray them to save himself? How could he ever live with himself? Worst of all, he realized he would be betraying Jesus, who died so he could have true life on Earth and an eternal life in heaven. How could he betray Jesus like that? If he did surrender to them and go back to his parents, he would have to forsake Jesus. That was impossible for him now; he could not live without Jesus, go back to worshiping those false gods.

I couldn't live such lie, he thought to himself. Living life knowing that he quit on the people and the things that meant the most to him, living like that till the day he died—and one day he would die—that would be worse than death. Giving up eternal life in exchange for a few years, just to escape some pain, that was madness, worse than madness. He'd have to be a fool to agree to those terms.

But what about your parents, the thought rushed into his mind? *See how you are hurting them?*

Now a saying of Jesus's rung through loud and clear, reaching through to his mind and heart. *"Whosoever he be of you that forsaketh not all that he hath, he cannot be my disciple."* Then another rang through his mind. *"If any man come to me and hate not his father, and mother and wife, and children, and brethren, and sisters, yea, and his own life also, he cannot be my disciple. And whoever does not bear his cross and come after me, cannot be my disciple."*

As soon as this crossed his mind, he heard Nero's voice.

"Anthony, my son, do you wish to be removed from this courtroom to a more private place where you may consider your decision?"

The Final Message to Rome

Nero's voice was no longer stern as it had been throughout the trial.

Anthony rose to his feet. "No, sire, I do not need more time to think. I have made my decision."

Fixing his gaze on Nero, he didn't want to see his parents' faces as he spoke. He feared it might discourage him.

"Sire, even though you may find me guilty of treason, I still maintain that neither I nor any of my friends are enemies of the state. As to your offer of a pardon, I will not renounce my faith in Jesus, and I will not turn on my friends, even though it will cost me my life."

He now turned his gaze to the watching spectators, and he began to walk about slowly and gently, yet firmly, as would make one think he was delivering an oration in a performance. With his gaze gliding from one end of the hall to the other, and then back, stopping now and then, a smile of exuberance of joy burst forth on his face like the water from a garden fountain.

"You call this Jesus a madman and dead. I tell you, he is not; he is alive and always will be. It is in this, that he rose from the dead, that he proved he was who he said he was, the Son of God."

When Anthony said this, he heard some giggles and low laughter come from the crowd. He smiled back, almost laughing.

"You may deny it or refuse to accept it, but you will never prevent him. It is Jesus, not Caesar, who is supreme. It is he who rules heaven and Earth, and someday all of you here will confess this, even as I do."

Nero bit his lip to restrain himself, almost drawing blood, when he heard this.

"I was not deceived or manipulated into joining the Christians. I became a Christian of my own free will, and so I remain. From the day the Christians rescued me from the great fire till now, they have never done me wrong. I will not betray them to their deaths."

He turned his gaze directly toward his parents, seated to his left. Both of them sat still as statues, gazing at him with a barren expression on their faces.

"To my mother and father, I love you both very much. I always will. I am sorry for the pain this causes you, but it is what I must do. There is no need to weep for me; it is for yourselves that you should weep. In

Christ, I have received eternal life that no one can take away from me. To die is nothing."

Anthony now turned his gaze back to Nero and the other judges.

"My life is in God's hands. You may do with me whatever you wish, but I am a Christian, and a Christian I remain."

Hearing this, Nero turned his head to the judges with his hands raised at his sides, palms up.

Speaking with an air of resignation Nero said, "You have heard his decision. Now we must make ours, and I fear that our duty leaves us but no choice. How do you find him, innocent or guilty?"

Anthony could see that there was some reluctance in them, but they all nodded in agreement. The verdict was guilty.

Seeing their decision, Nero turned back to Anthony, who had sat back down in the middle of the judgment hall. Nero was just about to address him, when one of the judges seated beside him reached over to him and whispered something in his ear.

Nero shrugged and then turned his attention back to Anthony.

"Having found you guilty of treason, it is the duty of this court to sentence you to death. Yet, we make one last appeal to you to come to your senses. Perhaps you do not fully understand where your treason will take you. We will let you see just what it is that you have chosen, and I hope you will choose life.

"Guards," Nero called out.

Anthony rose to his feet as two guards stepped forward and positioned themselves behind him.

"Escort the prisoner back to the dungeon, but do not return him to his cell. I'll have some official instructions sent down as soon as possible. See that you do nothing to him until you receive my orders."

"Yes, sire," they responded. Then, snapping to attention, they saluted him, accompanied with the shout "Hail Caesar!" Taking Anthony by the arms, they escorted him out of the courtroom.

His mother once again burst into tears as they led him away. Anthony hadn't noticed that other members of the senator's household were in the audience.

Chapter 13

Escape

Awakened by the voices of her two mistresses, Ariel, still partially asleep, sat up in her bed. She was just about to ask, in her usual manner, how she could serve them, when Gloria gently but firmly covered Ariel's mouth.

"Shh," she whispered. "Don't make a sound. Come with us, and walk quietly."

Still disoriented and confused, Ariel followed the two of them out of the servants' sleeping quarters and into the main house. Gloria and Floriana led her up to the third floor of the house, to their personal chambers, a place Ariel seldom went. There was no light in the room except for the moon and stars shining in through an open window. The two daughters shared a room. A basin of water was set at one end. The ladies permitted Ariel to quietly wash her face in the cool water and dry herself with a towel to help her wake up. Then they locked the door and led her to a small storeroom adjacent to their room and accessible only through a single door. Floriana went in first and lit a small candle. Gloria, standing behind Ariel, gently pressed her to enter. After the three were in, Gloria closed and locked the door. Immediately after the door was shut, Floriana placed the candle on a stand in the back corner of the room, elevated to enable full illumination of the closet. She then lit another candle and set it on another stand in the other corner at the back of the room.

Gloria and Floriana knelt down on the floor and drew Ariel down next to them in a small circle. Ariel was still wondering why they had brought her here at this hour of the night so secretly. Gloria spoke first.

"Ariel," she said, "you have been a cheerful and worthy servant the whole time you have served us, and we are very glad to have you here, but now you must tell us something. We are deeply concerned for your welfare and safety. Be honest with us, for your own sake. Don't lie to us. We must know. Are you a Christian?"

The question stunned Ariel. For several seconds, she didn't know what to say or even think. Her mind ran wild as she tried to collect her thoughts.

Why are they asking me this and so late at night? Both Anthony and I have kept our faith very hidden. What could have made them suspicious? What do they know? Hmmm, she thought to herself. *They don't know if I am a Christian, or they wouldn't be asking me like this. They also are trying to keep what I tell them to themselves. Otherwise, it would not be under these circumstances. I'll try to find out what they know first before I tell them what they want.*

"Why do you ask?" Ariel questioned, changing the expression on her face to look puzzled.

"Ariel, please, there is no time," Floriana entreated. "If you are a Christian, you must tell us. We are trying to help you; your life is in danger here. If you do not listen to us now, you may die tomorrow."

Looking into their faces, Ariel couldn't help but believe them. She saw only care and genuine desire to help, nothing hidden or deceptive, but still, she had to be sure.

"Very well," she said softly but firmly. "You say that my life is in danger. Suppose that I am a Christian. Tell me what danger I would be in."

Gloria and Floriana exchanged glances.

Floriana nodded. "Tell her what happened."

Still keeping her voice to a whisper, Gloria related to Ariel this tale.

"Ariel, do you remember the day that you were brought into this house as a servant and assigned to us?"

Ariel nodded. "I remember."

"The slave trader who delivered you brought you in with another slave, a boy a little older than you named Anthony. I know you have seen him working in the gardens. Shortly after he was brought in, they assigned him to wait on our father in the Roman Senate as a page, where he has been ever since. A short time ago, it was discovered that the boy was a Christian, and worse, a spy. The whole time he has been in the Senate, he has been collecting information of the emperor's plans against the Christians and passing it on to his associates. Nearly three weeks ago, a house where the Christians were known to meet was raided. The Christians put up a fight and kept the soldiers out till they all disappeared from the house. Nobody knows how they did it, but they did. Anthony, the boy you were brought in with, was helping the Christians in the house escape. He was shot by one of the archers, but he wasn't killed. Two soldiers recognized him as our father's page. They kept him alive and questioned him, but he refused to renounce his activities or tell them anything about the other conspirators. He was put on trial two days ago and found guilty on all charges. The sentence was death."

Ariel's heart, which had been sinking lower and lower as Gloria spoke, now felt as though it had been crushed. Her head hung low, but Gloria went on.

"The emperor tried one last time to get him to be reasonable. He offered him a full pardon if he would abandon his fellow conspirators and give what information he could to apprehend them, but Anthony refused. He insisted that neither he nor any of his friends had ever committed any treason against the state, yet he challenged the divinity of the emperor. He admitted to all the other charges of spying and resisting arrest, but he still refused to inform on his associates.

"His mother and father were there. They pleaded with him through tears to submit, but even though he cried before the open court, he still would not comply. The court found him guilty and sentenced him to death, but they did not specify how he would be put to death.

"Yesterday, at around noon, a public execution was set. They had captured probably the most prominent leader of the followers of the Way, as they call themselves, a man called Peter."

Ariel's heart stopped when she heard this. "What did you say his name was?"

"Peter," Gloria repeated, and then she paused to study Ariel's reaction. "So it's true. You are one of them."

"Please," said Ariel, managing to hold back her tears, "go on."

When they brought Peter out to be crucified, Anthony was brought out with him. Peter was nailed to a cross, but he requested that he be placed with his head down instead of up; they granted his request. A stake was set about a stone's throw away from the foot of the cross. Anthony was chained to the post and left there to watch as Peter died. They had hoped that this would bring him to his senses. We were there with our parents. We saw the whole thing. Anthony watched for several hours as Peter struggled on that cross. We had seen him cry at seeing his parents; now he was crying even harder. Then he stopped crying and watched in silence.

"Through the hours that passed, Peter and Anthony shouted some words to each other, but only a few times, and we could not hear what they said. At last, Peter's body fell limp on the cross as he stooped, struggling for breath. He was dead.

"Some soldiers now demanded that Anthony give up his futile efforts to protect the Christians. We saw him. His head was hung low, and he was weeping, but he shook his head and, through his tears, said no again.

"When he refused, the onlookers began shouting for him to be killed immediately. They said he was a traitor, a misguided fool, or a mad boy. 'Put him out of his misery,' they said. Nero acquiesced and called for the men to bring firewood. Yet, as soon as the men were sent, storm clouds began to gather over the plain. By the time they returned, it had already started to thunder. The rain would soon be upon them, and the fire still had not arrived. The people were enraged that the storm had rescued him, and they continued to shout for his death.

"Emperor Nero had to make a sudden departure due to the rain but left orders that Anthony was to be returned to the prison, tortured for information, and then beheaded. He said it was the most he could do to be merciful to this misused and beguiled youth. The soldiers cut him free from the stake, bound him with chains, and hurried him back to the prison. That was the last that we saw of him."

Ariel's mind and body felt numb. She was so sad but couldn't seem to cry. She sat there before her mistresses in total silence with her hands folded in her lap, her shoulders slumped, and a blank stare on her face.

Floriana reached out and gently shook Ariel by the shoulder. "Ariel," she said, "there is more, and this is why we have called you here. After the trial was over, our father and the overseer Claudio were called into a private meeting with the judges and Nero. We asked him what they wanted with him, but he told us that he could not say. Then tonight, just before we went to bed, we overheard the two of them talking in one of the rooms downstairs.

"In the meeting, Nero demanded of our father and Claudio where Anthony had come from. This whole affair has been one of the most embarrassing things that has happened in Rome. Having a spy operating in the Senate, right under everyone's noses, and releasing all their secret plans to their enemies, the whole thing infuriated the emperor. It made him and all the senators look like fools. Nero was especially angry with our father for bringing him in, but he still believed Father when he said that he didn't know that Anthony was a Christian. Nero demanded to know everything about Anthony.

"Claudio told him all he knew about Anthony and his family, which was not very much. Nero asked if there was anyone else in his house that might have a strong connection with Anthony. Both our father and Claudio said no; Anthony had not been a close friend with anyone in the house."

Ariel smiled to herself, feeling a little pride for herself and Anthony. They had done well at keeping their faith and friendship a secret.

"Then Claudio remembered that Anthony had been sold into the house on the same day as you, but he didn't know if the two of you had any prior relationship.

"Upon hearing your name, one of the judges asked about you. When Claudio told him what little he knew, the judge said that he knew your family and that your parents were still alive."

Ariel's mouth dropped open with a gasp, and she placed her hands over her heart as it started racing like a team of chariot horses.

Gloria continued, "The judge even went so far as to say where your parents are living in Rome. Senator Marcus confessed that he had made some inquiries into Anthony's family, and he told Nero where his mother and father lived. He was just in the process of getting in touch with Anthony's parents when Anthony disappeared from the house.

"Nero demanded to know if you were a Christian, but Father and Claudio could not say for sure. Nero ordered them to find out and told them that he was to have a full report of the matter by tomorrow evening at the latest. He told them that they were to find out everything they could about Anthony from you, Ariel, and if you were a Christian. If you were not a Christian and you told them what you knew about Anthony, if anything, you were to be returned home to your parents. By law, you are the daughter of a Roman citizen and should be freed from servitude. However, if you were found to be a Christian, you were to be handed over to the authorities for trial and punishment.

"Our father and Claudio were too exhausted to make any inquiries last night when they returned to the house, but they intend to make a full inquiry tomorrow morning.

I heard Father say to Claudio, 'If she is not a Christian, she is to be freed from service and returned to her parents; you will remember where they live. If she is a Christian, then the guards will take her into custody and deliver her to the prison.'

"Right then we leapt away from the door and ran quietly down the hallway. Father and Claudio didn't see us, so we snuck back up to our room and discussed what we should do."

"Ariel," Floriana said urgently, "now that you know what has happened, and since you are a Christian, you must leave this house tonight if you are to save your life. Tomorrow, they will interrogate you, and when they find that you are a Christian, you will most certainly be killed, just like Anthony."

Ariel had regained herself and had taken special note of everything that had been said.

"Thank you for the warning," she whispered. "You have saved my life. I will take your advice. I'll leave tonight."

Feeling free to converse with them as equals, Ariel reached out and touched their hands.

"Thank you for all the kindness you have shown to me. I will never forget you both. It has been an honor and pleasure to serve as your maid. I'm sorry I have to leave like this, but I hope to see you again someday, under better circumstances."

Gloria and Floriana's mouths dropped open. They sat there completely at a loss for what to do or say.

Shrugging her shoulders as she exhaled a short breath to relax herself, Ariel said, "Well, I don't have anything to take with me but my old clothes that I have kept. I'll change into those and be off. Good-bye, Gloria, Floriana. I shall miss you both very much."

As she was rising to her feet, Floriana reached out and gently took her hand, pulling her back down to the floor.

"Why?" she asked, pleading. "Why, Ariel? Why must you do this? You're only a child, you and Anthony. Why are you involved with these criminals? You're so innocent. Why must you hang on to whatever it is that you believe? It is useless. Why must you and so many others go to your deaths? It's only a matter of time, Ariel. Sooner or later they will find you. Why don't you just give it up? You could go back to your parents and have a normal, happy life again instead of living life as a criminal, always on the run. What makes you persist like this? You are all going to your deaths, giving your lives for a useless cause."

Ariel smiled. "From the very first day that we were brought into this house, God showed me that he had placed us here for a very special reason: to warn his followers of the danger that was coming. That is why we stayed; that is why Anthony did what he did, because it is what Jesus wanted.

"The innocence that you have seen in us is all because of the one who controls us. It is his virtue you saw, not ours. He loves using children, and other people like us, to carry out his plans. He does it to show that it is his strength that wins the battle, not ours.

"You may think it foolish that we are risking our lives for this Jesus. We owe him more than our lives. We were sinners; we were his enemies. We rebelled against him, broke his law. In his justice, he could have sentenced us to eternal punishment, which we deserved, but he didn't. He showed us mercy and took the punishment on himself. He died in our place so that we could be forgiven. He ransomed and empowered us to bring his kingdom to the world, conquering it for him. He bled for us; it only makes sense that we should bleed for him. Even if we die, what do we lose? Everyone will die someday, but with the promise of eternal life, we have nothing to lose. There is no need to be afraid.

"The same is true of the other followers of Jesus. Anthony and I should have died in the fire. It was the Christians who saved our lives. That's why Anthony would not turn on them. The emperor may call them criminals, but they are not.

"You think this is a lost cause, but it's not. Our God is more powerful than the emperor, and he will always be standing with us. The world could come to an end, and he would still be there. I don't understand everything that he does or why he allows some things to happen. I'm very sad over losing Anthony. He was the closest friend I had since my parents disappeared. All of us will be sad now that Peter is dead, especially now when times are so bad, when we need him most. I don't understand what God is trying to do, but I know that it is all a small part of his master plan. That is why we go on."

Gloria and Floriana did not know how to answer or how to ask another question.

Ariel took the initiative and recounted briefly what had happened to her and Anthony at the catacombs after the great fire: the people who had cared for them, how they had been healed, and the person Jesus they had grown to love. She told them about his life and the things he had done. Gloria and Floriana were especially confused when she told them that he had indeed died, but three days later, he rose again.

"It is in this that he proved that he was who he said he was, the Son of God," Ariel said. "The tomb is still empty. No man could do that; only God could."

Floriana asked, "How could you believe such an impossible thing? Whoever told you this must have been crazy or lying. Besides, anyone can steal a body from a tomb."

"The tomb was guarded for that very reason," Ariel answered with a smile. "I heard about this from my parents when I was just a little girl. They told me Jesus's disciples had stolen the body to fool the people, that his resurrection was a lie. They were wrong. No one stole the body. The people who watched him die also saw him alive a few days later. Many of the disciples have been tortured and killed because they will not stop speaking for him. Peter was one of them. You saw him die; you saw the pain he suffered. Tell me, would he have put himself through all of that just for a lie that he and some friends made up?"

Gloria and Floriana could not answer.

"No," Ariel went on, "Peter died because he knew that it was true. Jesus was the Son of God, he is alive, and he wants to give you eternal life and so much more."

Again Gloria and Floriana were overwhelmed and confused by everything they had heard, and they couldn't answer.

Ariel smiled. "It took a while for God to reveal it all to me. Just keep listening. He will come for you. He always does."

After a moment or two of silence, the three rose to their feet.

"Now I must go," Ariel said softly.

"Wait," Gloria said. "There is one last thing we have for you."

She reached in among a stack of parchment scrolls and drew one forth. Unrolling it on the floor, Ariel saw that it was a small map of Rome, almost identical to the one she and Anthony had used the first time they had snuck out of the senator's house. Two places in the city had been marked.

"When we overheard from our father that your parents were still alive, they also mentioned where they lived. We marked the place on this map," Gloria said, pointing to one of the marked places. "It may be useful to you someday. Even if you remain a Christian, we thought you'd want to know that your parents are alive and where they can be found. This other place here"—she pointed to the second marking—"is where Anthony's parents are living. Even though he's as good as dead, we thought we should put it down."

Ariel nodded. "That was good of you. Thank you."

Ariel rolled the scroll up as the two sisters extinguished the candles. Then the three of them quietly emerged from the closet. Ariel had kept the clothes that she had worn the night she and Anthony were kidnapped. Whenever she left the house, it was always in those clothes, to help her blend in with the other people on the street. She decided to change into those and leave her servants' clothes behind.

With Gloria and Floriana following, Ariel glided silently through the house to the storeroom where she and Anthony had hidden their clothes. She lit a small candle and placed it in a corner of the room. Slipping out of her servants' clothes, she folded them up and placed them under another pile of clothes and fabrics. With the light of the candle, she found her other clothes with no difficulty at all. Once changed, she extinguished the light and emerged from the closet, carrying the map and the key she had used to open the side door.

The three made their way to the side door as silently as a shadow. With the greatest care and gentleness, Ariel inserted the key and unlocked the door. She and Anthony had taken to oiling the hinges, ensuring it would not squeak when it was opened. The door didn't make the slightest sound as Ariel pulled it open and slipped out. Keeping in the shadows, she made her way to the corner of the house where the alleyway opened into the street. She knelt down close to the ground before inching her head out to scan the street. No one was about. She stood back and handed the key to Floriana.

"Good-bye," Ariel whispered. "I will always remember you in my thoughts and prayers."

Disregarding the social rules of the day, Ariel stepped forward and wrapped her arms around Floriana in a warm and prolonged embrace. Then she hugged Gloria. It didn't matter if it was unacceptable for a maid to embrace her mistresses; Gloria and Floriana received her gesture with as much warmth as they had ever shown to a close friend.

With a last smile, Ariel waved good-bye, peered out again to make sure the street was clear, then slipped around the corner and out of sight. Without another second's delay, she swiftly, yet silently and gracefully, glided across the street, into the shadows of the buildings.

The two sisters looked out after her to see where she had gone, but they couldn't find her. They glared out into the street, looking in every direction. Ariel had disappeared.

Realizing that they might be discovered, the two sisters slipped back into the house and locked the door. They returned to the storeroom and put the key back in its place with several others. Gloria suggested that, in the morning, people might be suspicious as to how she got out of the house. If all the doors were locked, they might realize that someone inside the house had helped her escape. However, she and Floriana decided to let the matter rest. Ariel had escaped, and that was all that mattered. The chances of them being accused of aiding her were very slim as long as no one saw them. With this thought in mind, the two carefully hurried back up to their room, realizing the danger that they were in.

Once back in their private chambers, they breathed a sigh of relief and composed to rest upon their beds. They slept soundly and awoke at their usual time, fully refreshed.

By the time they emerged from their room, the servants and overseers were in state of suppressed excitement and confusion at the disappearance of Ariel. The two sisters made themselves appear as ignorant and surprised as everyone else. The overseers could offer no explanation of how she had escaped or discovered the senator's plans. Senator Marcus was very morose when he left the house that afternoon to give his report to the emperor.

Gloria and Floriana giggled with each other that night; the agitated and befuddled state of Claudio and their father had been a sight to behold. They were glad to hear from their father that the emperor himself was baffled by the cunning of these seditionists and did not chide him too severely.

Still, they thought of Ariel and what she had said to them. As each of them fell asleep, they found themselves whispering a prayer, talking to this god. The words of each girl were different, but their petition was in essence the same.

"God, who are you? If you are real, show me who you are. I want to know."

Chapter 14

In Hiding

Maneuvering her way stealthily through the alleyways and passages, Ariel headed toward the south side of the city as silently as a tiger stalking its prey in the jungle. Her nerves were on edge, and her heart was pounding. She avoided the main roads as much as possible, keeping to the areas where she was less likely to be spotted. Both she and Anthony had become well acquainted with these shortcuts, but Ariel knew that robbers and other criminals also used these passages. Praying to God for protection, she hurried along, trying to stay as relaxed and confident as possible.

She had been on the road only a few minutes when she heard the rumble of thunder. At first, her heart fell.

Now I'll have to walk in the rain, she thought to herself despondently but then suddenly changed her mind. *With the rain out, more people will be driven into their houses. Even the robbers are likely to seek shelter. This is perfect.* She smiled to herself.

The storm came on quickly. Ariel hurried along as fast as she could, remembering that it would be far more difficult for her to navigate in the rain and getting lost could mean her life. The rain came in only a mist at first, but it quickly grew into a torrential downpour. Ariel hid the scroll underneath her tunic to protect it, if only for a little bit longer.

She had originally thought of going to the house just by the city walls in the hope of getting out of the city tonight, but with the storm and the darkness, finding the house would be a nightmare. She decided instead to go to another house much closer and easier to find. This was another place where the believers frequently gathered to pray and motivate each other.

Finding the house proved very difficult in the rain, and Ariel's clothes were completely soaked by the time she arrived. To her surprise and excitement, there was a light still burning inside the house. Creeping up to the door, she put her ear to the planks and listened. A murmur of voices could be heard inside. The believers had assembled there.

Ariel rapped on the door with her ear still on the planks. She smiled, almost laughing, as all the noise inside was hushed. She knocked softly once again. Finally, the door opened. The woman who answered the door was shocked to see Ariel kneeling on the threshold, dripping wet. The two had met several times before. The lady welcomed Ariel into the house instantly. She stepped into the front room, finding it full of people as she had guessed. They were startled to see her out in such weather.

Ariel removed the scroll she carried under her clothes. The woman who had answered the door moved to usher her away from the crowd and get her into some dry clothes, but Ariel stopped her.

"Wait," she said to the woman and then addressed the crowd. "I am not just here to meet with you; I am running for my life. I have to get out of Rome, and I need your help."

All the believers nodded in agreement that they would help her but insisted that she dry herself and put on some warm clothes before telling her tale. At this, the woman hurried her off. She showed Ariel into a closet and told her to take off her wet clothes as she went to fetch some dry ones. Ariel undressed and laid her wet garments aside along with the map, which was surprisingly dry. The woman returned with some towels and a set of dry clothes. Ariel was glad to dry herself off and put on the dry clothes, which were a bit large for a girl of her age. The lady insisted upon helping her to wring more of the water out of her hair, dry, and comb it before bringing Ariel back to the small gathering. The woman offered her some food, but Ariel refused to eat until she explained her situation.

Starting with the night of Anthony's arrest, she recounted everything that had happened at the senator's house, right up to that night. She related Anthony's trial, Peter's crucifixion, and how she had been warned to flee from the senator's house and get out of Rome as fast as possible.

One man in the crowd stood up. Ariel recognized him from the group that had escaped from the house with her the night Anthony was captured.

The man addressed the group. "That boy Anthony saved the lives of everyone in that house. He gave up his own life so we could escape. Most of us have heard about Peter's death. I was there also. I watched him die, though I didn't see Anthony. We should pray that God will grant him the strength not to deny our Lord Jesus or betray the other believers."

Everyone in the group knelt and thanked God for the life and service of Simon Peter, who had been among the three privileged disciples who were closest to Jesus. Tears came to everyone's eyes, as Peter's death was still fresh in their hearts. They then recalled and gave thanks for the warning messages Anthony had delivered and how he had risked his life to save the other believers. They prayed earnestly that he would receive strength from the Lord to remain true to Jesus and to his friends, even though it meant torture and death.

As Ariel listened to the heartfelt thanks and prayers for Anthony, she had never felt happier and was even a bit proud to have been his partner and friend. Though to her, he had always felt more like a brother.

When they finished praying, Ariel asked the group again, "I need to get out of Rome as soon as possible. Can you help me?"

The group offered and discussed several ways by which Ariel could escape from the city. Ariel suggested that using the tunnels might be the simplest and safest way.

A middle-aged man still in his prime raised his hand. "Using the tunnels would indeed be the simplest way, but it may not be the safest.

Over time, the Romans have started to learn our tactics of disappearing, and they are working harder than ever to find the tunnels we have built. They have also learned that we most frequently use the tunnels at night. More and more patrols are being sent out; they're everywhere. Every day it's becoming more and more dangerous to use the tunnels without being discovered. We use them only for emergencies."

Ariel nodded

"With all the soldiers about, it would be safer for you to simply walk out in broad daylight as normally as ever. They wouldn't be as suspicious as they would if they saw you trying to sneak out at night," another man offered.

"And they wouldn't be suspicious at all if they saw you leave the city in the company of your master," the lady of the house ventured with a smile of excitement and a sideways look in her eyes.

Ariel and other members of the group gasped at this suggestion.

"Her master! If he found her, and forbid it that he ever will, he would not take her anywhere but to the prison and have her executed," one of the men shot back.

"Not her old master, but what if she were in the company of a new master, a Christian one, better yet, in disguise," the woman expounded.

A murmur of voices broke from the assembly as the members exchanged glances.

"What specifically are you suggesting?" one of the elders inquired.

"I know a very wealthy family, a Christian family from India, who have been staying in Rome for several weeks," the woman said. "They are leaving Rome in a few days. If I introduced you and explained your situation to the master's wife, I think she would be willing to take you in. She would have no trouble disguising you and smuggling you out of the city, posing as one of her maids. If you wish to leave Rome completely, you could actually become one of her maids and return with her to India. You would be much safer there than here in Italy. Or, if you merely wish to escape back to the catacombs, I am sure that she would release you."

The believers smiled to each other and, after a bit more discussion, agreed that they couldn't think of any better plan for Ariel's safety. Ariel agreed to the plan. Deeply distressed over the news of Peter's crucifixion, Anthony's imminent death, and the danger to her, Ariel wanted nothing more than to get out of Rome as soon as possible.

The gathering of believers began to disperse as the storm outside began to lift. The believers said their last farewells to Ariel, whom they did not expect see again. However, as they were leaving, Ariel asked a few of them if they knew how Peter had been captured since he had agreed to flee from Rome. None of them could offer a single explanation. They, too, had heard that Peter had been finally convinced to flee from Rome and could only guess that he had somehow been overtaken and brought back.

Ariel spent the night in a spare bedroom. The lady, whose name was Abigail, promised to take her to see the family from India early the next morning and assured her that all would be well and she should not worry. Exhausted by the day's work in the senator's house, the excitement of her flight, and the lack of sleep, Ariel threw herself upon her bed and was sound asleep in less than a minute.

Awakened shortly after the sun had risen, Ariel found herself thoroughly relaxed and refreshed. At first, she was a bit surprised to find herself in a different environment than her usual place in the senator's house. She had temporarily forgotten what had happened the night before. It pained her as she thought back over the events that had forced her from the senator's house and drove her to escape the danger that had claimed so many of her friends. There was still more danger ahead. Ariel sat for several minutes on her bed, pondering these things. What was to come next?

Thrusting these thoughts aside, she arose and made herself useful helping Abigail prepare a morning meal for her husband and their three young children. As soon as the table was clear, Abigail gave Ariel back her old clothes, which were dry by now, and led her out to find this wealthy family that was to be her escort out of Rome.

Looking as inconspicuous as a mother with her daughter, Abigail and Ariel made their way through the city, heading north. By the time they left the house the inhabitants of Rome were stirring, and the streets were full of citizens, soldiers, and slaves going their separate ways. The road they were following was heading north and it took them through one of the districts of the city that had been rebuilt after being demolished by the fire. The two continued north until they came to another set of crossroads. From here they turned onto a road going east. They followed this road for at least half a mile, and then Abigail ventured off the main road and in among the many buildings beside the road. Judging from the ornateness and elegance of the structures, Ariel guessed that this was a fairly wealthy section of Rome.

At last, Abigail found the house she was looking for. It was surrounded by a brick wall about nine feet high, over which Ariel could see the branches of trees, some with fruit and some without. The two made their way to the front gate, but before knocking, Abigail paused to rearrange her appearance as best she could. She took a few moments to ensure that Ariel looked her best also.

"Now listen, Ariel," Abigail whispered. "Let me do the talking. The mother and daughter usually take their morning meal outside in the garden; they should be finishing right about now. I'll explain your situation to the mother, but if she asks anything of you, go ahead and answer her. She and her family are all believers. I don't foresee us having any problems here."

The two bowed their heads briefly and prayed for God to give them favor as they presented their request. Then Abigail knocked on the front gate. It was answered about a minute later by an armed guard. Observing the guard's appearance and clothes, Ariel concluded that he was obviously of Indian descent. Abigail introduced herself and politely asked to speak with the lady of the house. The guard knew Abigail and asked her to wait at the gate while he informed his mistress. He returned several minutes later and admitted the two ladies into the garden.

The house was of the same architecture as the senator's house, save that it had only two floors instead of three. The guard led Abigail and Ariel around the house to the back of the garden. The garden landscape reminded Ariel of the garden where she and Anthony had met secretly those many nights. The center area was paved with bricks and had a small fountain bubbling cheerfully in the midst of beds and hedges filled with colorful flowers and lush bushes. In one corner sat two women, a mother and a daughter, it would seem. A servant was just removing some small platters of bread and fruit, while another stood behind their couches, holding a fan.

Abigail and Ariel bowed courteously as the guard introduced them. The lady smiled graciously and motioned the guard and servants to retire. They withdrew into the house, leaving the four of them alone.

As soon as the guard and servants were out of sight, the lady and young girl rose up to greet them, a gracious act and informal for greeting someone of a lower status. The lady and Abigail embraced each other warmly, and then the lady turned her gaze toward Ariel.

"Greetings," she said cordially to Ariel. "And would this be your daughter?"

Ariel remembered to let Abigail do the talking.

"No," Abigail replied. "This is Ariel, one of the believers and a good friend of mine. I have come to ask you for help on her behalf."

With a smile, the lady stepped forward, tenderly wrapping her arms around Ariel, and kissed her on the forehead.

"I am pleased and honored to meet you, Ariel. My name is Aashritha. This is my daughter, Hashika," she said, motioning to girl about Ariel's age standing behind her.

With a beaming smile, Hashika embraced Ariel, making her feel more like a sister than a guest or a stranger.

"Please sit down," Aashritha said, directing them to a couch beside her own. "Would you like something to eat or drink?"

Abigail and Ariel declined her generous offer as they seated themselves.

"Very well," said Aashritha, most gently, as she and Hashika reseated themselves upon their couches. "How can we help you?"

Abigail proceeded to tell Aashritha everything that had happened the night before and that Ariel was an escaped slave running for her life because she was a believer. She further explained to Aashritha her idea that the best way for Ariel to escape would be for her to, in her house, disguise herself and then leave the city posing as one of her maids. She assured her of Ariel's character, devotion, and above all, her sweet, joyful attitude. Ariel felt a bit embarrassed and found it hard to keep her mouth shut, feeling that Abigail's praise bordered on flattery or outright falsehood, two things she and Anthony detested. They were both very modest and humble, especially when it came to themselves. Aashritha and Hashika listened intently and smiled as Abigail finished.

"Of course we will take her," Aashritha said. "Disguising her will be no problem at all. We won't be leaving for three days. Of course she may stay with us. She will be safer here in disguise than anywhere else."

Abigail agreed. Wasting no time, she said farewell to Ariel, Aashritha, and Hashika, gave each of them a parting embrace, and was escorted back to the front gate by the guard who had admitted her and Ariel.

Ariel watched her go, feeling rather sad over all the good-byes she had had to say and the many friends she was being separated from.

"We should waste no time, Ariel," Aashritha said, wrapping her arm around her shoulder. "The sooner we disguise you, the better. You can help us prepare to leave, and we'll even teach you some of our language to make you even more convincing as an Indian maid."

Ariel took a deep breath and nodded with a smile. "Very well," she said, "I am ready."

Ariel followed the two ladies into the rear of the house. Aashritha called for the servants to bring some special ointments, spices, clothes, and towels.

"Take her upstairs to your room, Hashika," Aashritha said. "We'll do everything up there."

Hashika led Ariel upstairs to her room, Aashritha then came up accompanied by two maids. Aashritha had strictly warned the two servants that they were not to speak of what was being done here to anyone. Ariel's transformation took a little over three hours. They began by applying several ointments to her face and arms to darken her skin. Aashritha and Hashika saw that the ointment was applied thoroughly to Ariel's entire body. Ariel rubbed the salve in wherever she could, and the servants attended to the other areas where she could not reach.

When Aashritha was satisfied that all her skin was thoroughly darkened, they turned their attention to Ariel's hair, which was dark brown. First, they washed her hair with another lotion to dye her hair black. This was repeated several times, after which Ariel was told to sit still for a time while the ointments took effect. Then at the appropriate time, the maids washed the ointments out again. Once Aashritha was certain that Ariel's hair was completely black, she anointed it with another oil to give it a shining gloss. Aashritha shaved off a few strands of hair that would have appeared a bit out of place for an Indian maid. She then combed and styled Ariel's hair in an Indian fashion.

Aashritha and Hashika assisted Ariel with putting on a set of Indian clothes. They were as opulent as anything Ariel had worn in the senator's house, but still appropriate for a maid. Hashika even offered Ariel some perfume. Ariel had almost forgotten the feeling of wearing such fine clothes, much less perfume. She could not even recognize herself when Hashika let her see her reflection in a small mirror. She gazed into the mirror for almost two minutes trying to find something that she remembered of herself. Finding nothing, she shook her head in bewilderment. Aashritha and Hashika smiled at her reaction.

"Now, Ariel, are you ready to begin your work as an Indian maid?" Aashritha asked.

"Yes, my lady," Ariel responded as sweetly as ever.

"Then you may help Hashika pack up her belongings in this room," Aashritha commanded.

Ariel bowed respectfully and hurried to her tasks. She proved to be an even finer servant than she first appeared. Her diligence and creativity significantly accelerated the progress of the packing. The ladies and other servants were surprised and pleased with her work. Ariel, however, had a little difficulty learning how to maneuver about in her new clothes, which were completely different than anything she had ever worn. Despite this challenge, the two girls succeeded in packing up almost everything in Hashika's room by the time supper was being served. Only a few necessary items were left out.

When the servants came up to announce supper, they brought with them a small couch for Ariel to sleep on that night. Aashritha had decided that Ariel and her daughter would sleep in the same room together. Ariel was very surprised to be sleeping in the same room as the daughter, but she said nothing.

When the meal came, Ariel was fully prepared to serve the meal with the other servants, but Aashritha insisted that she eat with her and her daughter. Aashritha's husband was not present that night but was expected to return in the next few days. When the meal was finished, Aashritha told Ariel and Hashika to come up to her room.

Aashritha had some lamps lit, as the light outside was fading fast. Once the three were seated, Aashritha asked Ariel to give her a full account of her life's history and who she was. Ariel recounted her life as the daughter of a Jewish family in Rome, the great fire, how she had become a believer. She related her association with Anthony, service as a maid, and the events that had forced her to flee for her life. Both ladies asked Ariel many other questions, among them, how she liked living with them. The three talked long into the night, until Ariel was exhausted. By the time Aashritha dismissed the two girls to bed, Ariel was half asleep.

The night passed quickly, and the next day proceeded in much the same fashion. On the third day, the master of the house, Sabal, returned shortly after noon and was pleased to find the whole house packed up and ready for departure. Aashritha presented Ariel to her husband as their guest, servant, and fellow believer. She related the specifics of Ariel's life and current situation to him in private. The family insisted that Ariel eat with them as she had on the previous nights. She felt a bit awkward and out of place, but they told her not to feel uncomfortable. As God had entrusted them with so much, he also commanded them to be hospitable, to entertain strangers, and do good to all men, especially to other believers.

The fourth day proceeded in a more relaxed manner than the previous three. Ariel was given only a few minute tasks to attend to. Most of her time that day was spent with the family, who insisted upon hearing more of her and her life. When evening came, Ariel insisted upon helping the other servants prepare the meal but, at the request of the family, ate it with them as a guest.

When the meal was over and the table was cleared, Ariel was called up to Sabal and Aashritha's room. She came immediately and found the whole family waiting for her. Sabal and Aashritha were seated on a couch beside each other, with Hashika sitting on another couch. They welcomed her in, directing her to sit on a small chair set before them. She seated herself, and Sabal began speaking.

"My wife has told me the specifics of your situation and the danger you are in," he said kindly. "I am also glad to have heard the story directly from you. In the few days that you have been here, you have shown yourself very diligent and reliable in helping us prepare for our departure. Both my wife and daughter have grown to love you, and with your consent, they would like to take you back with us to India as their adopted daughter and sister. Would you consider such an arrangement?"

Ariel was not completely taken by surprise at this offer. She had definitely seen how much Aashritha and Hashika had grown to like her. As they had already done so much to protect her life, it was only natural that they wished to do more. The generosity in their hearts was overflowing. Ariel liked that about them. The thought of having a family again, a Christian family, overwhelmed Ariel's heart with joy and excitement. She would be much safer with them in India than here in Rome. Ariel had always been intrigued and fascinated by different countries, people, and cultures. Still, was this the right choice? Thoughts of her parents came to mind. She had not seen them in a long time. What should she do? What would God have her do?

"I am honored and humbled," Ariel replied gracefully. "Thank you for your generous offer. If you will, let me consider it tonight, and I will give you my answer tomorrow."

"Of course you may," Sabal replied. "We are happy to help you. Even if you choose not to go with us, we will still be glad to help you in any way we can, not just in getting out of Rome."

Ariel smiled back at the three, bowed ceremoniously, and withdrew.

She walked down to the garden behind the house and sat down on one of the couches. The sun had almost completely disappeared behind the horizon, and the sound of the crickets and other night-loving creatures could be heard. She sat there, still and silent, as the daylight faded and the stars began to appear.

I would be much safer in India than here in Rome, Ariel mused to herself. *I would have a family again, something I have really missed. I love them just like they love me. They took me in because I was a believer in need. For the first time in my life, I would have a sister, but God, is this what you want for me, or do you want me to stay here in Rome?*

Her thoughts now turned to the many adventures she had shared with the believers. Even though the danger caused her concern, the thrill and excitement of being part of it all brought her great joy. She remembered Anthony, her brother. Even if he was dead, he had always been like a brother to her. Thinking of him brought tears to her eyes. She remembered how God had brought them to the senator's house to use them as spies, a high honor to be entrusted with such a decisive task.

Her thoughts now turned to when she had become a follower of Jesus. She had committed her whole life to Jesus, to follow him wherever he led her. She had put her faith in him, trusting that he would fulfill his promise to forgive her sin and give her eternal life. If she could trust him with eternal life, couldn't she trust him with her short life here?

"I will not go to India to escape the danger," she said to herself softly but firmly. "'Safety is of the Lord,'" she recalled from a psalm her father and mother had taught her. "It was God who kept us safe all this time. He was the one who saved us from the soldiers and warned me that I had to escape from the senator's house. The whole time it has been God protecting me. He can do it again."

She rose to her feet, turned her gaze skyward, and whispered, "The Lord is my shepherd; I shall not want. Lord Jesus, you are my true Father. Where do you want me? Call me; I will follow, to India or to Rome, to go or to stay. To the death, to the end of the world, you are with me, and I am yours."

She bowed her head for a few seconds and then looked back at the dark sky filled with sparkling stars. She smiled for a moment, then made her way back into the house. She slept peacefully that night, and when the morning came, she knew what she had to do.

Chapter 15

Return to the Catacombs

ARIEL ROSE EARLY, washed her face, combed her hair, and dressed herself to work as an Indian servant girl. Her skin and hair were still darkened, and instead of wearing the elegant clothes that she had first been given, she chose the apparel worn by all the other maids in the house. She put on no perfume or any ornaments that would appear ostentatious for a servant girl or hinder her ability to work. The family had not come down from their rooms, but Ariel was eager to make herself useful. She went to the kitchen and assisted the other servants in preparing the morning meal. The servants were a bit confused to see Ariel taking on such a role, but they were glad to have her help. Ariel smiled to herself at their reaction. She knew how to act both as the daughter of a wealthy family, in elegant clothes, or as a lowly servant girl in simple attire.

The sun had fully risen and the birds were singing when the family made their appearance. They had expected to find Ariel waiting for them at the table. When they did not find her there, they asked to have the meal brought out to the garden, thinking that Ariel may have been about the grounds.

They seated themselves, still wondering where Ariel could be. Ariel brought out two small platters, one with various fruits and the other with bread. They sent her back inside to fetch some additional items. Ariel smiled to herself again as she walked back to the house. They hadn't recognized her. The meal was half over before they finally did, and they, like the servants, were surprised to see her playing such a role.

Aashritha asked her why she was dressed the way she was.

Ariel replied in a soft but firm voice, "Today, I will serve you."

When the meal was ended, Sabal sent in one of the other maids to bring Ariel out to them and then retire, leaving them alone. The maid returned promptly, with Ariel following, and then withdrew to the house. Everyone would be leaving the next morning as early as possible. The morning meal had been fairly simple and brief. The servants were busy packing up the last few items in the house.

"Ariel," Sabal asked, "have you decided whether you would like to go with us back to India or stay here in Rome?"

Ariel had already prepared how she would answer when the question came. "It is God's will that I remain here in Rome," she replied. "I thought and prayed about your offer last night. I would be just as content to live with you in India as I would to live here in Rome, provided that I knew it was where God wanted me. You have all shown me so much kindness, especially your wife and daughter. Thank you. You've saved my life. I will never forget what you have done for me, and I know that I'm going to miss you."

At this, Aashritha interjected, "Are you sure you will be safe here, Ariel? You know the danger you are in as an escaped slave and a Christian."

Ariel smiled. She had specifically prepared herself to answer this concern, to herself and anyone else.

"My safety is God's concern; it is not mine to carry. The Lord is my Father, and he can protect me just as well in Rome as in India. He has already done it for me many times. He saved my life in the fire, rescued my soul, and brought me into the senator's house with Anthony so we could warn the believers. He was the one who let me find favor with the senator's daughters and moved them to warn me. He brought me safely to your house so that I could return to the catacombs."

Her voice turned a bit graver. "He gave courage and strength to Anthony when he was tried, and he will be with Anthony when he dies, if he has not passed already.

"When the senator's daughters told me I had to flee, they also gave me a map showing where Anthony's parents and mine are living in Rome. Both Anthony and I thought they had been killed in the fire, but God kept them alive too. He did this for a reason. It was no accident that I should find out where they are, and I am convinced that Jesus wants me to go back and tell them about him and what he has done for me. I really miss them, and I know they miss me. I am not exactly sure how they will receive me, but I suspect they will be disappointed, if not very angry, with me. In becoming a Christian, I have not only become a wanted criminal, I have also betrayed my family's Jewish heritage and law. I remember them telling me that Jesus was an imposter and a deceiver that he and his followers sought to corrupt and destroy the Law of Moses with false teaching. They raised me to be very faithful to our traditions and laws. They will almost certainly be furious that I have been following their archenemy. Going back to them will be dangerous, but I feel this is what God wants me to do.

"I think he may also want me to speak to Anthony's parents. His mother was heartbroken at his trial. Hearing from me may help her understand a little of why he refused to submit, also that he still loves them. Anthony spoke a great deal of his mother and father in the time I knew him."

Hashika now broke in. "Ariel, you could die doing that."

"I know," Ariel replied, "but if I am doing God's will, I can be sure he will either protect me or give me strength to face whatever I must suffer. I am doing what he told me to do; he's not going to betray me when I need him the most."

"And will you be all right without family?" Aashritha asked.

A smile broke across Ariel's face.

"I am not without a family," Ariel replied. "I never was. When I lost my parents, the Lord adopted me and made me his daughter. With him, I never have to be alone again. The family of believers he has given me is more than enough, though I will always miss my parents. If I truly need another real family of my own, God will either bring them to me or bring me to them. Until then, he wants me to stay here in Rome.

"I will miss each of you, but I will see you again, if not in this life, then in the next. God will take care of me, but I have to be where he wants me."

Sabal nodded as his lips widened into a smile. He rose to his feet, strode up to her, and placed his hand on her shoulder.

"Then let us waste no time in getting you out to the catacombs," he said. "But how will you get back without being seen? Getting out of the city will be no problem, but people on the road, it will be impossible for you to leave the caravan without attracting attention."

"Yes, yes," admitted Ariel, nodding her head, "I see what you mean. Let me think about that for a while. I'll find a way. I'll come up with some kind of a plan."

Ariel paused for a moment to collect her thoughts.

"If I may be excused, sir?" she inquired, tilting her head slightly downward to show respect.

Sabal tilted his head downward and spread out his arms to his sides with his hands open, palms up. "But of course you may," he said.

Ariel bowed respectfully and withdrew back up to Hashika's room, where she had slept that night. She paced back and forth trying to think of the best way to get back to the catacombs without attracting the attention of the other passersby. She was up in her room for almost a quarter of an hour before she came back down. Sabal and his family were double-checking everything around the house so they would be ready to leave the next morning.

"I have thought about it," Ariel replied, "and I have a plan that I think can get me back to the catacombs safely and yet do so without attracting attention or raising suspicion. The place where Anthony and I usually went is about half a mile from the outer city walls. The people there know me well. Of course, I doubt that even they would recognize me as I am now. Still, this area is a bit too close to Rome, and the risk of being spotted is great. However, there is another place where I could go. When Anthony and I started serving with the believers, they took us to another set of caves that are on the same road but it is much farther from the city. I think this would be the best place for me to slip away. There won't be as many people about that far away from the city. Most of them will be travelers themselves, going to and from the city. They won't be especially interested in the activities of the other people on the road. They'll be focused on getting to where they're going. We'll act as casually as ever, just as we will when we leave the city. Besides this, the area is wooded. It is not a dense forest, but it will provide more than enough cover to hide us from anyone on the road. As long as we aren't looking conspicuous or mysterious, no one will think twice of us. I understand that you, Aashritha and Hashika, will each be riding in a litter."

Ariel now directed her attention to Sabal. "If it pleases you, sir, let the caravan be arranged as follows. You will lead, riding a horse in front with a few packhorses behind you, then the two litters, the rest of the packhorses, and some guards protecting the rear. Let me lead the last horse in the first group in front of the two litters so your wife and daughter will be able to see me. I will be watching for the place where we need to stop when we are as close as the road can take us."

Now Ariel turned her attention to Aashritha and Hashika. "As an Indian maid, I will be wearing a veil or shawl covering my head. When you see me take it off, revealing my hair and wiping my brow as if to remove sweat, you will know that we have come to the place. Call out to Sabal and ask for a rest.

"You will grant it," Ariel said, turning to Sabal.

"We will step off to the side of the road for a brief drink and rest. Aashritha, you and your daughter will leave the litters, acting as if you are stretching your legs. Call me to follow you, and I will show you the way to the caves. I'll keep the sack with my old clothes on the horse that I am leading and then bring it with me as I leave. Once we leave the city, keep going. Do not stop for anything. The servants carrying the litter will be getting tired and thirsty, so they will be ready for a rest. We'll leave the caravan, acting as normal as ever; everyone else will stay behind to distract anyone who might be passing by. The caves are not too far from the road, and there are plenty of trees, bushes, and dips in the ground that we can use to hide our movements. We'll disappear from sight, go to the entrance of the caves, and explain who I am. Then you two will go back to the caravan acting as if nothing happened."

Sabal nodded approvingly. "Well done, Ariel. It's an excellent plan. I love it. It shall be done just as you have said. We'll be ready to leave first thing in the morning."

With a smile, Ariel bowed and got to work, making sure everything was ready for their early departure the next day. They day passed quickly for everyone in the house. Ariel's mind was perfectly at ease thinking about the coming day. She had become accustomed to taking risks like this, and the danger of being spotted while leaving the road was only minimal.

Ariel's assistance in packing up the family's furniture and possessions proved crucial. In the late afternoon, all was in readiness for their early departure the next day. True to her word, Ariel assisted the other servants in preparing and serving the evening meal. The family commended Ariel for her willingness to help. She could tell that they were very sorry that she would not be coming with them to India.

Thinking back over the events of the past few days, she considered that she simply could have walked out of the city gates in a crowd. She and Anthony had encountered no trouble getting around in the city before being enslaved. Their clothes were very simple, and walking about in the streets had covered the two of them with dust. They looked just like any other homeless children searching or begging for food. She could have tried to escape the city like that. It was unlikely that the guards would be able to identify her as an escaped slave, as she bore no marks of enslavement. The slaves and freemen of Rome were indistinguishable by their clothing or appearance. Still, God had brought her here, to be with this family. This was his way for her to get out.

As she lay down to sleep that night she told herself, *"I have to be where God wants me, though I, too, will miss them."*

EVERYONE AROSE JUST before the crack of dawn the next morning and the whole house exploded with activity. They gulped down a rapid meal and made haste to assemble the caravan.

The Final Message to Rome

Sabal instructed the servant in bringing the chests, sacks, and other items to the front gate and loading them onto a train of packhorses waiting outside. Aashritha and Hashika took Ariel aside and did a final inspection of her appearance to ensure she would not attract suspicion. Satisfied, they joined the servants in securing the last of the family's property on the horses, and in less than two hours, they were ready to start out.

Sabal took care to see that the caravan was arranged in the formation Ariel had described to them. He, with one of his armed attendants, led the way on horseback. Behind them were three packhorses loaded with food, water, and other items that would be essential for the journey. Ariel took her strategically planned position leading the third horse behind Sabal and his attendant. Behind Ariel came the two litters bearing Aashritha and her daughter, each one borne on the shoulders of four powerful men, exactly according to the plan. If ever a man bearing the litter needed rest, he would switch out with one of the men leading a horse. Behind them came the train of packhorses led by servants, male and female alike. Other male and some female servants were laden down with some baggage that the horses had been unable to carry. These servants walked along beside the second train of packhorses. To the rear and on either side were more armed attendants, on horseback or on foot, to protect them from robbers or any other possible threat.

The family had packed Ariel's clothes in a small sack that she would carry with her once she left the train. In addition, they had packed some special clothes for her, some money, and a few spices and ointments. The sack was on the horse that Ariel would be leading and had been secured so that it was accessible and easily removable. They had given these additional items to her, without her knowledge, as a thank-you for the sunshine and energy that Ariel had brought to them, something she carried with her wherever she went. Gloria and Floriana had seen it too. This was among the chief beauties of Ariel's soul and spirit, which overflowed with the spirit of the Lord.

Ariel found her place in the caravan as Aashritha and Hashika climbed into their litters. Atop his black stallion, Sabal looked over the caravan, ensuring that everything was in position. He nodded approvingly.

"Onward," he declared in a strong yet calm tone, "back to India."

He turned his stead and trotted down the street with his attendant beside him. The caravan followed. They were on their way. Ariel would soon be back with her friends, provided God willed it to be so.

Noting the expressions and stride of the other servants, Ariel did her best to mirror them. No one in the family would speak to her again until the city was out of sight and there were no passersby. The city was vibrant with activity, and the streets were filled with people. Fortunately, the streets were not as congested as Ariel had seen them on other days. The caravan followed the road that Abigail had taken when she had brought Ariel to the family's house, heading west back toward the section of the town that had been consumed by the fire.

At the next set of crossroads, the caravan turned southward, heading toward what once had been the Circus Maximus. They reached the crossroads beside where the gigantic structure had once stood and turned left, heading toward the southern, outer side of the city. They passed through the busy streets without attracting the slightest attention. Now it was on to the gates and then off into open country, until the road passed by the catacombs. Ariel knew this part of the city very well. It seemed to her a very long time since she had traveled these streets.

Ariel could not see far ahead of her, as the streets were crowded, and there were so many horses from the caravan in front of her. Keeping herself as relaxed as possible, she walked along as normally as ever, thrusting aside the thought that she was a runaway slave and criminal making her escape. They had walked nearly two-thirds of a mile when they finally reached the outer gate. The caravan came to a stop as soldiers on duty approached Sabal.

Sabal dismounted as the two guards walked up and began questioning him. The servants bearing the two litters set them down on the ground for a brief rest. Aashritha and Hashika got out to stretch their legs. The soldier speaking with Sabal took a few moments to glance over the caravan before gesturing with his hand that they were free to move on. Sabal mounted his horse again and beckoned for everyone to move on. Aashritha and Hashika climbed back into their litters as the servants bearing them switched out with others who had been leading horses. Acting as nonchalantly as ever, Ariel led her horse on through the gate, looking straight ahead to avoid the eyes of the guards. Ariel remembered this gate from the first time she and Anthony had snuck out of the city. The train passed through the gate without harm or hindrance and down the road southward. The midmorning sun was streaming down on the convoy as they traveled along the well-paved roads leading toward the catacombs.

Using the map she had received from Gloria and Floriana, Ariel had advised them which road would lead to the caves before they had left the house. There were no crowds of people on the highway, but still a few people coming or going to and from the city. The place where Ariel would leave the caravan and sneak back to the catacombs was well over two miles down the road, but she kept a close eye on the layout of the land. She wasn't going to take any chances that they might miss the area.

They had traveled almost a full mile from the city when everyone's attention was alerted by the clatter of hooves from behind. They turned to see a company of mounted Roman soldiers riding down upon them. The caravan quickly moved off to the side of the road. Ariel hoped that they would ride by. They did not. The band rode up just parallel to the train and stopped. The soldiers scanned the people, showing no sign of finding what they were looking for.

Sabal walked his horse over to the officer at the head of the column, who obviously commanded the highest rank. Ariel looked up at the soldier seated upon a mighty stallion, nostrils flaring. That soldier looked very familiar to Ariel somehow, but from where, she couldn't remember. The two met just a few yards beside where Ariel was standing; she heard every word.

"Good morning, sir," Sabal greeted him. "Is there something I can do for you?"

"Yes, tell me, how long have you been on the road today?" the soldier inquired.

"We left city just after dawn, not a half an hour ago. Is there something wrong?" Sabal asked.

"Who has been on the road today, going out of the city?" the Roman asked.

"A few people," Sabal responded, "not many, most of them slaves with their masters. Are you looking for someone in particular?"

"Yes." The soldier nodded. "A runaway slave, a Jewish girl in her teen years who we believe to be in league with the Christians."

Suddenly, it hit Ariel like a blast of hot air from a furnace. She knew who this soldier was. He was the same one who had called on Senator Marcus to come to the prison and identify Anthony. Her heart froze inside her. She had heard and seen him at the door, and he must have seen her. For a second, she forgot that she was disguised, as her first impulse was to hide her face. She checked herself and kept her composure while still looking up at the two men.

"Can you describe her?" Sabal inquired.

The officer offered a brief description of Ariel as she had been as a maid.

A fairly thorough description, Ariel thought to herself. *They probably got it from Julia.*

"We haven't seen anybody like that all morning, sir," Sabal replied.

The soldier's shoulders drooped as he exhaled a fast breath.

"Well, thank you for your help, sir. You may be on your way," he said. "Off with us!" he shouted over his shoulder to his troop.

Spurring his steed onward, the officer galloped away with his troop following him down the road, heading away from Rome. The train moved back onto the highway and proceeded on their way. Ariel breathed a sigh of relief as her heart regained its normal rhythm.

This is why God had me leave the city in disguise, Ariel thought to herself. *If I had left Rome as I am, I very likely would have been caught.*

They still had a good distance to cover before they reached the place where Ariel would try to slip away. Having mounted patrols out and about would make it more difficult to leave the road undetected. Ariel decided not to think about what could or might happen. Everything would be over in less than an hour, and it would not help to worry. She had made the best plan she could think of. Now it was time to put it to the test.

The Final Message to Rome

Moving along at a good pace, the train continued down the stone-paved road heading south. As God would have it, there was no one in close proximity to them as they journeyed along. In the distance, about a mile ahead, they could see a small group of travelers who had left the city a good while before them. Because of her position toward the front of the train, Ariel could not see if there was anyone close behind them. Reminding herself of the many ways God had protected her, she began to hum several tunes of praise to the Lord with a smile on her face.

With the stopping place getting nearer and nearer, Ariel continued to scan the right side of the road, searching for the landmarks that would lead her to the entrance of the caves. As the train made its way farther and farther south, the land adjacent to the road gradually began to change. When they had left Rome that morning on the Via Latina, the country was fairly open, with only a few bushes and trees, but now, two miles south of Rome, there were many more trees beside the road. Farther off the road, the trees grew thicker, making concealment much easier. Ariel had planned on this, and now she could finally see some of the landmarks that told where they were. She could tell that they were in the general vicinity of the cave, but the entrance was too deep into the trees to be seen. She decided to give the signal now. It might take the two ladies a while before they noticed that she had removed her shawl.

While still holding the reins of the horse she was leading, she removed the shawl from her head, wiping her brow, and brushing over her hair in a combing motion. Aashritha and Hashika were more observant than she thought they were. In less than half a minute, Aashritha was calling for a rest. Sabal, at the head of the column, raised his hand and reined in his horse. The train halted and stepped off to the side of the road. The riders dismounted, and the ladies stepped out of their litters. Ariel put the shawl back on. They had stopped just where she had hoped they would, and there wasn't a single traveler in sight. Ariel was almost home.

She watched as Sabal dismounted from his horse and the two ladies approached him, asking leave to venture off the road to stretch their legs. Sabal nodded in approval. Bowing with respect, the two ladies turned and walked back down the length of the column to their litters, passing by Ariel. Ariel stood still, holding the horse's reins. She knew that when the time was right, they would call her to follow them. The family had taken as many measures as possible to keep their interactions with her a secret from the other servants and wished to keep it as such.

Having a maid accompany them off the road may not appear strange to the other servants, Ariel thought to herself, *but they would begin to wonder when the three were gone for such a long time.*

When the ladies returned without Ariel, the servants would surely see through the whole façade. They would know that their masters had been helping this girl escape. Fortunately, none of the servants knew much about her. They didn't know her history, where she was from, or even if she truly was a slave, but it wouldn't make any difference to think about that now. The servants would not question the decisions of their masters, and whatever they thought or did after she escaped was the concern of the family, not her. She couldn't do anything about that. It was up to her to stay hidden for a time and try to help the other believers.

As the two steeped off to the side of the road, Aashritha glanced over her shoulder at Ariel.

"You," she said, speaking as she would to any other servant, "come with us, and bring that sack." She pointed to the sack on the horse that contained Ariel's clothes.

Another servant stepped forward and took the reins from Ariel. Hoisting the sack over her shoulder, Ariel followed the two ladies off into the small foothills with trees here and there. The trees grew thicker as they ventured farther out. To Ariel's surprise, the sack seemed much heavier than she thought it would be. She didn't know that Aashritha had generously included some special gifts for her.

Acting as casual as ever, the two ladies led the way looking this way and that, admiring the beauty of the fields, hills, trees, the singing of the birds, and the gentle breeze. They changed their direction two or three times, moving into the thicker parts of the trees to screen their movements. Ariel kept her focus on their position in proximity to the entrance of the cave. They were moving in more or less the right direction. She felt an urge to look over her shoulder back at the road but checked herself. The slightest gesture could arouse suspicion. She glanced about the fields; there was not a soul in sight.

They had gone nearly 150 yards from the road when Aashritha glanced over her shoulder at Ariel. She didn't say a word, but Ariel knew exactly what she was thinking, or rather, asking.

Ariel nodded in reply. "Keep going straight ahead."

Seeing Ariel's response, Aashritha quickened her pace. They were out of sight from the road now, but there were other people about. Though Ariel couldn't see them, she knew they were there. If they got too close, the entrance would be discovered. They had to act fast.

They walked on as fast they could for another hundred yards. The trees grew still thicker, and it was almost impossible to walk in a straight line. The believers had always taken care to avoid walking the same route for fear a trail could be detected. Ariel knew they were almost there. Gently, she pursed her lips together and let out a soft whistle to get the ladies' attention. Both slowed their pace and glanced back at her.

Motioning with her head, she whispered softly, "Bear left."

They adjusted their course, still moving at a brisk pace. By now, Ariel could see the entrance to the cave. It was a welcome relief for her as her mind raced back over the events of the past few weeks. Filled with joy at the thought of seeing her friends again, Ariel almost laughed, then quickly changed back to a sober mood.

She whistled again softly. "Head for those bushes at the foot of that hill. That's where the entrance is."

When they reached the bushes, the ladies stopped and let Ariel take the lead. She looked around one last time and then gathered up her skirt and crawled into the bushes with the two ladies following. Seen from the outside, the bushes were thick, but farther in, they thinned out, and there it was, a large stone that was laid over the entrance. Ariel picked up a large rock and rapped on the boulder and the rock wall of the cave, then waited. After about a minute, she repeated the procedure. Still no answer came. Everyone began to get a bit worried.

"What if no one answers?" Hashika offered.

Ariel let out a long breath. "Then you must return to the road. I will have to stay here till someone does come."

Her answer shocked the two ladies, but Ariel's expression remained unchanged.

She knocked again. The sooner Aashritha and Hashika got back to the caravan, the better. Ariel was about to tell them to return, when she heard a noise from inside the cave. She crouched close to the stone and listened. With a low rumble, the stone began to move. Aashritha and Hashika seemed more relieved than Ariel.

"Let's help them," Ariel said, throwing her shoulder against the stone.

In less than half a minute, the opening was clear, and they were met with the stares of four men. Ariel could tell that they were very surprised to see three Indian women.

"Who are you?" they asked.

Everyone must be on edge with the news of Peter's death, Ariel thought to herself.

Ariel explained who she was and what had happened to her over the past few weeks, how Anthony had been captured, convicted, and how she had been forced to flee for her life. They didn't remember her at first, but fortunately, Ariel knew all of their names and a few facts about them. It didn't take her long to convince them that she was one of the believers who had been there before. Ariel refreshed their memories to the few times she and Anthony had visited this part of the catacombs, and the messages they had brought of what was happening in Rome. Immediately, the men recalled the events, but her appearance and disguise had completely baffled them.

Ariel now introduced her new friends who had saved her life in hiding her and helping her get out of Rome. Other believers from inside the cave joined the four men at the entrance. All welcomed and embraced the three visitors. What a joyful reunion it was. Ariel felt that her mistress and her daughter should return to the road as quickly as possible.

Aashritha and Hashika knew that Ariel was right, but they were very sorry to leave. In less than a week, they had fallen in love with her as they had with few others. Ariel walked out to the cave's entrance with them. Aashritha wrapped her arms around Ariel in a warm embrace and kissed her on the forehead. Hashika did the same. Ariel began to cry. She tried to restrain herself, but it was useless. Aashritha and Hashika embraced her again.

"It's all right," Aashritha said. "Go ahead and cry."

Ariel did, for at least a minute or two. Finally, she regained herself and wiped away her tears.

Aashritha smiled at her most lovingly and said very gently, "We will meet again, Ariel. Don't forget that, no matter how long we are apart, if not in this life, then in the next. You are right where God wants you to be. That is all that matters. Until then, we will all remember and pray for you."

"I will too," Ariel said, choking back more tears.

The three embraced one last time and then parted. The two ladies knelt down and disappeared into the bushes. They faded from sight, and Ariel heard the rustling of the bushes cease. She walked back into the cave, and the stone was returned to its place.

Chapter 16

REUNITED

Turning from the sealed entrance, Ariel followed the men farther into the cave. She and Anthony had been here a few times and knew some of the people. Only a few were present at this time, and Ariel had met only two of them. The people were very surprised to see an Indian girl coming in and immediately asked the men who this strange girl was. Ariel smiled to herself. Aashritha and Hashika had disguised her well. The men who had greeted Ariel at the entrance introduced her and explained why she was disguised. The few that remembered her embraced her immediately.

They asked her to tell them what had happened to her. The last they had heard, she had disappeared several days ago and had not been heard from since. Ariel let her sack down off her shoulder. She and about six ladies seated themselves next to the wall of the cave. Beginning with the warning she had received from the senator's daughters, Ariel related everything that had happened to her up to her days with the family from India and her return to the catacombs.

A few of the ladies seemed a bit puzzled by her story. "Why, Ariel?" one of them asked. "What made you decide to stay?"

"Because God told me this is where he wants me," Ariel said. "Nothing is more important in this life than knowing that he is pleased with me. He laid it on my heart to find my parents and tell them about

Jesus and what he did for me. Whether I live or I die, it doesn't matter anymore. Someday, I will die. We all will. But I want to die knowing that when I do meet Jesus; he will be pleased with me. I want to truly live my life, not just stay alive. Jesus himself said, 'Anyone who tries to save his life will lose it, but those who lose their life for my sake will save it.'"

"So what are your plans?" another lady asked.

"I'm not sure yet," Ariel replied. "I know I want to go back into Rome and visit my parents, but I haven't made a plan for how to do it."

She paused for a moment to collect her thoughts and then went on.

"I think I'll go back to the caves that are closest to the city on this road. Anthony and I went there as often as we could. I know the caves and the people fairly well."

Then, dropping her gaze and speaking almost as if she were talking to herself, she said, "It's also where we found ourselves after the fire. They are the closest friends I have now that Anthony is gone."

Giving her a smile of understanding and sympathy, one of the ladies reached out and took her hand. "He's not gone yet, dear," she whispered gently. "There's still hope."

Ariel recalled the Emperor's final orders concerning Anthony: that he was to be tortured for information until he complied or until he was dead. Of course she knew that as soon as the Romans had gotten what information they could from Anthony, he was of no more use to them and they would certainly kill him. As she thought on these things, tears filled her eyes.

"They'll torture him till they get what they want, and then they will kill him," she said in despair.

"Oh, you don't know," the lady said. "I forgot, you've been in Rome the whole time."

"I-I don't understand. What are you talking about?" Ariel stammered, wiping away her tears, her lip quivering.

"Anthony is not dead, Ariel. He's alive, at least for now," the lady said.

Ariel couldn't believe her ears. "What...what did you say?" she asked feeling very confused.

The woman repeated herself.

"What? But how?" Ariel said in disbelief as her mouth dropped open. "The last I heard, he had been taken back to the prison to be tortured till he gave them the information they wanted. The Romans have always followed the same practice when dealing with Christians. Once they have outlived their usefulness to them, they kill them."

The lady smiled ever so gently. "He was taken back to the prison, and he was tortured," the lady replied, "but somehow he got out. Two days ago, we had gone to see the believers in the caves you mentioned, and they told us that he was there. They don't know how he got out of the prison, only that he was brought in three days ago by several other believers. He was badly injured, almost dead, when they brought him in, but they said he was still alive."

"But how did he escape from the prison?" Ariel asked. The whole thing sounded impossible, too good to be true.

"We asked," the lady replied, "but they couldn't tell us. The men who brought him in either didn't know themselves or refused to say."

"Did you see him?" Ariel pressed with hope and excitement.

"No, we didn't," another lady chimed in, "and from how bad they said he was hurt, I think it was best that we didn't."

"Well, if you didn't see him," Ariel questioned, "how can you be sure that it was him?"

"They said his name was Anthony, that he was a servant to a Roman senator, and that he had been acting as a spy with a girl named Ariel, bringing important messages to the catacombs," the woman replied.

Ariel exhaled a long breath of relief. It was Anthony; he was alive. Then a horrible thought occurred to her. Much could have changed in two days. If Anthony's injuries were as serious as they said they were, by now he could be dead.

Rising to her feet, Ariel declared, "I must go to him."

The ladies nodded with small smiles. "We knew you would," one of them said. "One of us will take you there as soon as it gets dark."

At first, Ariel was about to protest waiting for over half a day to go to see Anthony, but then she hesitated as she considered the dangers of going there in the middle of the day. The roads were still full of people coming and going to and from the city, not to mention soldiers who had been out searching for her. Jeopardizing the lives of the believers hiding there was not worth it, just so she could see Anthony half a day sooner.

Ariel nodded in agreement.

"You should also get out of that disguise," another lady suggested. "It was perfect for you when you were with that Indian family, but without them around, you would attract attention from everyone."

"Of course, do you have a place where I could wash myself?" Ariel inquired.

"Come with us. We'll take you there," one of the ladies said, rising to her feet.

Shouldering up her sack, Ariel followed one the ladies into a deeper part of the caves she had never seen before. She led her to a small room where, in one corner, there was a small spring of water bubbling out from the rock wall. The water flowed down into a small rock bowl cut into the wall of the cave and spilled down, disappearing into a crevasse beneath it. Ariel set her sack down on a shelf of rock and unpacked the contents. She had guessed from the first that Aashritha had been exceptionally generous. Now she saw just how generous. Focusing on the task at hand, Ariel set aside the specific oils that Aashritha had told her to use to remove the skin coloring. Presently, the two other ladies joined them, one carrying a basin and the other two old cloaks, which would be used as towels.

After laying her Indian apparel aside, Ariel began applying the ointments to remove the oil that they had used to darken her skin. Ariel scrubbed most of the areas she could by herself, and the ladies assisted her with the places she could not reach. The whole procedure lasted for a little over an hour before Ariel and the ladies were content that her skin had regained its natural color. Ariel washed herself one last time and then put on her old clothes.

As for her hair, Ariel washed it through once but knew that time would have to change that. Aashritha had told her that the dark oil had been absorbed into her hair. It would be a week or two before the oil would fade and her hair would return to its normal color. Still, Ariel changed the style of her hair so as to look more like a simple girl in Italy.

The Final Message to Rome

As she looked at the clothes, a whole flood of emotions and memories washed over her. She remembered that these clothes had been made and given to her by the believers when she and Anthony had recovered from their injuries in the great fire. She had been wearing them the night Anthony and her had been seized and sold as slaves. Also, when they were sneaking out to the gardens or out of the city. She recalled the night Anthony had saved her life and the lives of all the other believers, her meeting with Senator Marcus's daughters, and her escape from Rome. So much had happened. It seemed to have been so long ago, but she remembered it as if it was yesterday.

After putting on her clothes, Ariel returned to the large room closest to the entrance. She asked them briefly about what had been happening since she had last seen them. They told her that the entire body of believers, both in the catacombs and in the city, was still grieving the loss of the apostle Peter. His crucifixion had frightened some, while it had inspired others, but all were deeply sad. The believers had managed to recover Peter's body and had buried it in one of the catacombs. Ariel also felt the pain of losing Peter. His boldness, courage, and faithfulness had been an example and an inspiration to her, especially when she was serving in the senator's house separated from the other believers. Now he was gone, at least she could hope that Anthony was not dead yet.

"*I should go to where they buried him to say good-bye,*" Ariel promised herself.

The ladies also noted that his death had convinced quite a few believers to either leave Rome completely or, at the very least, move out of the city. Emperor Nero, along with his associates and many of the citizens of Rome, were celebrating that they had finally captured and done justice to the leader of these dangerous seditionists. In spite of this, many of the citizens of Rome were becoming more and more sympathetic to the tragic plight of the people, who did not seem as dangerous as the emperor said.

By now, the day must have been getting into the afternoon, and Ariel was becoming a bit anxious as the minutes dragged by. The ladies advised her that she should try to rest and even sleep, as she would be out late that night.

With nothing better to do, Ariel briefly explored the catacombs and found a secluded spot where she could rest without being disturbed or causing any inconvenience. Using her clothes, she managed to make a small mattress and pillow and went to sleep.

It was late in the afternoon when she awoke. After putting her few belongings back into her sack and laying it aside, she inquired of the ladies as to how she could serve or assist them. The ladies enlisted her help in preparing a meal for the believers that would be gathering there that night. Staying busy helped the time pass quickly and prevented Ariel from worrying about Anthony. She also took initiative to fill some water jugs and basins for the men to wash in and refresh themselves with after completing a day of hard work.

The people began to arrive as the sun was disappearing behind the horizon. One of the ladies, whose name was Lydia, told Ariel that as soon as twilight came, she could take her back to the catacombs where Anthony could be found.

The stone at the entrance of the tunnel was moved just slightly to enable one person to pass at a time. Ariel crawled out of the cave, looking up at the sky as the sun's light faded. She took care not to expose herself, and lay on her stomach underneath the bushes that covered the entrance. She saw the people—men, women, and some children—cautiously approaching, all coming from different directions. Ariel greeted the new arrivals as warmly and cheerfully as ever. At last, one of the ladies informed her that it was dark enough for the two of them to leave. Ariel said farewell to her friends and thanked them for all their help.

Crawling out from among the bushes with her sack, Ariel followed Lydia back toward the city, taking care to keep a safe distance from the road. There were plenty of bushes and trees about to hide their movements, and there was just enough light left for them to move without making any unnecessary noise. They stopped for a moment in some bushes to listen. In the distance, Ariel could hear a few faint sounds coming from the direction of the road, but nothing closed upon them but the chirping of the crickets.

The two moved on at a brisk pace still watching and listening all around. Ariel glanced at the sky as the celestial host of stars began to

The Final Message to Rome

make their appearance. It was only a little over a mile to their destination, and they covered the distance in just over a quarter of an hour. As they drew nearer to the city, the trees and bushes began to get thinner, and they were forced to slow their pace and proceed with greater caution. By now, all the travelers and passersby on the road had vanished, and all sound had ceased. The two could just make out the outline of the road stretching across the plain toward the walls of Rome. Ariel recognized the grounds. They had circled around and were approaching the catacomb entrance from the west. Now they would have to move back toward the road. Each woman pulled up the front of her skirt slightly and tucked it in along the waist to enable her to crawl. It was difficult for Ariel to crawl with a sack on her shoulder, but she managed it well.

They were now entering the collection of small foothills that surrounded the entrance. Keeping to the valleys, the two crawled their way through the mounds, heading in the direction of the road. Once or twice, Lydia stopped to pick up their bearings. Ariel was beginning to worry that they might have missed the entrance, when she spotted a tiny glimmer of light shining out of the ground at the base of a large rock.

"Lydia, look," she whispered, pointing to the rock. "See that tiny ray of light coming out beneath that rock? I think we found it."

After straining her eyes for a few moments, Lydia smiled approvingly. "Well done, Ariel," she whispered. "I would have completely missed that."

The two crawled carefully up to the boulder, and as before, Ariel picked up a small rock from beside the boulder and knocked.

A murmur of voices was faintly heard beneath the stone, and the glimmer of light they had seen was doused. Then came a creak and a grind; the mouth of the cave was open. Lydia and Ariel knelt down in front of the stone so they could be seen by the people inside without silhouetting themselves against the sky. The believers recognized Lydia almost immediately, and they welcomed the two in. A few shadowy figures brushed past them and hauled the boulder back to its resting place. Now there was absolute blackness.

A sharp scrape was heard and a small spark appeared as one of the band struck a nail to the side of a flint stone. A moment later, the cavern was illuminated with the light of a torch. Ariel looked about her; it was still just as she had remembered it. She was glad to be back with her friends where she could feel at home. She recognized nearly all of the people standing about, but they did not know her until she began to talk. Briefly she explained what had happened to her. They gasped at first, then surrounded and embraced her with a warm welcome. Lydia looked on with a smile.

Ariel had been very anxious to ask about Anthony, but before she could say anything, one of the ladies took her by the hand and hurried her into the main part of the catacomb.

"Come and meet the others," she said.

The rest of the group, along with Lydia, followed. Two of men stayed at the entrance. They followed the passage leading down into the largest cavern, where the believers frequently met. On this particular night, there were nearly thirty people gathered in the main cavern who were just beginning to disperse when the woman appeared, leading Ariel behind her.

Raising her hands and elevating her voice slightly, she said, "Listen to me, please. Everyone, listen to me."

All faces turned toward her.

"Many of you remember that several days ago, our young friend and informer Anthony was brought in after being terribly tortured in the prison. We had learned from sources inside the city that his associate, Ariel, had disappeared. We thought she had been arrested or even killed by the Romans, but just this morning, she came back to the caves farther south on the road, disguised as an Indian maid."

The crowd looked at each other, gasping in amazement, confusion, while others stood completely dumbfounded and shocked in total disbelief.

"It's true," the woman affirmed, "and here she is." She gently presented her so all could see her. Eyebrows were raised and foreheads wrinkled as the people studied her in bewilderment. Ariel smiled when she saw their reaction.

"*I guess I really don't look like myself with my hair black,*" she laughed to herself. "*Or maybe my skin is still a bit dark.*"

Raising her hands with a smile, Ariel stepped forward and addressed the crowd. "You do not recognize me. That is because I was disguised, and I still am, but what you have just heard is true. I am Ariel, and I have come very close to death these last days, but God kept me alive and brought me back home."

Smiles broke on the faces of the people as they heard and recognized her voice. Ariel proceeded to tell again the whole story of how she had been warned by Marcus's daughters, hidden, and rescued out of the city by the Indian family who were also believers. The crowd raised their hands, releasing a breath of relief and exuberance. Others flew off the ground, leaping for joy, forgetting how low the ceiling of the cave was. Then they all converged on Ariel, embracing her and welcoming her back. The emotional waterfall washed over her once again as tears streamed down her cheek. She was home—or was she?

Then the thought hit her—Anthony. He was the reason she had come here. Now, more than anything, she wanted to see him alive and well.

Raising her hands to get the attention of the people, Ariel spoke up. "Please, the main reason I came back tonight is because I had heard that my friend Anthony was still alive. The senator's daughters told me that he had been condemned to be tortured and then executed. When I left the city, I assumed that he was dead, but when I came back, Lydia told me that he was still alive. She also told me that he was here in this cave, though he was very close to death. Tell me, is he still alive?"

A lady standing behind her, whose name was Elizabeth, answered, "He is. We have been nursing him since he was brought in three days ago."

"How is he?" Ariel pleaded, almost afraid to hear the answer.

"The Romans tortured him very badly. He lost a lot of blood. He is still very weak and has fallen into a fever. He has been delirious since last night; he drifts in and out, and he hasn't stirred since the morning."

"Please," Ariel said, choking back her tears, "may I see him?"

"Of course you may," Elizabeth replied. "Come with me."

Taking her by the hand, Elizabeth led Ariel out of the main cavern and into another passage at the far end. Another woman, who had also been watching over Anthony, followed them. The passage sloped downward and became narrower. The walls had a few small candles set up on the rocks for illumination. Now, at last, the floor leveled off, and the walls opened up. In this part of the cave, there were several openings on either side of the passage, like small doors in a corridor or hallway. The woman in front led Ariel into the last opening on the right. The three had to stoop down slightly to enter because of the low arch. The room was a small one, only about ten or twelve feet in length and width, with oil lamps set around the perimeter of the wall. A large slab of stone, seven feet in length, was set against the back wall, covered with blankets so as to make a sort of bed. There, on the bed, lay Anthony.

He was lying motionless, faceup, with his eyes closed, his upper and lower body covered by a blanket with only his head showing. His face, which was covered with numerous cuts and bruises, had swelled significantly. His chest rose and fell only slightly under the blanket as he breathed. They could not tell if he was unconscious or asleep, but he was indeed alive.

Ariel stood frozen in her tracks. It seemed such a long time ago that she had last seen him. She had come to believe that he was dead, and here he was alive, at least for the moment. A flood of thoughts and emotions swept over her, too many to count or express. Elizabeth placed her hand on Ariel's shoulder. Ariel looked up at the woman. Her face seemed filled with understanding, empathy, and care.

After a few moments of silence she asked, "We are going to redress his wounds. Would you like to help us?"

Ariel was silent for a moment and then replied very faintly, "Yes, yes, I would like that."

Elizabeth turned to the other two ladies standing behind them. "This is Adria and Hannah," she said. "Go with them. Help them bring back the ointments with some bandages and water."

Ariel nodded obediently and followed the two back into another part of the caves. Hannah sent her to get some water from an underground spring in the caves. Ariel knew exactly where it was and hurried off on her own. She found a small jar, filled it with water, and carried it back to Anthony's room. Hannah and Adria were only just returning with the other necessary items.

Elizabeth had removed Anthony's clothes along with many strips of cloth that had been used as bandages. He was laid facedown now, still unconscious. Ariel nearly gasped, horrified at the awful sight. Countless wounds covered Anthony's back. Rough gashes and jagged piercings blanketed his back from the shoulders to his waist. Sear marks, left by piercings from a hot iron, could be seen here and there, some superficial and others quite deep. On his wrists, circular burn marks caused by a rope could be seen, left by intense stretching of the limbs and body, another cruel form of Roman torture. Elizabeth wet a small cloth in the water Ariel had brought and began ever so gently to wash the wounds on his back. Hannah uncovered his legs and did the same. They, too, were severely lacerated. Ariel cringed when she saw that the soles of Anthony's feet were covered with numerous stabbing and burn marks.

She wondered, *Can he possibly live, and even if he does, will he ever walk again?*

Adria interrupted her thoughts. "Elizabeth," she said, "I'm afraid we are out of cloth to use for bandages."

"Is there anything else we can use?" Elizabeth asked. "He really needs it."

"Hannah and I looked, but we couldn't find anything but the few rags we have here."

Elizabeth shook her head as she looked down at the few available strips of cloth. "That won't be enough to cover all his wounds," she said with a serious look.

"Wait," Ariel piped up. "I know where we can find some. I'll be right back."

She hurried back up to the main chamber of the caves where all the believers had gathered. Now it was almost empty, as most of the people had gone to other passages or slipped out of the caves. She found her sack just where she had left it. Aashritha had given her some additional clothes. Looking up at the ceiling of the chamber, Ariel smiled, thinking of Aashritha and Hashika.

"You gave these to me because you thought I'd need them. Well, now I do. I don't think you'll mind," Ariel laughed to herself.

Finding the garment made of the fabric best suited for bandages, she put the other items back in the bag and hurried back to the ladies. The ladies were delighted when she showed them the garment but were curious as to its origin since it seemed a bit more elegant than the typical clothes worn by most in Italy, and certainly by the followers of the Way. Briefly, Ariel explained how they had been given to her. The ladies were fascinated by her story and moved by her generosity. Ariel helped Adria cut the clothes into strips for bandages. Hannah and Elizabeth then applied them to Anthony's wounds, along with a salve to help the healing. When the ladies rolled him over onto his back, Ariel saw that his chest and belly had suffered the same injuries as his back. Anthony did not stir even the slightest bit through the whole procedure.

"We'll dress his wounds again tomorrow night," Elizabeth said to Ariel. "Until then, there is nothing we can do but wait and let him rest."

The three ladies collected the nursing supplies, along with the water jug, and began to leave. Seeing that Ariel was still preoccupied with Anthony's condition, Elizabeth asked her if she would like to stay with him that night. Ariel eagerly replied that she would. After helping the three ladies return the items they had brought down to their proper places, Elizabeth gave Ariel a blanket, as the cave could get very cold at night. The three of them bade her good night and hurried off to another section of the catacombs where their families awaited them.

Ariel took up her sack and brought it with the blanket back to Anthony's room. Using the additional clothes and sack, she made a small mattress and pillow on the floor at the foot of Anthony's bed. Still, before lying down, Ariel could not resist taking a last look at Anthony. He remained motionless except for his faint breathing. Kneeling down beside his bed, Ariel laid her right hand gently on Anthony's chest while softly brushing over his hair with her left hand.

"Good night, Anthony," she whispered with a smile.

Then, rising to her feet, she blew out all but one small oil lamp in the room, lay down on her bed, and fell asleep.

Chapter 17

A Last Request

ARIEL AWOKE THE next day feeling somewhat drained and not as energetic as she usually felt early in the morning. Despite her weariness, she got up and lit the candles in the room. She had hoped that Anthony would be awake, or at least show some indication of improvement, but there he was, just as he had been last night, no change whatsoever.

The catacombs were used primarily as a hiding place and occasionally as a meeting place for the believers to worship and connect with each other. Few people lived there. The more people and activity that went on only increased the risk of being discovered. Ariel had learned from her time at the catacombs that if food was to be found, it would be found in the homes of other believers who lived close by. This was not a serious concern, for the believers knew all too well the plight of their friends who were being hunted and were extremely generous.

Making her way to the main chamber of the caves, she found a small group of people gathered there looking as if they were about to leave. Among the group were Hannah, Elizabeth, and Adria. Ariel asked where they were going.

"We are all going to different places," Elizabeth answered, "but we are all going out to work."

"May I come with you and help?" Ariel begged.

The party exchanged glances with one another. A few of the ladies smiled and shrugged their shoulders.

"She can help us," Adria offered. "We need some additional help with preparing meals and making the clothes."

"Of course you may come," Elizabeth said with a welcoming smile.

Ariel had already dressed herself so she would be ready for work and so followed along with the group as they made their way out of the cave. They did not leave all at once. A few of the men moved the stone to allow them to leave and then slipped out in silence. The next few people waited for a few minutes before venturing out. Ariel and the three ladies were the last of the group to emerge from the cave. Once out, they reset the stone with the assistance of two men who remained behind. The four split up. Adria and Hannah went out first, heading southeast along the road, away from Rome. Elizabeth and Ariel waited a minute or two then headed due south. They were all going to the same place but taking different routes.

The sun was just starting to make its appearance on the eastern horizon. A cool breeze swept gently over the countryside mingled with the chirping of birds. It was a beautiful morning. Elizabeth and Ariel walked for nearly a mile, heading south, when they came in sight of another road running southwest away from the city. There were only a few people on the road, and Ariel and Elizabeth got onto it and followed it away from the city. They walked on for half a mile. Up until now, the two had both been totally quiet, fixated on watching to ensure they had not been seen and were not being followed. Now on the road, Ariel asked Elizabeth where they were going and what they would be doing.

"We are going to the estate of a landowner and farmer. He is a member of the Roman nobility, and he has hundreds of servants, but he also hires on other people and allows them to work on his estate. He lives in the city and only rarely visits the estate. He has other people who oversee and manage it. He gives us a meal for our work, and some small wages. This is what we must do to feed our families and those who have to stay hidden. Adria, Hannah, and I, we were all forced to flee from the city with our husbands. That's why we are living at the catacombs until the men can find a better place for us to live."

"What of your husbands?" Ariel asked. "Are they also working?"

"Yes, yes, they are," Elizabeth, responded in a low tone.

"Is the landowner one of us?" Ariel asked. "Is he a follower of Jesus?"

"No," said Elizabeth, shaking her head, "he is not. He worships the emperor, like any other loyal Roman citizen, along with the host of idols they have made. Still, he is fairly honest, and he treats his servants well."

"What is your story, Elizabeth?" Ariel asked. "How did you learn of Jesus and end up out here?"

"I am Jewish like you." Elizabeth smiled. "I grew up in Israel, but because of heavy taxes that my father could not pay, the publicans and Romans took me from my parents when I was even younger than you. They kept me at Jerusalem. I worked there for several years, more than enough to pay my father's debts, but my Roman master didn't want to let me go. My father even tried to buy me back, but my owner refused. He wanted me for life. I knew about everything that was happening with my father. The Romans, my master especially, was afraid that I would try to escape, so he sent me and several other servants off to Rome. He made us work on his estate there. I was a few years older than you when it happened, and I've never seen my family since.

"I was broken and hopeless, and then I met a man who had actually seen and been with Jesus. He was also a slave like me, but he was filled with so much joy, power, and faith. What he told me gave me hope like nothing else. So I gave my life over to Jesus. He was everything I had hoped for and so much more. About a year later, that same man who had told me about Jesus asked me to be his wife. I couldn't dream of anything better. We stayed together working on the estate for many years, telling the other servants about Jesus. A few months ago, we had to flee for our lives when the owner found out we were followers of the Way."

"Do you know anything about Hannah and Adria?" Ariel asked curiously.

"I do." Elizabeth nodded. "Hannah was an orphan. She never met her mother or father. No one knows what happened to them. A wealthy Jewish family took her in. At first, she was a slave, but she grew up to become very favored by the family. She spent most of her childhood in Rome. Even with all that, she was still brokenhearted and empty until Jesus became her Father. The family had intended to have her marry one of their sons, but when they found out that she was a believer, they disowned her. As for Adria, both she and her husband were Roman citizens, but they were persuaded that Jesus was the true God, not the emperor or idols. They were able to live for almost five years without being discovered. Then, when word got out that they were followers of the Way, they lost all their lands and wealth. Now they are hunted just like the rest of us."

These stories deeply moved Ariel, but she could see something strange and beautiful in each of these women. Even though they had suffered so much pain, it had not made them sorrowful or despondent, Elizabeth especially. She was not reserved, silent, or somber as so many other servants were, and she did not look at herself as a degraded slave. She saw herself as a woman who belonged to Jesus, a daughter of the King of Kings.

"Now look there," said Elizabeth, pointing on the left side of the road, toward some fields. "That's where we are going. The overseer will be waiting for us in the small house they have here. They give us a meal and our instructions for the day. Stay close to me today, and when they give us our meal, if you have some extra bread, save it for the others back in the caves. Now, from here on, we act like normal servants. Don't say anything that might arouse suspicion."

Ariel nodded, and the two women turned off the road onto the path leading into the fields. Several others on the road were taking the same path, and the two mingled in as inconspicuously as ever. They gathered together with all the others, who were eating a simple meal for servants. Ariel did not see Adria and Hannah among the crowd and decided that it would be best not to look for them.

On this particular day, Elizabeth and Ariel were sent out to work in the fields. They were out there most of the day but occasionally went into the house to bring water to the other workers. The day's work was cut short in the afternoon when a storm came up. As the clouds grew thicker and darker, the overseer called the servants in early, gave the workers their meal, and dismissed them just shortly before the rain began to fall.

After leaving the estate, Elizabeth told Ariel that they would have to take the road back to the caves, as the risk of getting lost in a storm was too great. The two hurried along the road as quickly as they could, heading back toward the city. The rain came down first softly, then in torrents. The ladies all made it back to the catacombs utterly exhausted, with their hair and clothes dripping wet. Retiring to a private room, the ladies discarded their garments and hurriedly dried themselves before changing into some dry clothes.

Ariel had just barely finished changing her clothes and was attempting to wring more water out of her hair when Hannah came rushing into the small chamber filled with suppressed excitement.

"Ariel," Hannah said with urgency in her voice, "you must come quickly. Anthony is awake, and he is pleading to see you."

Ariel gasped.

"How did he know I am even here?" she asked, utterly confused.

"We don't know," Hannah replied, "but you must come now. He says he must speak to you, and he could lose consciousness at any moment."

Rising to her feet, Ariel hurried after Hannah as fast as she could through the passageway back to the small room where Anthony was kept. Wheeling around the corner and into the room, she saw him. His eyes were open, and he was moving. Ariel fell to her knees beside his bed and grasped his outstretched hand. He was burning with fever, writhing in pain, and seemed a bit delirious. Pulling with what little strength he had, Anthony sat himself up in the bed.

"Ariel, Ariel," he gasped, "listen to me. I have to tell you something. This is very important. Not too long ago, Peter was crucified, and now all the believers are mourning his death. Before he died, he gave me a message to deliver to the rest of the church. I am afraid that I may not live to give it, so I am entrusting it to you. Listen carefully, and pass this message on to those who are mourning his death."

Hannah had left the room. It pained Ariel to see Anthony like this, fighting so hard to stay awake, giving, as it seemed, his last words. She did her best to stay calm but could not restrain her tears. She grasped his hand as he spoke and supported his back with her left hand. Ariel listened with her full attention, fearing that she was hearing Anthony's last words.

Anthony talked for nearly five minutes, struggling in pain to get the words out. Ariel was afraid that he might lose consciousness, but he managed to hang on and finish his report.

When at last he did finish, Anthony relaxed a bit and smiled at her as tears clouded his eyes.

"I'm glad I got to see you again," he whispered, struggling for breath. "I really missed you."

"I missed you too, Anthony," Ariel sobbed. "I thought you were dead."

"Then you will know how to deliver the message," Anthony said, "Won't you?"

Ariel nodded, choking back her tears. "Yes, yes, I will."

"I love you, Ariel," Anthony said. "Don't forget what Peter said, no matter what happens, whether I live or die. Don't ever forget..."

At this, Anthony's voice trailed off. He seemed to become delirious and lost. He was still conscious but had lost awareness of everything around him. Ariel, looked on, wide-eyed and breathless, waiting to see what would happen next. Anthony's body fell limp, and his head began to wag as he whispered the word "love." He seemed to speak as if he was talking to himself and was completely oblivious to Ariel's presence. He slumped back onto the bed, and his eyes closed.

Ariel thought that he was dead. She held her breath, unsure of herself. At last, she breathed a sigh of relief when she saw that Anthony was still breathing. Then, overcome with feelings of grief, love, pain, and too many others to name, she laid herself on his chest and wept, as she had never done before. There she lay, sobbing uncontrollably, for she knew not how long.

Yet, as she wept, she also prayed. "Lord, spare him, please. Jesus, please don't let him die."

When she seemed to run out of tears, she pulled herself back to where she knelt beside his bed, looking down on him. He was still breathing but only faintly.

"I love you, Anthony," she cried. "I love you so much."

Then, turning her gaze up to the ceiling of the chamber, she whispered, "He belongs to you, Lord. Thank you for taking care of him..." Pausing in midsentence, Ariel hesitated, glanced back down at Anthony and then back up at the ceiling. "With your love," she finished.

Utterly exhausted, she rested her head on the side of the bed for a bit longer. Then, finding her strength, she rose up and walked out of the room, giving one last glance at Anthony.

She returned to the main area of the cave, expecting to find some of the believers, but it was empty and silent. She went from passage to passage and looked into some of the rooms where she knew the believers would be. They were there, but they were all asleep. The time had passed much faster than she had thought; it was now late at night. Everyone else had gone to sleep.

Realizing that she would need to work the next day, as well as deliver Anthony's message, she returned to his room. Nothing had changed. She made out her bed on the floor and lay down. Exhausted by the day's activities and the ordeal with Anthony, she fell asleep much easier than she thought she would.

It's just as well, waiting till tomorrow, she thought to herself as she drifted off. *It will give me time to understand it. Now that I have done my grieving, I will be able to deliver it better. I just hope the others are ready for it. This may not be easy for them to hear.*

Chapter 18

THE SECRET REVEALED

THE MORNING CAME in what seemed like a few minutes. Ariel awoke fully refreshed and ready to tackle the challenges of the day. She would be going out that morning to work in the fields as she had the day before. Today, she had a plan to deliver Peter's message. Anthony had done his part; now it was up to her.

Waiting no time, she washed her face, took a short drink of water from the spring, and joined her friends at the entrance of the cave. It was just before sunrise, and they were all getting ready to proceed to their places of employment. Dawn was fast approaching, and they would have to leave soon.

Ariel immediately addressed the group.

"Pardon me," she said, "but I recently received a very important message that I have to pass on to the rest of the believers in Rome. I need your help. Please, spread the word to all the other believers in this area and also those that you work with, every last one of them. Tell them to come to this cave at sunset. I have to get the word out as soon as possible, and the more people who hear it, the better. Will you all please help me?"

At first, the others were a bit skeptical of Ariel's intentions. What could she know that would be so important for so many people to hear and why not tell them here and now? Why call them all together tonight?

"What is this message that you say you must deliver?" one of them questioned. Their faces seemed cynical, nonchalant, uninterested.

"If you will meet me here, I will tell you. I received it from Anthony. Before Peter was crucified, he and Anthony were kept in a cell together for a short space of time. While they were there, Peter entrusted Anthony with a very important message and told him to pass it on to the rest of the believers. Peter said that this would be his final message and that it was to be given to every believer in Rome and was especially important for them to receive as they mourned his death."

Hearing this, every eye in the group widened, mouths dropped open, and a long pause of silence fell over the whole company before Hannah finally spoke up.

"Of course we'll help you, Ariel. Forgive us. We'll all be here," she said earnestly.

"Not just us," one of the men broke in. "To everyone here, if you meet any of the other followers of the Way today, tell them what she said and urge them to come listen. This is very important if Peter wants everyone in Rome to hear this. Spread the word."

All nodded in agreement, and the small band stealthily headed off in their separate directions. Today, Ariel joined with Hannah, and the two ladies took a different route to the fields where they would be working. The route they took was a bit longer than the one Ariel had taken the day before, and they moved along at a rather brisk pace. Fortunately, Ariel had always been a very strong girl and was able to keep pace with Hannah without the slightest difficulty. The two arrived in the fields just as the sun made its full appearance on the horizon. The activities of the day were very similar to those of the previous one. The workers met together for their meal and headed out into the fields. Today, Ariel and the three ladies were called to assist with some household duties at the master's house. Ariel, who was quite familiar with the workings of a Roman household, had no trouble at all making herself useful, and she quickly caught the attention of the household staff. Adria overheard some of what was being said and informed Ariel. Ariel's heart sank.

This will complicate things, Ariel thought to herself, laughing rather sarcastically. *If the people here really like my work, they'll start asking questions: who I am, where I'm from, and who I belong to. The more they ask, the more difficult it will be to keep them from finding out that I am a Christian. How do you hide something like that?*

The thought then struck her. *But I am not supposed to hide it. Jesus told us that we are the light of the world. We are a light far superior to the sun, the moon, and the stars. Nothing can be hid from us, and we cannot be hid from the eyes of anybody in the world. Nobody lights a candle just to hide it under a bushel basket. The light, the hope that Jesus brought, he gave to us freely, and he expected us to do the same. He didn't expect us to hide it. If you hide a candle under a basket, it will go out. Jesus commanded us to let our good works be open so that people would see them and they would give praise to the Father. But how to stay alive when we are being hunted? If they find out that I am a Christian, as they call us, they'll do the same thing that Senator Marcus did.*

Then another thought hit her. *I will do the same thing I did with Gloria and Floriana. They warned me because they cared about me. They, well...loved me,* Ariel thought to herself with amusement. *I captured their hearts by my work, my joy—no, not me, it was really the Spirit that they saw, and they were drawn to that. I keep being myself. I keep working hard and letting them see Jesus in me, but then there are the others who don't care.*

Ariel smiled to herself again, amused, as God seemed to answer her questions as quickly as she could think of them.

This is why you warned us to be as shrewd as snakes and as innocent as doves. We must be, and not just appear to be, but truly be as innocent as a baby who could not understand the word "evil," and as sly as a fox evading the hunters. I will not let them know that I am a follower of the Way, who I am living with, or where I am from. If they ask, I will tell them as much as they need to know, without being evasive or drawing suspicion to myself or anyone else.

The day flew by for Ariel. While her hands and feet were racing to carry out her assigned tasks, her mind was constantly rehearsing Anthony's message and how she would deliver it to the others. When evening finally came and the workers were released, Ariel tarried about for a few extra minutes before heading to the rendezvous point that she and the other believers had agreed upon before they had left the catacombs. Adria and Hannah were waiting on the northwest corner of the field. Elizabeth and the other men were standing around the rendezvous point at different distances, some barely a stone's throw, others beyond shouting distance. They were all waiting, looking as inconspicuous as ever. Some were sitting down, observing the sunset, and others were talking with each other. It was time to move out. Adria raised her hands high above her head as if she were stretching; this was the signal everyone had been waiting for. Then, with Hannah leading the way, the three ventured out onto the road heading northeast toward the city.

The believers standing about followed. One by one, they left their places and followed. They did not do this all at once. The three women left first. A few others followed them at a safe distance, then a few others followed them, and the others after them, like a long, spread-out caravan. Some walked on the road; others stayed off the road. Some followed close; others were almost out of sight. The sun was drawing near to the horizon. Everyone was scanning the countryside to ensure they were not being followed. There were no patrols anywhere in sight. The road was completely deserted except for the usual people returning to their homes. They were fortunate that the land the road cut through was filled with trees and hills. Though not a dense forest, it was ideal to screen their movements and allow them to detect anyone who might be shadowing them.

Ariel noticed that the believers were frequently changing direction and randomly adjusting their pace. No more than three of them walked together. Everyone was watching to protect each member of the group, yet acting as casual as anyone who would be going home after a day of work. Indeed, this was just a typical day for any believer in Rome who wished to stay alive. Vigilance and caution were essential for each person's survival. This had become an intricate part of their lives that was as routine as eating or sleeping. All of the members had mastered it well. As they drew near to their destination, Ariel noticed that the believers were dispersing even more.

The Final Message to Rome

Ariel entered the caves as routinely yet cautiously as ever. Numerous people who had come from other areas were waiting inside. Ariel hurried back to Anthony's room, hoping he had awakened. He had not. He was alive but still unconscious and very weak. Ariel knelt beside his bed and, in silent prayer, thanked God for giving Anthony to her as a friend when she so desperately needed one.

"Speak through me, Lord, to everyone here," she whispered. "Give them hope."

After a few more minutes of thought and reflection on what Anthony had said to her, she stood up and walked back to the main chamber, where she found the small group of believers waiting for her. As several more groups would be arriving, Ariel decided to wait a bit longer.

At length, one of the men slipped out and circled around the cave's entrance. He returned shortly after and reported that the sun had almost completely set and there was not a soul in sight. Ariel rose to her feet. This was her time. She was about to speak what could be the most important words of her life.

She began by explaining briefly who she was and what had happened to her since the great fire up to her return to the catacombs.

"All this time I thought he was dead," Ariel continued, speaking of Anthony, "and he may still die, but he gave me this message. I have to tell it, for him, for Peter, and for Jesus. As many of you know, just a few days ago, our dear friend and brother Simon Peter was crucified. He lived and died for his faith and the love he had for our Savior, Jesus. What some of you may not know is that he had been warned that the emperor was planning an all-out effort to find him. Anthony himself discovered what they were planning and snuck out to warn Peter what was coming. The believers, and the elders especially, entreated Peter that he should leave Rome. At last, he was finally persuaded, and he agreed to leave Rome.

"Anthony was captured shortly after delivering that warning. They tried him for being a Christian and found him guilty, but they still wanted to use him to get information. To break him, they decided to make him watch as they crucified Peter. They put the two of them in a cell together and kept them there until they were ready to crucify Peter.

While they were together, Peter gave Anthony a message that he was to deliver to the rest of the believers in Rome.

"Even after Peter's death, Anthony still refused to recant his faith and inform on the believers he knew, so the Romans tortured him. They almost killed him, but God saved his life and somehow got him out of the prison and back to the caves. I don't know how God did it, but he did.

"When the two of them were together in the cell, Anthony asked Peter how the Romans had managed captured him. To his surprise, Peter responded that he had purposefully come back to Rome knowing that he would be captured. Anthony was shocked and asked him why. Peter told him that as he was leaving Rome he encountered Jesus who was coming back into Rome. He couldn't tell if he was seeing a vision or a real person, but he knew it was Jesus, that he was there. He ran to Jesus and asked him where he was going.

Jesus answered, "I am coming to be crucified again."

Peter didn't understand him, but he knew Jesus was trying to tell him something. Then Peter remembered that Jesus had told him before and after his death and resurrection that one day Peter would follow him. Jesus was speaking of the cross. Then Peter understood. Jesus was telling him that his time had come. It was Peter's time to die. Jesus wanted him to go back to Rome, so he did and he was arrested shortly thereafter.

Ariel continued, "Peter told Anthony he wanted him to tell the other believers about his encounter with Jesus, along with a final message to all the believers of Rome.

To those of you who have heard this, you may feel a bit confused, especially hearing this after Peter's death. You are wondering why. Why did Jesus send him back? He was sending him to his death, and why now? There is so much more that Peter could have done for Jesus, especially now when we are suffering like never before. Now is the time when we would need him the most. Why take him away? It doesn't make sense.

"This may not be the answer that you are looking for; in fact, it may not be an answer at all, but this is what Jesus was telling Peter: he missed him. They hadn't seen each other in over thirty years, and like any friends who have been apart for such a long time, they missed each other. This could possibly be the reason he called Peter home, though I cannot be sure that it was. When the disciples ate the Passover with Jesus, the night he was arrested, he told them, "It is expedient for you that I go away." They were all very sorry to see him go, and they knew that Jesus felt it, too. Still, Jesus had to leave because it was the best thing for everyone, though it may not have seemed like it at the time. Jesus left his Father, his throne in heaven to become a man and finish what had been planned out from before the world began. Then, after he finished what he had been sent to do, he returned to his Father to make intercession for us. He has done this day and night now for over thirty years.

"Still, there is a longing in him for us to be with him. Late that same night in the garden, he prayed and told his Father that he desired that the people who had been given to him would be with him, where he was, so that they could see his glory. He was not just speaking about those who had been with him those three years. He was speaking about all the people that would believe in him, us included.

"He came to Earth to win us, just as a husband wins his bride. Indeed, we know that we are his bride, and as his bride, he misses us. Just as a husband longs desperately to be united with his future wife, so Jesus, our husband, longs to be united with us, his bride. He promised, as a husband does, "I go to prepare a place for you, and I will come back to receive you as my own, so that you may be with me where I am." The same night he ate the Passover, he gave the disciples a cup of wine and told them to divide it among themselves, but he didn't drink any of it and said that he wouldn't until the kingdom of God had come. He has waited these many years, and he is still waiting as patiently as only Jesus can. Yet, as he waits, he is still longing for the day when we all will be reunited with him and his Father.'

"Many of you are asking God, why did you let this happen? You are asking this question because you wonder if, or even fear that, you or Peter may have somehow fallen out of God's love, that God may have forgotten Peter or deserted him to his death. Peter has not fallen out of

God's love because the Lord sent him back to die, and neither have we. On the contrary, it is because of God's love for Peter that he did this. He loved Peter, he missed Peter, and he wanted him to come home. To die is nothing. Anthony saw Peter die, the pain was awful, but it was only for a moment, and then all his pain was gone, forever. He is home now; he is with Jesus, where he belongs, where we all belong. We don't belong here on Earth; we belong in the glorious kingdom that is coming.

"Peter was telling us not to be afraid, even now, in the midst of such disaster; when everything around us seems to be collapsing, trust God's love. He loves us, and nothing can separate us from his love, certainly not death. If anything, death unites us with his love. Don't be afraid, and don't doubt his love. It is still there. Even though we may not always see it, it is always there.

"If you are hurting or still in pain, take your pain to Jesus. He never intended for you to carry it alone. You will not be disappointed when you take your sorrow to him. He is there to carry your burdens with you and to heal your broken heart."

The small group was silent. Some of the people were smiling, some were nodding, and a few were crying. Everyone seemed at a loss for what to do next. Sensing this, Ariel began to pray aloud.

"Lord Jesus," she prayed, "we love you, and we trust your love. We are what dominates your thoughts. We thank you for coming to Earth to show us your love and give us hope. We thank you for giving to us your friend and servant Peter, for all the time we had with him. You gave, and you have taken away. May your name be praised."

One by one the believers joined her. Some offered up more prayers of thanks to God; others began to sing songs of praise and adoration to the Lord. Ariel sang a song she had made up from one of the Hebrew psalms that she had memorized as a little girl, "Trust in him at all times; pour out your heart before him: God is a refuge for us." Many in the crowd were still weeping through the whole ordeal, even Ariel herself cried a little. The believers continued in their prayers, songs, and giving of thanks late into the night, but to them it seemed like no time at all.

When at last the group finally began to disperse, Ariel was exhausted and eager to retire. Still, before going to sleep, she made another visit to Anthony's bedside. She had hoped that his condition would have improved, but there was no change. He remained unconscious and very weak.

Ariel knelt beside the bed, looking down at Anthony's pale face. Her mind raced back to the very first time she had seen him when they had been injured in the great fire. She remembered the night they had both been kidnapped and the challenges of serving in the senator's house, sneaking out to the gardens and caves at night, and then the last time she had seen him, defending the house while the believers made their escape. She smiled down on him, feeling so proud of him as her friend and brother, and knew that Jesus felt the same way. He was truly a real hero. He had always been a hero; in his heart, he had always had the character and spirit. Even though few had seen it until now, it had always been there.

Gently, she laid her hand on his warm forehead and brushed over his black hair. Anthony did not stir.

"Well done, Anthony," she whispered softly. "The message Peter gave you has been delivered. We haven't lost hope. We never will. The work will continue. The Lord and Peter are so proud of you, and so am I. You finished what they gave you to do. You did it, Anthony. Well done."

There were so many other things that Ariel wanted to say to Anthony, but she couldn't think of the words, and it all didn't seem to matter anymore.

"Good night, Anthony," she said, then crawled over to her bed, curled up under the blankets, and in a few minutes was asleep.

Chapter 19

Persecuted, But Not Forsaken

THE NEXT MORNING seemed uneventful for Ariel. She awoke a bit later than she usually did but hurriedly prepared for the day's work and was off with her friends in the morning light. She worked as hard as she always did, with a smile on her face and a song in her heart. On several occasions, a few of the people who had seen her at the cave the previous evening thanked her for what she had said. It had given them such courage and strength of heart. Graciously, Ariel reminded them that the message was from Jesus and that she, Anthony, and even Peter, though willing, were only the messengers, normal people that God had used.

When the day's work was complete, Ariel returned with the other believers to the caves and was surprised and overjoyed to hear that Anthony had awakened and that the fever had left him. Hearing this, Ariel scurried down the passage to the chamber where Anthony had been resting. Coming into the room, she saw him sitting upright on the bed, awake with a smile on his face, but she could tell that he was still very weak. The two embraced each other as warmly as they had ever done, laughing and crying, unable to restrain themselves. Shortly after the exhilarating reunion, Elizabeth reminded Ariel that Anthony's wounds would have to be redressed. Taking the initiative, Ariel volunteered to attend to his wounds herself, and Elizabeth graciously consented.

Ever so gently, Ariel removed Anthony's tunic and proceeded to wash and dress his wounds. Despite the intense pain, he remained still and silent throughout the whole procedure. After treating Anthony, Ariel hurried away to another part of the caves and returned with what food she could find. Because of his wounds and weakness, his appetite was greatly reduced.

After the meal, the two sat together on Anthony's bed and learned what had befallen the other since his capture. Their conversation continued long into the night. Anthony was especially interested to hear if Peter's message had been delivered and was glad to hear Ariel's report. When at last both began to yawn and wag their heads, they composed to sleep again. However, on this night, Ariel moved her bedroll and spent the night in another section of the caves. The two arose the next day feeling fully rejuvenated. Anthony continued to recover from his wounds and regain his strength, while Ariel resumed her work with the three ladies in the fields.

Nearly a week passed before Anthony was able to stand up and walk about. Two weeks later, he was able to join Ariel and the other believers at work in the fields.

The news of Peter's death spread among the Christians like a wildfire. His loss had left a terrible void in the hearts of the believers, but as God would have it, his last message to the church also spread. The message did not erase the pain of Peter's loss—he had never intended that it should—but it did give them hope, knowing that even in death, Peter had not fallen out of God's love, but rather it was because of God's love that he called Peter to the place he had been preparing for him. He was not being separated from God's love by death, but united with God's love through death. There was no reason to be afraid. Peter had suffered in pain but only for a moment. Now his pain was over forever. Even in the pain, Jesus had not abandoned Peter; he was with Peter all through the pain.

Around seven years before the great fire, the apostle Paul had written a letter to the church in Rome at the time of its infancy. In that letter, he affirmed that God intended everything they would face as followers of Christ for their benefit. Even in the midst of such catastrophe and evil, he was still working out his grand plan when he made the world. Paul had been held in Rome under house arrest for some time, but he was released and had departed for Spain nearly a year before the great fire.

Both the children continued working in the fields of the landowner or went from house to house offering their services wherever they could find work. This went on for several weeks. Then one day when their services were not required by the landowner, the two choose not to look for work elsewhere and went with a group of friends to visit Peter's grave, located in one of the other cave networks outside the city. As always when they were going somewhere in public, they exercised due caution to ensure they did not attract attention and were not being followed.

His tomb was underground, in the caves of one of the many hills, and with some help from the few that were there, the believers had no trouble finding it. Reminiscing of the many things Peter had said and done, everyone was quiet for a long time. The assembled group shed tears recalling the sacrifice Peter had made for the one he loved. They would all remember and miss him.

After a long moment of silence, Anthony stood up before the group. Over the past weeks, in spite of the hope his message had brought them, he could sense that many of them were becoming more complacent and even fearful. The fear that had set in from Peter's death had caused many to lose their boldness and concern themselves more with surviving Nero's terror. A feeling came over Anthony that now was the time to speak.

"Friends," he declared resolutely, "we are not beaten! The battle is not over. It will go on. As long as we still have hope, it will go on. Before our Savior died, he told his disciples, time and time again, that he would die, and indeed that he must, but he did not leave them hopeless. He told them that on the third day, he would rise again. When he ascended back to heaven, he did not leave us hopeless or alone. He left us with the promise that he would send us the Holy Spirit and that he himself would be with us always even unto the end of the world. The Holy Spirit came, and it has not left us. Jesus is gone, but he is still here, and he lives on in us. He left us with another promise that the works that he had done, we would do, and even greater works than his because he would intercede for us to his Father. Even without his physical presence, he knew we would be more effective with the Holy Spirit.

"We are not at a disadvantage; all power in heaven and in Earth is on our side. Though it may appear otherwise, we are to trust his promise no matter what happens, no matter how hopeless it gets. Though Peter is gone, our strength was not in him, and he would not want us to live in fear of what men can do to us. He would tell us to stand up and fight harder for our king, King Jesus. We should not stay out of Rome, hiding from the battle; we should go back into Rome, where the fight is. God does not rely on numbers or appearances to win his battles, nor should we. The battle will be won, as we trust in his strength. No matter how many of us they may kill, it will not hinder God's plans. It will only enable him to show even more of his power, and he will show it. We can be sure of that.

"Be of good hearts, my friends. Do not fear what we may suffer. Be strong, and put trust in the Lord. It is an honor and privilege to suffer for Jesus. He bled for us; it is only right that we should bleed for him. I have. I know what it is like. It is hard to suffer, but even as I suffered, I saw his love and the rewards of suffering. I love Jesus; I always have, since the day I became his son. But only as I suffered for him did I see how much he meant to me. I love Jesus even more now that I have been tortured for him, because it required something of me; it almost cost me my life. It has enlarged my heart, and I would do it again for him. If following him was easy, we would not love him as much, and he would not be so precious to us, not nearly as we are to him. He embraced the cross for us because he loved us. Suffering for him, giving for him makes me love him all the more. Jesus said, 'Where your treasure is, there will your heart be also.' We are all in his hands, and no man, not the emperor nor the entire empire of Rome, can snatch us out of his hands. His will shall be done, here on Earth as it is done in heaven, but whether you will be a part of it is for only you to decide. As for me, I am going back into Rome."

The Final Message to Rome

Anthony could not determine the general response of those listening. The hearts of some received strength and joy; others were cynical, who had already given way to despair. Sensing the Lord's voice, Anthony glanced over his shoulder one last time at Peter's grave, and then strode off down the tunnel in the direction of the exit.

Ariel, who had been deeply moved and motivated by what Anthony had said, rose up quickly and followed him. She caught up with him in the tunnel and, gently taking him by the arm, asked, "Where are you going, and what are you going to do?"

Turning to her with a smile, he pulled out from a small pouch strapped to his belt a scroll. Unrolling it, Ariel immediately recognized it as the map of Rome that had been given to her by Gloria and Floriana.

Pointing to the two markings that showed where their parents lived, he answered, "I'm going to find my parents, find where they live and then find a way to get through to them."

Ariel's face beamed with joy, excitement, and satisfaction. "I'll go with you," she said with an exuberant smile.

Anthony nodded and smiled in reply, and so it was that the two children went back into Rome.

Epilogue

History tells us that the horrific persecution of the Christians in Rome and throughout the world continued. Many more courageous believers paid with their lives for worshiping Jesus as their king, rather than Caesar. The emperor continued to arrest, imprison, torture, and kill all those who claimed the name of Christ.

Sadly, in addition to the dangers outside, all was not well inside the church. A large percentage of the church was comprised of Jews. They had accepted Jesus as their Messiah but had not accepted his fulfillment of many of the statutes and practices handed down by the Law of Moses. Because of this, they proceeded to criticize those who did not keep all of the law, just as they had before Christ had come. Others of Gentile descent looked down on their Jewish brethren for being legalistic and not morally sinful, or overzealous about trivial things. The two children saw these divisions firsthand, especially Anthony. He was shunned by many who regarded his commitment to Christ with skepticism because of his Roman ancestry. Others refused to eat with him and forbade him to eat in their houses.

A large number of the believers who had been former Jews deserted the church. At the time, the Jewish religion was recognized by the state and granted protection under Roman law, but not those who worshiped Jesus. Because of this, many believers of Jewish background separated from the church and went back to their old life in the synagogues.

Despite these many hardships, the worst enemy the church faced was not the persecution of Rome from without, but the false doctrine and false teachers from within. The apostle Peter had warned that just as there were false prophets in Israel before Christ, there would be false teachers among the church. By the Spirit's inspiration, Peter read the future only too well when he wrote that letter to the churches of Asia Minor. False teachers did creep into the church, and by their doctrine and influence, many were deceived.

Still, the church pressed on. Despite their many divisions, persecution, and false teachers, they found unity in loving Christ. The persecution carried out by Nero eventually came to an end in 68 AD, four terrible years after the great fire. Though for a time the city was willing to abide Nero's cruel and incessant ways, they gradually turned against him. Declaring him insane and an enemy of Rome, the Senate ordered him tracked down and executed. Nero, emperor of Rome, who was once the most powerful man in the world, found himself fleeing for his life, hunted by Rome, just as he had hunted the Christians. He had exalted himself as God and had been humbled by the God he had sought to destroy. He had been the hunter, and now he had become the hunted.

He did not face death with the courage that the Christians had shown. Rather than be captured and face the consequences of his actions, he took his own life, like the coward he had always been. In Paul's epistle to Rome, he had reiterated the Lord's promise to his people, "Vengeance is mine; I will repay, saith the Lord."

Nero was gone and remembered only with great disdain, shame, and hatred. The church remained and continued to thrive and expand, just as Jesus had said it would. No one could prevail against his church, not the full might of Rome, not even hell itself. Unshakable, it remained faithful and true to its God until the day when he returned as he had promised he would, faithful and true.

As for Anthony and Ariel, they went back into Rome and tried to reach their parents with the good news of Christ. They continued to meet with other believers to strengthen them and find strength for themselves. It is unknown what became of these two brave soldiers of the Cross. There have been lots of legends and stories told about these two children, all of them different. Some say they gave their lives as so many others had, in the arena; others suggest they left Rome and continued the work somewhere else. Others still say they stayed in

Rome and lived to see the end of Nero's evil reign. Exactly how their story ended will remain a mystery, especially because it is believed that, shortly hereafter, they changed their names. This made confirmation of the many stories next to impossible. Still, in every story, one thing was for sure.

Whatever the danger, they pressed on, loyal and fiercely committed to the mission entrusted to them by their Lord and Savior. They both knew that any day could be their day in the arena, but this did not shake them, for they knew well the love of Jesus Christ. They were more than conquerors through Christ who loved them, and nothing could separate them from his love.

The End

PS: But, there may be some of you who are wondering one thing more. Did Anthony and Ariel get married? Well, even that is beyond what we know, although it is not outside the realm of possibility. They loved each other like a brother and a sister, and indeed they were. Whether that love progressed into something deeper is unknown. However, had they seen such a union as advancing the kingdom, thought they could serve God better married than single, marriage would not only have been probable but likely. Oh, and as for the tunnel, the one that God prevented the Romans from discovering, they never found it, and the children and other believers succeeded in putting it to good use.

John 17:24

"Father, I will that they also, whom thou hast given me, be with me where I am; that they may behold my glory, which thou hast given me: for thou lovedst me before the foundation of the world."

Afterword

The historical context of this story centers around the last four years of the reign of Emperor Nero, from 64 to 68 AD. These last four years have been referred to by Biblical scholars and historians as the First Persecution. The church had been birthed barely thirty years previous. During that first thirty years, the Body of Christ had experienced a great deal of adversity, but they had never faced anything so cruel as what they would endure during those last four years. Despite the many hardships they faced, the Lord's people did not falter or fail. They remained faithful and bold. They knew, as Jesus had told them, that no one, not even the gates hell itself, could prevail against them. We read in Revelation, chapter twelve, verse eleven, "They overcame him by the blood of the Lamb and by the word of their testimony; and they loved not their lives unto the death."

Well before he went to the cross, Jesus had warned his disciples that "in the world you will have tribulation: but be of good cheer; I have overcome the world" (John 16:33, King James Version). The apostle Paul told Timothy, whom he referred to as his son in the faith, "This know also, that in the last days, perilous times shall come" (2 Timothy 3:1, KJV). As followers of Christ, we should always be mindful of this and remember that when persecution, tragedy, or disaster cloud our path, it does not mean that God has forgotten us. The Lord used those terrible years to test and refine his church, and while the oppressor Nero faded away into a distant and shameful memory, the church emerged glorious and triumphant. Nothing that God allows into our lives is intended for our ruin. He has a purpose for everything, and he works all things together for good to those who will love him and follow him with all their heart wherever he may lead them. For the church, there will be a season of ease and of persecution, even as there is a time for peace and a time for war. We should not fear the hard times or feel betrayed when they arise. As the author Ralph Toliver wrote, *Gold Fears No Fire*. For we who follow Christ, there are no accidents, and there are no true tragedies, except that we should lose faith and heart.

I have struggled with keeping this in mind as much as anyone else, especially as I see the events in the world unfolding. As I hear of wars, rumors of wars, famines, earthquakes, diseases and wicked rulers, he reminds me, "I love you, don't lose heart. Jesus told us that these are the beginning or sorrows, but he also told us not to be afraid. God has used writing this story to comfort me and remind me of these things.

Persecution comes in many forms. We hear a lot about the persecution that has happened throughout history, in the times of Rome, the Reformation, and the atrocities that took place behind the Iron Curtain. Despite these terrible times, there is more persecution going on today than at any other time in history. This is not cause for discouragement, for the Lord says that "we are more than conquerors through him that loved us" (Romans 8:37, KJV), and "If God be for us, who can be against us?" (Romans 8:31, KJV).

Acknowledgements

I say a big thank you to my family members who have supported me through the long process of writing the book and also for their assistance in proof reading and offering advice for the story.

I give a special thanks to my brother, Philip Goppelt for the photo shop work and modifications on the map.

Thank you to Erin Bogdon and the publishing team at www.createspace.com. A big thank you to the editor for helping perfect the manuscript and prepare it for publishing.

Thank you to all the brethren down through history, who have suffered for their faith. For the courage you give us by your example, we will never forget you. We will always remain faithful to the Lord.

Best of all, thank you to God for entrusting me with the responsibility of telling this story, for the joy you gave me as I wrote it, and the strength to persevere when I was tempted to quit.

Bibliography

Astoria, Dorothy. *The Name Book,* Bethany House Publishers, 1997.

Bunyan, John. *Pilgrim's Progress,* adaptation. Orion's Gate, 1990.

Foxe, John. *Foxe's Book of Martyrs.* 1559. Baker Book House, 1978.

Grant, Myrna. *Vanya: A True Story.* Charisma House, 1974.

Morgan, Julian. *Leaders of Ancient Rome: Nero: Destroyer of Rome.* The Rosen Publishing Group Inc., 2003.

Nardo, Don. *Life in Ancient Rome.* Lucent Books, Inc., 1997.

Tacitus. *The Annals of Tacitus.*

Toliver, Ralph. *Gold Fears No Fire.* Overseas Missionary Fellowship (IHQ) Ltd., 1986.

Talk, D.C. and Voice of the Martyrs. *Jesus Freaks,* Bethany House Publishers, 1999.

Viola, Frank. *The Untold Story of the New Testament Church.* 2004.

Wikipedia.org.

Williams, Brian. *Ancient Roman Homes.* Heinemann Library, 2003.

Wurmbrand, Richard. *Tortured for Christ.* Living Sacrifice Book Company, 1998. (Original work published in 1967).

Wurmbrand, Richard. *If Prison Walls Could Speak.* Living Sacrifice Book Company, 2000. (Original work published in 1972).

Wurmbrand, Richard. *With God in Solitary Confinement.* Living Sacrifice Book Company, 2001. (Original work published in 1969).

Wurmbrand, Richard. *In God's Underground.* Living Sacrifice Book Company, 2004. (Original work published in 1968).

Image:

Unknown (H. Jordan). G. Droysens Allgemeiner Historischer Handatlas, (Map of Rome during Antiquity), www.wikipedia.org. Public Domain.1885.

(Photo modifications courtesy of Philip Goppelt.)